THE MAN WHO
COULDN'T SLEEP

I could feel the sting of the powder smoke on my up-thrust wrist

THE MAN WHO COULDN'T SLEEP

By Arthur Stringer

WILDSIDE PRESS

This book was published by
Wildside Press LLC.
www.wildsidebooks.com

To Harvey, of the dome-like pate,
  The dreamy eye, the Celtic wit
And kindly heart, I dedicate
  This blithe romance conceived and writ
By one of that triumvirate
  Who knew Defeat, yet conquered it.

The Man Who Couldn't Sleep

CHAPTER I

RUNNING OUT OF PAY-DIRT

TO begin with, I am a Canadian by birth, and thirty-three years old. For nine of those years I have lived in New York. And by my friends in that city I am regarded as a successful author.

There was a time when I even regarded myself in much the same light. But that period is past. I now have to face the fact that I am a failure. For when a man is no longer able to write he naturally can no longer be reckoned as an author.

I have made the name of Witter Kerfoot too well known, I think, to explain that practically all of my stories have been written about Alaska. Just why I resorted to that far-off country for my settings is still more or less a mystery to me. Perhaps it was merely because of its far-offness. Perhaps it was because the editors remembered that I came from the land of the beaver and sagely concluded that a Canadian would be most at home in writing about the Frozen North. At any rate, when I romanced about the Yukon and its ice-bound trails they bought my stories, and asked for more.

And I gave them more. I gave them blood-red fiction about gun-men and claim-jumpers and Siwash

1

queens and salmon fisheries. I gave them supermen of iron, fighting against cold and hunger, and snarling, always snarling, at their foes. I gave them oratorical young engineers with clear-cut features and sinews of steel, battling against the forces of hyperborean evil. I gave them fist-fights that caused my books to be discreetly shut out of school-libraries yet brought in telegrams from motion-picture directors for first rights. I gave them enough gun-play to shoot Chilcoot Pass into the middle of the Pacific, and was publicly denominated as the apostle of the Eye-Socket School, and during the three-hundred-night run of my melodrama, *The Pole Raiders*, even beheld on the Broadway sign-boards an extraordinarily stalwart picture of myself in a rakish Stetson and a flannel shirt very much open at the throat, with a cowhide holster depending from my Herculean waist-line and a very dreadful-looking six-shooter protruding from the open top of that belted holster. My publishers spoke of me, for business reasons, as the Interpreter of the Great Northwest. And I exploited that territory with the industry of a badger. In my own way, I mined Alaska. And it brought me in a very respectable amount of pay-dirt.

But I knew nothing about Alaska. I had never even seen the country. I "crammed up" on it, of course, the same as we used to cram up for a third-form examination in Latin grammar. I perused the atlases and sent for governmental reports, and pored over the R. N. W. M. P. Blue Books, and gleaned a hundred or so French-Canadian names for half-breed villains from a telephone-directory for the city of Montreal. But I knew no more about Alaska than a Fiji Islander knows about the New York Stock Exchange. And that was why I could romance so freely, so magnificently, about it!

I was equally prodigal of blood, I suppose, because I had never seen the real thing flow—except in the case of my little niece, when her tonsils had been removed and a very soft-spoken nurse had helped me out of the surgery and given me a drink of ice-water, after telling me it would be best to keep my head as low as possible until I was feeling better. As for firearms, I abhorred them. I never shot off an air-rifle without first shutting my eyes. I never picked up a duck-gun without a wince of aversion. So I was able to do wonderful things with firearms, on paper. And with the Frozen Yukon and firearms combined, I was able to work miracles. I gave a whole continent goose-flesh, so many times a season. And the continent seemed to enjoy it, for those airy essays in iron and gore were always paid for, and paid for at higher and higher rates.

While this was taking place, something even more important was taking place, something which finally brought me in touch with Mary Lockwood herself. It was accident more than anything else, I think, that first launched me in what is so indefinitely and often so disparagingly known as society. Society, as a rule, admits only the lions of my calling across its sacred portals. And even these lions, I found, were accepted under protest or the wing of some commendable effort for charity, and having roared their little hour, were let pass quietly out to oblivion again. But I had been lucky enough to bring letters to the Peytons and to the Gruger-Philmores, and these old families, I will be honest enough to confess, had been foolish enough to like me.

So from the first I did my best to live up to those earlier affiliations. I found myself passed on, from one mysteriously barricaded seclusion to the other. The tea-hour visit merged into the formal dinner, and the formal dinner into the even more formal box at the Horse-Show, and then a call to fill up a niche at the Metropolitan on a Caruso-night, or a vacancy for an Assembly Dance at Sherry's, or a week at Tuxedo, in winter, when the skating was good.

I worked hard to keep up my end of the game. But I was an impostor, of course, all along the line. I soon saw that I had to prove more than acceptable; I had also to prove *dependable*. That I was a writer meant nothing whatever to those people. They had scant patience with the long-haired genius type. That went down only with musicians. So I soon learned to keep my bangs clipped, my trousers creased, and my necktie inside my coat-lapels. I also learned to use my wits, and how to key my talk up to dowager or down to débutante, and how to be passably amusing even before the champagne course had arrived. I made it a point to remember engagements and anniversaries, and more than once sent flowers and Millairds, which I went hungry to pay for. Even

my *pourboires* to butlers and footmen and maids stood
a matter, in those earlier days, for much secret and
sedulous consideration.

But, as I have said, I tried to keep up my end. I
liked those large and orderly houses. I liked the
quiet-mannered people who lived in them. I liked
looking at life with their hill-top unconcern for triviali-
ties. I grew rather contemptuous of my humbler
fellow-workers who haunted the neighborhood theaters
and the red-inkeries of Greenwich Village, and orated
Socialism and blank-verse poems to garret audiences,
and wore window-curtain cravats and celluloid blinkers with big round lenses, and went in joyous and cara-
mel-eating groups to the "rush" seats at *Rigoletto.* I
was accepted, as I have already tried to explain, as an
impecunious but dependable young bachelor. And
I suppose I could have kept on at that rôle, year after
year, until I developed into a foppish and somewhat
threadbare old *beau.* But about this time I was giving North America its first spasms of goose-flesh with
my demigod type of Gibsonian engineer who fought
the villain until his flannel shirt was in rags and then
shook his fist in Nature's face when she dogged him
with the Eternal Cold. And there was money in
writing for flat-dwellers about that Eternal Cold, and
about battling claw to claw and fang to fang, and
about eye-sockets without any eyes in them. My in-
come gathered like a snow-ball. And as it gathered I
began to feel that I ought to have an establishment—
not a back-room studio in Washington Square, nor a
garret in the Village of the Free-Versers, nor a mere

apartment in the West Sixties, nor even a duplex overlooking Central Park South. I wanted to be something more than a number. I wanted a house, a house of my own, and a cat-footed butler to put a hickory-log on the fire, and a full set of *Sèvres* on my mahogany sideboard, and something to stretch a strip of red carpet across when the landaulets and the limousines rolled up to my door.

So I took a nine-year lease of the Whighams' house in Gramercy Square. It was old-fashioned and sedate and unpretentious to the passing eye, but beneath that somewhat somber shell nested an amazingly rich kernel of luxuriousness. It was good form; it was unbelievably comfortable, and it was not what the climber clutches for. The cost of even a nine-year claim on it rather took my breath away, but the thought of Alaska always served to stiffen up my courage.

It was necessary to think a good deal about Alaska in those days, for after I had acquired my house I also had to acquire a man to run it, and then a couple of other people to help the man who helped me, and then a town car to take me back and forth from it, and then a chauffeur to take care of the car, and then the service-clothes for the chauffeur, and the thousand and one unlooked for things, in short, which confront the pin-feather householder and keep him from feeling too much a lord of creation.

Yet in Benson, my butler, I undoubtedly found a gem of the first water. He moved about as silent as a panther, yet as watchful as an eagle. He could be ubiquitous and self-obliterating at one and the same time. He was meekness incarnate, and yet he could coerce me into a predetermined line of conduct as inexorably as steel rails lead a street-car along its predestined line of traffic. He was, in fact, much more than a butler. He was a valet and a *chef de cuisine* and a lord-high-chamberlain and a purchasing-agent and a body-guard and a benignant-eyed old god-father all in one. The man *babied* me. I could see that all along. But I was already an overworked and slightly neurasthenic specimen, even in those days, and I was glad enough to have that masked and silent Efficiency always at my elbow. There were times, too, when his activities merged into those of a trained nurse, for when I smoked too much he hid away my cigars, and when I worked too hard he impersonally remembered what morning horseback riding in the park had done for a former master of his. And when I drifted into the use of chloral hydrate, to make me sleep, that dangerous little bottle had the habit of disappearing, mysteriously and inexplicably disappear-ing, from its allotted place in my bathroom cabinet.

There was just one thing in which Benson disap-pointed me. That was in his stubborn and unreason-able aversion to Latreille, my French chauffeur. For Latreille was as efficient, in his way, as Benson him-self. He understood his car, he understood the traffic rules, and he understood what I wanted of him. Latreille was, after a manner of speaking, a find of my own. Dining one night at the Peytons', I had met the Commissioner of Police, who had given me a card to stroll through Headquarters and inspect the

machinery of the law.   I had happened on Latreille as
he was being measured and "mugged" in the Identification Bureau, with those odd-looking Bertillon forceps
taking his cranial measurements.   The intelligence of
the man interested me; the inalienable look of respectability in his face convinced me, as a student of
human nature, that he was not meant for any such
fate or any such environment.   And when I looked
into his case I found that instinct had not been amiss.
The unfortunate fellow had been "framed" for a car-
theft of which he was entirely innocent.   He explained all this to me, in fact, with tears in his eyes.
And circumstances, when I looked into them, bore
out his statements.   So I visited the Commissioner,
and was passed on to the Probation Officers, from
whom I caromed off to the Assistant District-Attorney,
who in turn delegated me to another official, who was
cynical enough to suggest that the prisoner might possibly be released if I was willing to go to the extent
of bonding him.   This I very promptly did, for I was
now determined to see poor Latreille once more a free
man.

Latreille showed his appreciation of my efforts by
saving me seven hundred dollars when I bought my
town car—though candor compels me to admit that I
later discovered it to be a used car rehabilitated, and not
a product fresh from the factory, as I had anticipated.
But Latreille was proud of that car, and proud of his
position, and I was proud of having a French chauffeur, though my ardor was dampened a little later
on, when I discovered that Latreille, instead of hailing

from the *Bois de Boulogne* and the *Avenue de la Paix*, originated in the slightly less splendid suburbs of Three Rivers, up on the St. Lawrence.

But my interest in Latreille about this time became quite subsidiary, for something much more important than cars happened to me. I fell in love. I fell in love with Mary Lockwood, head-over-heels in love with a girl who could have thrown a town car into the Hudson every other week and never have missed it. She was beautiful; she was wonderful; but she was dishearteningly wealthy. With all those odious riches of hers, however, she was a terribly honest and above-board girl, a healthy-bodied, clear-eyed, practical-minded, normal-living New York girl who in her twenty-two active years of existence had seen enough of the world to know what was veneer and what was solid, and had seen enough of men to demand mental camaraderie and not "squaw-talk" from them.

I first saw her at the Volpi sale, in the American Art Galleries, where we chanced to bid against each other for an old Italian table-cover, a sixteenth-century blue velvet embroidered with gold galloon. Mary bid me down, of course. I lost my table-cover, and with it I lost my heart. When I met her at the Obden-Belponts, a week later, she confessed that I'd rather been on her conscience. She generously offered to hand over that oblong of old velvet, if I still happened to be grieving over its loss. But I told her that all I asked for was a chance to see it occasionally. And occasionally I went to see it. I also saw its owner, who became more wonderful to me, week by week. Then I lost my head over her. That *apheresis* was so complete that I told Mary what had happened, and asked her to marry me.

Mary was very practical about it all. She said she liked me, liked me a lot. But there were other things to be considered. We would have to wait. I had my work to do—and she wanted it to be *big* work, gloriously big work. She wouldn't even consent to a formal engagement. But we had an "understanding." I was sent back to my work, drunk with the memory of her surrendering lips warm on mine, of her wistfully entreating eyes searching my face for something which she seemed unable to find there.

That work of mine which I went back to, however, seemed something very flat and meager and trivial. And this, I realized, was a condition which would never do. The pot had to be kept boiling, and boiling now more briskly than ever. I had lapsed into more or less luxurious ways of living; I had formed expensive tastes, and had developed a fondness for antiques and Chinese bronzes and those *objets d'art* which are never found on the bargain-counter. I had outgrown the Spartan ways of my youth when I could lunch contentedly at Child's and sleep soundly on a studio-couch in a top-floor room. And more and more that rapacious ogre known as Social Obligation had forged his links and fetters about my movements. More than ever, I saw, I had my end to keep up. What should have been a recreation had become almost a treadmill. I was a pretender, and had my pretense to sustain. I couldn't afford to be "dropped." I had my frontiers to protect, and my powers to placate. I couldn't ask Mary to throw herself away on a no-body. So instead of trying to keep up one end, I tried to keep up two. I continued to bob about the fringes of the Four Hundred. And I continued to cling hungrily to Mary's hint about doing work, glori-ously big work.

But gloriously big work, I discovered, was usually done by lonely men, living simply and quietly, and dwelling aloof from the frivolous side-issues of life, divorced from the distractions of a city which seemed organized for only the idler and the lotos-eater. And I could see that the pay-dirt coming out of Alaska was running thinner and thinner.

It was to remedy this, I suppose, that I dined with my old friend Pip Conners, just back to civilization after fourteen long years up in the Yukon. That dinner of ours together was memorable. It was one of the mile-stones of my life. I wanted to furbish up my information on that remote corner of the world, which, in a way, I had preempted as my own. I wanted fresh information, first-hand data, renewed in-spiration. And I was glad to feel Pip's horny hand close fraternally about mine.

"Witter," he said, staring at me with open admi-ration, "you're a wonder."

I liked Pip's praise, even though I stood a little at a loss to discern its inspiration.

"You mean—this?" I asked, with a casual hand-wave about that Gramercy Square abode of mine.

"No, sir," was Pip's prompt retort. "I mean those stories of yours. I've read 'em all."

I blushed at this, blushed openly. For such commendation from a man who knew life as it was, who knew life in the raw, was as honey to my ears.

"Do you mean to say you could get them, up *there?*" I asked, more for something to dissemble my embarrassment than to acquire actual information.

"Yes," acknowledged Pip with a rather foolish-sounding laugh, "they come through the mails about the same as they'd come through the mails down here. And folks even read them, now and then, when the gun-smoke blows out of the valley!"

"Then what struck you as wonderful about them?" I inquired, a little at sea as to his line of thought.

"It's not *them* that's wonderful, Witter. It's *you*. I said you were a wonder. And you are."

"And why am I a wonder?" I asked, with the drip of the honey no longer embarrassing my modesty.

"Witter, *you're a wonder to get away with it!*" was Pip's solemnly intoned reply.

"To get away with it?" I repeated.

"Yes; to make it go down! To get 'em trussed and gagged and hog-tied! To make 'em come and eat out of your hand and then holler for more! For I've been up there in the British Yukon for fourteen nice comfortable years, Witter, and I've kind o' got to know the country. I know how folks live up there, and what the laws are. And it may strike you as queer, friend-author, but folks up in that district are uncommonly like folks down here in the States. And in the

Klondike and this same British Yukon there is a Firearms Act which makes it against the law for any
civilian to tote a gun. And that law is sure carried
out. Fact is, there's no *need* for a gun. And even
if you did smuggle one in, the Mounted Police would
darned soon take it away from you!"

I sat staring at him.

"But all those motion-pictures," I gasped. "And
all those novels about—"

"That's why I say you're a wonder," broke in the
genial-eyed Pip. "You can fool *all* the people *all* the
time! You've done it. And you keep on doing it.
You can put 'em to sleep and take it out of their pants
pocket before they know they've gone by-by. Why,
you've even got 'em tranced off in the matter of every-
day school-geography. You've had some of those hero-
guys o' yours mush seven or eight hundred miles, and
on a birch-bark toboggan, between dinner and supper.
And if that ain't genius, I ain't ever seen it bound up in
a reading-book!"

That dinner was a mile-stone in my life, all right,
but not after the manner I had expected. For as
I sat there in a cold sweat of apprehension crowned
with shame, Pip Conners told me many things about
Alaska and the Klondike. He told me many things
that were new to me, dishearteningly, discouragingly,
devitalizingly new to me. Without knowing it, he
poignarded me, knifed me through and through. Without dreaming what he was doing, he eviscerated me.
He left me a hollow and empty mask of an author.
He left me a homeless exile, with the iron gates of

Fact swung sternly shut on what had been a Fairy Land of Romance, a Promised Land of untrammelled and care-free imaginings.

That was my first sleepless night. I said nothing to Pip. I said nothing to any one. I held that vulture of shame close in my arms and felt its unclean beak awling into my vitals. I tried to go back to my work, next day, to lose myself in creation. But it was like seeking consolation beside a corpse. For me, Alaska was killed, killed forever. And blight had fallen on more than my work. It had crept over my very world, the world which only the labor of my pen could keep orderly and organized. The city in which I had seemed to sit a conqueror suddenly lay about me a flat and monotonous tableland of ennui, as empty and stale as a circus-lot after the last canvas-wagon has rumbled away.

I have no intention of making this recount the confessions of a neurasthenic. Nothing is further from my aims than the inditing of a second City of Dreadful Night. But I began to worry. And later on I began to magnify my troubles. I even stuck to New York that summer, for the simple reason that I couldn't afford to go away. And it was an unspeakably hot summer. I did my best to work, sitting for hours at a time staring at a blank sheet of paper, set out like tangle-foot to catch a passing idea. But not an idea alighted on that square of spotless white. When I tried new fields, knowing Alaska was dead, the editors solemnly shook their heads and announced that this new offering of mine didn't seem to have the snap and go of my older manner. Then panic overtook me, and after yet another white night I went straight to Sanson, the nerve specialist, and told him I was going crazy.

He laughed at me. Then he offhandedly tapped me over and tried my reflexes and took my blood pressure and even more diffidently asked me a question or two. He ended up by announcing that I was as sound as a dollar, whatever that may have meant, and suggested as an afterthought that I drop tobacco and go in more for golf.

That buoyed me up for a week or two. But Mary, when she came in to town radiant and cool for three days' shopping, seemed to detect in me a change which first surprised and then troubled her. I was bitterly conscious of being a disappointment to some-body who expected great things of me. And to escape that double-edged sword of mortification, I once again tried to bury myself in my work. But I just as well might have tried to bury myself in a butter-dish, for there was no effort and no activity there to envelope me. I was coerced into idleness, without ever having acquired the art of doing nothing. For life with me had been a good deal like boiling rice: it had to be kept galloping to save it from going mushy. Yet now the fire itself seemed out. And that prompted me to sit and listen to my works, as the French idiom expresses it, which is never a profitable calling for a naturally nervous man.

The lee and the long of it was, as the Irish say, that I went back to Doctor Sanson and demanded something, in the name of God, that would give me a good night's sleep. He was less jocular, this time. He told me to forget my troubles and go fishing for a couple of weeks.

I *did* go fishing, but I fished for ideas. And I got scarcely a strike. To leave the city was now more than ever out of the question. So for recreation I had Latreille take me out in the car, when a feverish thirst for speed, which I found it hard to account for, drove me into daily violations of the traffic laws. Twice, in fact, I was fined for this, with a curtly warning talk from the presiding magistrate on the second occasion, since the offense, in this case, was complicated by collision with an empty baby-carriage. Latreille, about this time, seemed uncannily conscious of my condition. More and more he seemed to rasp me on the raw, until irritation deepened into positive dislike for the man.

When Mary came back to the city for a few days, before going to the Virginia hills for the autumn, I looked so wretched and felt so wretched that I decided not to see her. I was taking veronal now, to make me sleep, and with cooler weather I looked for better rest and a return to work. But my hopes were ill-founded. I came to dread the night, and the night's ever-recurring battle for sleep. I lost my perspective on things. And then came the crowning catastrophe, the catastrophe which turned me into a sort of twentieth-century Macbeth.

The details of that catastrophe were ludicrous enough, and it had no definite and clear-cut outcome, but its effect on my over-tensioned nerves was sufficiently calamitous. It occurred, oddly enough, on Hallow-e'en night, when the world is supposed to be given over to festivity. Latreille had motored me out to a small dinner-dance at Washburn's, on Long Island, but I had left early in the evening, perversely depressed by a hilarity in which I had not the heart to join. Twice, on the way back to the city, I had called out to Latreille for more speed. We had just taken a turn in the outskirts of Brooklyn when my swinging headlights disclosed the figure of a man, an unstable and wavering man, obviously drunk, totter and fall directly in front of my car.

I heard the squeal of the brakes and the high-pitched shouts from a crowd of youths along the sidewalk. But it was too late. I could feel the impact as we struck. I could feel the sickening thud and jolt as the wheels pounded over that fallen body.

I stood up, without quite knowing what I was doing, and screamed like a woman. Then I dropped weakly back in my seat. I think I was sobbing. I scarcely noticed that Latreille had failed to stop the car. He spoke to me twice, in fact, before I knew it.

"Shall we go on, sir?" he asked, glancing back at me over his shoulder.

"*Go on!*" I shouted, knowing well enough by this time what I said, surrendering merely to that blind and cowardly panic for self-preservation which marks man at his lowest.

We thumped and swerved and speeded away on the wings of cowardice. I sat there gasping and clutching my moist fingers together, as I've seen hysterical women do, calling on Latreille for speed, and still more speed.

I don't know where he took me. But I became conscious of the consoling blackness of the night about us. And I thanked God, as Cain must have done when he found himself alone with his shame.

"Latreille," I said, breathing brokenly as we slowed up, "did we—*did we kill him?*"

My chauffeur turned in his seat and studied my face. Then he looked carefully back, to make sure we were not being followed.

"This is a heavy car, sir," he finally admitted. He said it coolly, and almost impersonally. But the words fell like a sledge-hammer on my heart.

"But we couldn't have killed a man," I clamored insanely, weakly, as we came to a dead stop at the roadside.

"Forty-two hundred pounds—and he got both wheels!" calmly protested my enemy, for I felt now that he was in some way my enemy.

"What in heaven's name are you going to do?" I gasped, for I noticed that he was getting down from his seat.

"Hadn't I better get the blood off the running-gear, before we turn back into town?"

"Blood?" I quavered as I clutched at the robe-rail in front of me. And that one word brought the horror of the thing home to me in all its ghastliness. I could see axles and running-board and brake-bar dripping with red, festooned with shreds of flesh, maculated with blackening gore. And I covered my face with my hands, and groaned aloud in my misery of soul.

But Latreille did not wait for me. He lifted the seat-cushion, took rubbing-cloths from the tool-box and crawled out of sight beneath the car. I could feel the occasional tremors that went through the frame-work as he busied himself at that grisly task. I could hear his grunt of satisfaction when he had finished. And I watched him with stricken eyes as he stepped through the vague darkness and tossed his telltale cloths far over the roadside fence.

"It's all right," he companionably announced as he stepped back into the car. But there was a new note in the man's demeanor, a note which even through that black fog of terror reached me and awakened my resentment. We were partners in crime. We were fellow-actors in a drama of indescribable cowardice, and I was in the man's power, to the end of time.

The outcome of that catastrophe, as I have already said, was indefinite, torturingly indefinite. I was too shaken and sick to ferret out its consequences. I left that to Latreille, who seemed to understand well enough what I expected of him.

That first night wore by, and nothing came of it all. The morning dragged away, and my fellow-criminal seemingly encountered nothing worthy of rehearsal to me. Then still another night came and went. I went through the published hospital reports, and the police records, with my heart in my mouth. But I could unearth no official account of the tragedy. I even encountered my good friend Patrolman Mc-

Cooey, apparently by accident, and held him up on his beat about Gramercy Park to make casual inquiries as to street-accidents, and if such things were increasing of late. But nothing of moment, apparently, had come to McCooey's ears. And I stood watching him as he flatfooted his way placidly on from my housefront, with one of my best cigars tucked under his tunic, wondering what the world would say if it knew that Witter Kerfoot, the intrepid creator of sinewy supermen who snarl and fight and shake iron fists in the teeth of Extremity, had run like a rabbit from a human being he had bowled over and killed?

I still hoped against hope, however, trying to tell myself that it is no easy thing to knock the life out of a man, passionately upbraiding myself for not doing what I should have done to succor the injured, then sinkingly remembering what Latreille had mentioned about the weight of my car. Yet it wasn't until the next night, as I ventured out to step into that odiously ponderous engine of destruction, that uncertainty solidified into fact.

"*You got him,*" announced my chauffeur out of one side of his mouth, so that Benson, who stood on the house-steps, might not overhear those fateful words.

"Got him?" I echoed, vaguely resenting the man's use of that personal pronoun singular.

"Killed!" was Latreille's monosyllabic explanation. And my heart stopped beating.

"How do you know that?" I demanded in whispering horror. For I understood enough of the law of the land to know that a speeder who flees from the

victim of his carelessness is technically guilty of man-
slaughter.

"A man I know, named Crotty, helped carry the
body back to his house. Crotty's just told me about
it."

My face must have frightened Latreille, for he
covered his movement of catching hold of my arm by
ceremoniously opening the car door for me.

"Sit tight, man!" he ordered in his curt and con-
spiratorial undertone. "Sit tight—for it's all that's
left to do!"

I sat tight. It was all there was to do. I endured
Latreille's accession of self-importance without com-
ment. There promptly grew up between us a tacit
understanding of silence. Yet I had reason to feel
that this silence wasn't always as profound as it
seemed. For at the end of my third day of self-
torturing solitude I went to my club to dine. I went
with set teeth. I went in the hope of ridding my system of self-fear, very much as an alcoholic goes to a
Turkish-bath. I went to mix once more with my fellows, to prove that I stood on common ground with
them.

But the mixing was not a success. I stepped across
that familiar portal in quavering dread of hostility.
And I found what I was looking for. I detected myself
being eyed coldly by men who had once posed as my
friends. I dined alone, oppressed by the discovery
that I was being deliberately avoided by the fellow-
members of what should have been an organized com-
panionability. Then I took a grip on myself, and for-

lornly argued that it was all mere imagination, the vaporings of a morbid and chlorotic mind. Yet the next moment a counter-shock confronted me. For as I stared desolately out of that club window I caught sight of Latreille himself. He stood there at the curb, talking confidently to three other chauffeurs clustered about him between their cars. Nothing, I suddenly remembered, could keep the man from gossiping. And a word dropped in one servant's ear would soon pass on to another. And that other would carry the whisper still wider, until it spread like an infection from below-stairs to above-stairs, and from private homes to the very housetops. And already I was a marked man, a pariah, an outcast with no friendly wilderness to swallow me up.

I slunk home that night with a plumb-bob of lead swinging under my ribs where my heart should have been. I tried to sleep and could not sleep. So I took a double dose of chloral hydrate, and was re-warded with a few hours of nightmare wherein I was a twentieth-century Attila driving a racing-car over an endless avenue of denuded infants. It was all so horrible that it left me limp and quailing before the lash of daylight. Then, out of a blank desolation that became more and more unendurable, I clutched fever-ishly at the thought of Mary Lockwood and the autumn-tinted hills of Virginia. I felt the need of getting away from that city of lost sleep. I felt the need of "exteriorating" what was corroding my in-most soul. I was seized with a sudden and febrile ache for companionship. So I sent a forty-word wire to the only woman in the world I could look to in my extremity. And the next morning brought me a reply. It merely said, "Don't come."

The bottom seemed to fall out of the world, with that curt message, and I groped forlornly, frantically, for something stable to sustain me. But there was nothing. Bad news, I bitterly reminded myself, had the habit of traveling fast. *Mary knew.* The endless chain had widened, like a wireless-wave. It had rolled on, like war-gas, until it had blighted even the slopes beyond the Potomac. For Mary *knew!*

It was two days later that a note, in her picket-fence script that was as sharp-pointed as arrow-heads, followed after the telegram.

"There are certain things," wrote Mary, "which I can scarcely talk about on paper. At least, not as I should prefer talking about them. But these things must necessarily make a change in your life, and in mine. I don't want to seem harsh, Witter, but we can't go on as we have been doing. We'll both have to get used to the idea of trudging along in single harness. And I think you will understand why. I'm not exacting explanations, remember. I'm merely requesting an armistice. If you intend to let me, I still want to be your friend, and I trust no perceptible gulf will yarn between us, when we chance to dine at the same table or step through the same *cotillion.* But I must bow to those newer circumstances which seem to have confronted you even before they presented themselves to me. So when I say good-by, it is more to the Past, I think, than to You."

That was the first night, I remember, when sleeping-powders proved of no earthly use to me. And this would not be an honest record of events if I neglected to state that the next day I shut myself up in my study and drank much more *Pommery-Greno* than was good for me. I got drunk, in fact, blindly, stupidly, senselessly drunk. But it seemed to drape a veil between me and the past. It made a bonfire of my body to burn up the debris of my mind. And when poor old patient-eyed Benson mixed me a bromide and put me to bed I felt like a patient coming out of ether after a major operation. I was tired, and I wanted to lie there and rest for a long time.

CHAPTER II

IT was a week later, and well after two, in the dullest ebb of earth's deadest hour, when Benson lifted the portière and stepped into my room.

I put down the book at which my brain had been scratching like a dog scratching at a closed door. It was a volume of Gautier's *nouvelles*. I had just reached that mildly assuaging point in *Une Nuit de Cléopâtre* where the mysterious arrow, whistling through the palace window of a queen bored almost to extinction, buries itself quivering in the cedar wainscoting above her couch.

But the incident, this time, seemed to have lost its appeal. The whole thing sounded very empty and old, very foolish and far-away. The thrill of drama, I cogitated, is apt to leak out of a situation when it comes to one over a circuit of two thousand moldering years. So I looked up at my servant a little listlessly and yet a little puzzled by what was plainly a studied calmness of appearance.

"Benson, why aren't you in bed?"

"If you will pardon me, sir," began the intruder, "I've a gentleman here."

He was so extraordinarily cool about it that I rose like a fish at the flash of something unusual.

"At this time of night?" I inquired.

25

"Yes, sir."

"But what *kind* of gentleman, Benson?"

Benson hesitated; it was the sort of hesitation that is able to translate silence into an apology.

"I think, sir, it's a burglar."

"A what?" I demanded, incredulously.

"The fact is, sir, I 'appened to hear him at the lock. When he forced the door, sir, not being able to work the lock, I was waiting for him."

The dropped aspirate was an unfailing sign of mental disturbance in Benson. I closed my book and tossed it aside. It was only drama of the second dimension, as old and musty as a mummy. And here, apparently, was adventure of the first water, something of my own world and time.

"This sounds rather interesting, Benson. Be so good as to show the gentleman up."

I sat down, with a second look at the dragging hands of the little French clock on my mantel. But Benson still seemed a trifle ill at ease.

"I—I took the liberty of tying him up a bit, sir," explained that astute old dissembler, "being compelled, as it were, to use a bit of force."

"Of course. Then untie him as much as necessary, and fetch him here. And you might bring up a bottle of *Lafitte* and a bite to eat. For two, if you please."

"Yes, sir," he answered. But still he hesitated.

"The revolver, sir, is in the cabinet-drawer on your left."

There were times when old Benson could almost make me laugh; times when the transparencies of his obliquities converted them into something almost respectable.

"We won't need the revolver, Benson. What I most need I fancy is amusement, distraction, excitement, anything—anything to get me through this endless hell of a night."

I could feel my voice rise on the closing words, like the uprear of a terrified racehorse. It was not a good sign. I got up and paced the rug, like a castaway pacing some barren and empty island. But here, I told myself, was a timely footprint. I waited, as breathless as a Crusoe awaiting his Friday.

I waited so long that I was beginning to dread some mishap. Then the portière parted for the second time, and Benson led the burglar into the room.

I experienced, as I looked at him, a distinct sense of disappointment. He was not at all what I expected. He wore no black mask, and was neither burly nor ferocious. The thing that first impressed me was his slenderness—an almost feline sort of slenderness. The fact I next remarked was that he was very badly frightened, so frightened, in fact, that his face was the tint of a rather soiled white glove. It could never have been a ruddy face. But its present startling pallor, I assumed, must have been largely due to Benson's treatment, although I was still puzzled by the look of abject terror which gave the captive's eyes their animal-like glitter. He stood before me for all the world as though a hospital interne had been practising abstruse bandaging feats on his body, so neatly and yet so firmly had the redoubtable Benson hobbled him and swathed his arms in a half-dozen of my best Irish linen table-napkins. Over these, again, had been wound and buckled a trunk-strap. Benson had not skimped his job. His burglar was wrapped as securely as a butcher wraps a boned rib-roast.

My hope for any diverting talk along the more picturesque avenues of life was depressingly short-lived. The man remained both sullen and silent. His sulky speechlessness was plainly that of a low order of mind menaced by vague uncertainties and mystified by new surroundings. Blood still dripped slowly down the back of his soiled collar, where Benson's neat whelp had abraded the scalp.

Yet his eyes, all the time, were alert enough. They seemed to take on a wisdom that was uncanny, the inarticulate wisdom of a reptile, bewildering me, for all their terror, with some inner sense of vicious security. To fire questions at him was as futile as throwing pebbles at an alligator. He had determined, apparently, not to open his lips; though his glance, all this time, was never an idle or empty one. I gave up, with a touch of anger.

"Frisk him," I told the waiting Benson. As that underworld phrase was new to those respectable Anglian ears, I had to translate it. "See if he's carrying a gun. Search his pockets—every one of them."

This Benson did, with an affective mingling of muffled caution and open repugnance. He felt from pocket to pocket, as gingerly as small boys feel into ferret holes, and with one eye always on the colorless and sphinx-like face beside him.

The result of that search was quite encouraging. From one pocket came an ugly, short-barreled Colt. From another came two skeleton keys and a few inches of copper wire bent into a coil. From still another came a small electric flashlight. Under our burglar's coat, with one end resting in his left-hand waistcoat pocket, was a twenty-inch steel "jimmy." It was a very attractive tool, not unlike a long and extremely slender stove lifter, with a tip-tilted end. I found it suggestive of tremendous leverage-power, tempting one to test its strength. It proved as inviting to the hand as a golfer's well-balanced "driver."

From the right-hand waistcoat pocket Benson produced a lady's gold watch, two finger rings, a gold barrette, and a foot or two of old-fashioned locket chain, of solid gold. There was nothing to show who the owner of this jewelry might be.

"I suppose you just bought this at Tiffany's?" I inquired. But the needle of antiphrasis had no effect on his indurated hide. His passivity was beginning to get on my nerves. He might have been a wax figure in the Eden Musée, were it not for those reptiliously alert and ever exasperating eyes. I stood up and confronted him.

"I want to know where this stuff came from."

The white-faced burglar still looked at me out of those sullen and rebellious blinkers of his. But not a word passed his lips.

"Then we'll investigate a little farther," I said, eying his somewhat protuberant breast-bone. "Go on with the search, Benson, and get everything." For it was plain that our visitor, before honoring us that night, had called at other homes.

I watched Benson with increased interest as his fastidiously exploring hand went down inside the burglar's opened waistcoat. I saw him feel there, and as he did so I caught a change of expression on our prisoner's face. He looked worried and harassed by this time; he seemed to have lost his tranquil and snake-like assurance. His small, lean head with the pathetically eager eyes took on a rat-like look. I knew then the end toward which my mind had been groping. The man was not snake-like. He was rat-like. He was a cornered rat. Rat seemed written all over him.

But at that moment my eyes went back to Benson, for I had seen his hand bringing away a small vase partly wrapped in a pocket-handkerchief. This handkerchief was extremely dirty.

I took the vase from his hand, drawing away the rag that screened it. Only by an effort, as I did so, was I able to conceal my surprise. For one glance at that slender little column of *sang-de-boeuf* porcelain told me what it was. There was no possibility of mistake. One glimpse of it was enough. It was from the Gubtill collection. For once before my fingers had caressed the same glaze and the same tender contours. Once before, and under vastly different circumstances, I had weighed that delicate tube of porcelain in my contemplative hands.

I sat back and looked at it more carefully. I examined the crackled groundwork, with its brilliant mottled tones, and its pale ruby shades that deepened into crimson. I peered down at the foot of enameled white with its slowly deepening tinge of pale green. Then I looked up at the delicate lip, the lip that had once been injured and artfully banded with a ring of gold. It was a vase of the K'angshi Period, a rare and beautiful specimen among the Lang Yao monochromes. And history said that thirty years before it had been purchased from the sixth Prince of Pekin, and had always been known as "The Flame."

Both Anthony Gubtill and I had bid for that vase. Our contest for it had been a spirited one, and had even been made the subject of a paragraph or two in the morning papers. But an inexplicably reckless mood had overtaken that parsimonious old collector, and he had won, though the day after the Graves sale I had been a member of that decorously appreciative dinner party which had witnessed its installation between a rather valuable peach-bloom amphora of haricot-red groundwork, with rose spots accentuated by the usual clouds of apple-green, and a taller and, to my mind, much more valuable ashes-of-roses cylindrical Lang Yao with a carved ivory base. We had looked on the occasion as somewhat of an event, for such things naturally are not picked up every day. So the mere sight of the vase took me back to the Gubtill home, to that rich and spacious house on lower Fifth Avenue where I had spent not a few happy evenings. And that in turn took my thoughts back to a certain Volpi sale and an old Italian table-cover of blue velvet. From the table-cover they flashed on to Mary Lockwood and the remembered loveliness of her face as we stood side by side staring down at the gold galloon along the borders of that old vestment. Then I drew memory up short, with a wince, as I suddenly realized that the wanderer had been penetrating into strictly forbidden paths.

I put the vase down on my table and turned away from it, not caring to betray my interest in it, nor to give to the rat-like eyes still watching me any inkling of my true feelings. Yet the thought of such beauty being in the hands of a brute like that sickened me. I was angered by the very idea that such grace and delicacy should be outraged by the foul rags and the even fouler touch of a low-browed sneakthief. I resented the outrage, just as any normal mind would resent a jungle ape's abduction of a delicate child.

I turned and looked the criminal up and down. I noticed, for the first time, that his face was beaded with sweat.

"Might I inquire just what you intend doing with this?" I asked, gazing back, against my will, at the fragile little treasure known as The Flame.

The man moved uneasily, and for the first time. For the first time, too, he spoke.

"Give it to its owner," he said.

"And who is its owner?"

He looked from me to the vase, and then back again.

"It belongs to a pal o' mine over t' Fifth Avenue," he had the effrontery to assert.

"And where did you get it?"

"Out o' hock!"

I couldn't restrain a touch of impatience as my glance fell on the all too eloquent implements of burglary.

"And you expect me to swallow that?" I demanded.

"I don't give a dam' what you swallow. I know the trut' when I'm sayin' it!"

"And you're telling me the truth?" I found it hard to keep my anger within bounds.

"Sure," was his curt answer.

"That's a cowardly lie!" I cried out again. "You're a coward and a liar, like all your sneaking kind, that skulk about dark corners, and crawl under beds, and arm yourself to the teeth, and stand ready to murder innocent women, to strike them down in the dark, rather than be found out! It's cowardice, the lowest and meanest kind of cowardice!"

The sweat stood out on his face in glistening drops.

"What's eatin' you, anyway?" he demanded. "What 'ave I done?"

I pushed the cluster of women's jewelry closer to him.

"You've done some of the meanest and dirtiest work a man can stoop to. You've skulked and crawled and slunk through the dark to rob women and children!"

"Who's given *you* a license to call me a coward?"

"Do you dare to intimate there's anything but low and arrant cowardice in work like this?"

"Just try it," he said with a grin that made his face hideous.

"Why should I try it?" I demanded. "Do you

suppose because I don't carry a jimmy and gun that I can't face honest danger when I need to?"

I glanced round at my den walls, studded with trophies as they were, from the bull moose over the fireplace to the leopard pelt under my heels. The other man followed my glance, but with a lip-curl of contempt. He had jumped to the conclusion, of course, that those relics of encounter in the open stood as a sort of object-lesson of bravery which belonged to me in person.

"Bah," he said, apparently glad to crowd me off into some less personal side-issue, "*that's* all play-actin'. Get up against what I have, and you'd tone down your squeal. Then you'd walk into the real thing."

"The real thing, black-jacking chambermaids and running like a pelted cur at the sight of a brass button!"

I could see his sudden wince, and that it took an effort for him to speak.

"You'd find it took nerve, all right, all right," he retorted. "And the kind o' nerve that ain't a cuff-shooter's long suit."

My movement of contempt brought him a step or two nearer. But it was Benson who spoke first.

"Hadn't we better have the police, sir?" he suggested. The burglar, with his eyes on my face, stepped still closer, as though to shoulder any such suggestion as Benson's out of the issue.

"You just go out in the middle of the night," he went on, with derisive volubility. "Go out at night

and look at a house. Stand off, and look at it good
and plenty. Then ask yourself who's inside, and what's
doin' behind them brick walls, and who's awake, and
where a shot's goin' to come from, and what chances
of a getaway you'll have, and the size of the bit you'll
get if you're pinched. Just stand there and tell yourself you've got to get inside that house, and make
your haul and get away with the goods, that you've
got to do it or go with empty guts. Try it, and see
if it takes nerve."

I must have touched his professional pride. I had
trifled with that ethical totem-pole that is known as
honor among thieves.

"All right," I said, suddenly turning on him as the
inspiration came to me. "We'll try it, and we'll try
it together. For I'm going to make you take this
stuff back, and take it back to-night."

I could see his face cloud. Then a sudden change
came over it. His rat-like eyes actually began to
twinkle.

"I think we ought to have the police, sir," reiterated Benson, remembering, doubtless, his encounter
below-stairs. "He's an uncommon tricky one, sir."

I saw, on more sober second thought, that it would
be giving my friend too much rope, too many chances
for treachery. And he would not be over-nice in his
methods, I knew, now that I had him cornered. A
second idea occurred to me, a rather intoxicating one.
I suddenly felt like a Crusader saving from pollution
a sacred relic. I could catch the whimper of some
unkenneled sense of drama in the affair.

"Benson," I said, "I'm going to leave this worthy gentleman here with you. And while you look after him, I'm going to return this peach-bloom vase to its owner."

"He ain't in town to-night," broke in my troubled burglar.

"And to demonstrate to his somewhat cynical cast of mind that there's nothing extraordinary in his particular line of activity, I propose to return it in the same manner that it was taken."

Benson looked troubled.

"I beg pardon, sir, but mightn't it get us all into a bit of trouble? Couldn't we leave it until morning, sir, and talk it over quiet-like with your friend Mr. McCooey, or with Lieutenant Belton, sir, or the gentleman from the Pinkerton office?"

"And have a cuff-shooter running for help over such a triviality? Never, Benson, never! You will make yourself comfortable here with this gallant gentleman of the black-jack, and keep this handsome Colt of his quite close about you while you're doing it. For I'm going to take this piece of porcelain back where it belongs, even though I have to face a dozen lap-dogs and frighten every housemaid of Twelfth Street into hysterics."

Nobody, I have more than once contended, is altogether sane after midnight. This belief came back to me as I stood before that gloomy-fronted Fifth Avenue house, in that ebb-tide hour of the night when even Broadway is empty, wondering what lay behind the brownstone mask, asking myself what dangers lurked

about that inner gloom, speculating as to what sleepers stirred and what eyes, even as I stood there, might
be alert and watching.

As Benson had suggested, I might have waited
decorously until daylight, or I might have quietly
ascended the wide stone steps and continued to ring
the electric push-bell until a sleepy servant answered
it. But that, after all, seemed absurdly tame and
commonplace. It was without the slightest tang of
drama, and I was as waywardly impatient to try that
enticing tip-tilted instrument of steel on an opposing
door as a boy with a new knife is to whittle on the
nursery woodwork.

There was a tingle of novelty even in standing before
a grimly substantial and altogether forbidding-looking
house, and being conscious of the fact that you had
decided on its secret invasion. I could no longer deny
that it took a certain crude form of nerve. I was
convinced of this, indeed, as I saw the approaching
figure of a patrolman on his rounds. It caused me,
as I felt the jimmy like a staybone against my ribs,
and the flashlight like a torpedo-head in my pocket,
to swing promptly about into Twelfth Street and walk
toward Sixth Avenue. I experienced a distinct glow
of satisfaction as the patrolling footsteps passed northward up the quietness of the avenue.

But the house itself seemed as impregnable as a
fortress. It disheartened me a little to find that not
even a basement grill had been disturbed. For the
second time I turned and sauntered slowly toward
Sixth Avenue. As I swung eastward again I found

that the last house on the side-street, the house abutting the Fifth Avenue mansion which was the object of my attack, was vacant. Of that there could be no doubt. Its doors and windows were sealed with neatly painted shutters.

This, it occurred to me, might mark a possible line of approach. But here again I faced what seemed an impregnable position. I was backing away a little, studying that boarded and coffin-like front, when my heel grated against the iron covering of a coal-chute. This coal-chute stood midway between the curb and the area railing. I looked down at it for a moment or two. Then something prompted me to test its edge with the toe of my shoe. Then, making quite sure that the street was empty, I stooped down and clutched at the edge of the iron disk. It was quite heavy. But one tug at it showed me that its lock-chain had been forced apart.

It took but a moment to lift the metal shield to one side of the chute-head. It took but another moment to lower myself into the chute itself. I could see that it was a somewhat ignominious beginning. But I felt buoyantly sure that I was on the right track. It took an effort to work the iron disk back over the opening. It also required many strange contortions of the body to worm my way down into that narrow and dirty tunnel.

My rather peremptory advent into the coal-bin resulted in a startling amount of noise, noise enough to wake the soundest of sleepers. So I crouched there for several seconds, inhaling dust, and listening and wondering whether or not the walls above me harbored a caretaker. Then I took out the pocket searchlight, and, with the pressure of a finger, directed my ray of illumination against a wooden partition bisected by a painted wooden door.

A distinct sense of disappointment swept through me as I stooped down to examine this door and found that it had already been forced open. I knew, however, that I was following in the footsteps of my more experienced predecessor. Then came a storeroom, and then a laundry-room, with another jimmied door at the head of the stairway leading to the first floor.

Here I stood waiting and listening for some time. But still again nothing but darkness and silence and that musty aroma peculiar to unoccupied houses surrounded me. I felt more at home by this time, and was more leisurely in my survey of the passage upward. I was, of course, confronted by nothing more disturbing than ghost-like furniture covered with ticking and crystal-hung chandeliers encased in cheesecloth. I began to admire my friend the burglar's astuteness in choosing so circuitous and yet so protected a path. There was almost genius in it. His advance, I felt sure, was toward the roof. As I had expected, I found the scuttle open. The lock, I could see, had been quite cleverly picked. And, so far, there had not been a mishap.

Once out on the housetop, however, I foresaw that I would have to be more careful. As I clambered up to the higher coping-tiles that marked the line of the next roof, I knew that I had actually broken into the enemy's lines. Yet the way still seemed clear enough. For, as I came to the roof-scuttle of the second house I found that it, too, remained unlocked. My predecessor had made things almost disappointingly easy for me. Yet, in another way, he had left things doubly dangerous. I had to bear the brunt of any mis-step he may have made. I was being called to face the responsibility of both his intrusion and my own.

So it was with infinite precaution that I lifted the scuttle and leaned over that little well of darkness, inhaling the warmer air that seeped up in my face. With it came an odor quite different to that of the house I had just left. There was something expository in it, something more vital and electric, eloquent of a place inhabited, of human beings and their lairs and trails, of movement and life and vaguely defined menaces. It was, I fancied, a good deal like that man-smell which comes down-wind to a stalked and wary elk.

I stepped down on the iron ladder that led into the uncertain darkness, covering the trap after me. I began to feel, as I groped my way downward, that the whole thing was becoming more than a game. I was disturbed by the thought of how deep I had ventured into an uncertainty. I began to be oppressed by the thought of how complicated my path was proving. I felt intimidated by the undetermined intricacies that still awaited me. A new anxiety was taking possession of me, a sort of low fever of fear, an increasing impatience to replace my precious porcelain, end my mission, and make my escape to the open.

It began to dawn on me, as I groped lower and lower down through the darkness, that a burglar's calling was not all beer and skittles. I began to feel a little ashamed of my heroics of an hour before.

Then I drew up, suddenly, for a sound had crept to my ears. The tingle that ran through my body was not wholly one of fright. Yet, as I stood there in the darkness with one hand against the wall, I caught the rhythm of a slow and muffled snoring. There was something oddly reassuring in that reiterated vibration, even though it served to emphasize the dangers that surrounded me. It was not unlike the sound of a bell-buoy floating up to a fog-wrapped liner's bridge.

I was no longer a prey to any feeling of hesitancy. I was already too deep in the woods to think of turning back. My one passion now was to complete the circuit, to emerge on the other side.

I began to wonder, as I felt for the stair banister and groped my cautious way down the treads, just how the burglar himself had effected that final exit from the house. And the sooner I got away from the sleeping quarters, I felt, the safer I would be. Every bedroom was a shoal of dangers, and not all of them, I very well knew, would be equipped with the same generous whistling-buoy as that I had just left behind me. There was, too, something satisfying in the knowledge that I was at least getting nearer and nearer the ground-floor. This was due, not so much to the fact that I was approaching a part of the house

with which I was more or less familiar, but more to
the fact that my descent marked an approach to some
possible pathway of escape. For that idea was now
uppermost in my mind, and no aviator with a balky
motor ever ached to get back to earth more eagerly
than I.

The utter darkness and silence of the lower halls
were beginning to get on my nerves. I was glad to feel
the newel-post, which assured me that I had reached the
last step in my descent. I was relieved to be able to
turn carefully and silently about to the left, to grope
toward a door which I knew stood before me in the
gloom, and then cautiously to turn the knob and step
inside.

I knew at once, even before I took the flashlight
from my pocket, that I was in the library. And the
room that opened off this, I remembered, half cabinet-
lined study and half informal exhibition-room, was
the chamber wherein Anthony Gubtill treasured his
curios. It would take but a minute or two, I knew,
to replace his priceless little porcelain. And another
minute or two, I felt, ought to see me safely out and
on my way home.

I stood with my back to the door, determined that
no untimely blunder should mar the end of my adventure. My first precaution was to thrust out my
flashlight and make sure of my path. I let the incan-
descent ray finger interrogatively about the massively
furnished room, resting for a moment on marble and
metal and glass-fronted book-shelf. I remembered,
with almost a smile of satisfaction, the little *Clytie*

above the fireplace, and the *Hebe* in bronze that stood beside the heavy reading-lamp. This lamp, Gubtill had once told me, had come from Munich; and I remembered his chuckle over the fact that it had come in a "sleeper" trunk and had evaded duty.

Then I let the wavering light travel toward the end of the glimmering and dark-wooded reading-table. I stood there, picking out remembered object after object, remarking them with singular detachment of mind as my light continued to circle the end of the room.

Then I quietly made my way to the open door in the rear, and bisecting that second room with my spear of light, satisfied myself that the space between the peach-bloom amphora and the ashes-of-roses Yang Lao with the ivory base was indeed empty.

I stood listening to the exotic tick of a brazen-dialed Roumanian clock. I lingered there, letting my bald light-shaft root like a hog's-snout along that shelf so crowded with delicate tones and contours. I sighed a little enviously as I turned toward the other end of the room.

Then, of a sudden, I stopped breathing. Automatically I let my thumb lift from the current-spring of my storage-lamp and the light at once went out. I stood there with every nerve of my body on edge. I crouched forward, tingling and peering into the darkness before me. For I had suddenly discovered that I was not alone in the room.

There, facing me, picked out as distinctly as a baby spot-light picks out an actor's face, I had seen the owner of the house himself, not ten paces from me.

He was sitting in a high-backed armchair of green leather. He must have been watching me from the first, every moment and every movement. He had. made no effort to interrupt or intercept me. He had been too sure of his position.

I waited for what seemed an interminable length of time. But not a sound, beyond the querulous tick of the clock, came to my ears. Not even a movement took place in the darkness.

The undefined menace of this silence was too much for me. The whole thing grew into something strangely like a nightmare. I moved away, involuntarily, wondering what I should say, and after what fashion I should begin my foolish explanation. I crouched low and backed off obliquely, as though some value lay in the intervention of space, and as though something venomous were confronting me. I fell slowly back, pawing frenziedly about me for some sustaining tangibility to which to cling. As I did so my body came in contact with some article of furniture— just what I could not tell. But I shied away from it in a panic, as a colt shies at a fallen newspaper.

My sudden movement threw over a second piece of furniture. It must have been some sort of collapsible screen, for it fell to the floor with an echoing crash. I waited, holding my breath, with horripilations of fear nettling every limb of my body, knowing only too well that this must indeed mark the end.

But there was no movement, no word spoken, no slightest sound. I stared through the darkness, still half expectant. I tried to tell myself that it may have been mere hallucination, that expectant attention had projected into my line of vision a purely imaginary figure. I still waited, with my heart pounding. Then the tension became more than I could endure. I actually crept forward a step or two, still peering blindly through the darkness, still listening and waiting.

Then I caught my breath with sudden new suspicion, with a quick fear that crashed, bullet-like, through the film of consciousness. It was followed by a sickening sense of shock, amounting almost to physical nausea.

I once more raised the flashlight. This time my hand shook perceptibly as I turned the electric ray directly in front of me. I let the minute circle of illumination arrow through the darkness, direct to the white face that seemed to be awaiting it. Then I let it come to a rest.

I remember falling back a step or two. I may have called out, but of that I am not sure. Yet of one thing I was only too certain. There before me sat Anthony Gubtill. *He was quite dead.*

My first feeling was not altogether one of terror. It was accompanied by a surge of indignation at the injustice, at the brutality, of it all. I was able to make note of the quilted dressing-gown that covered the relaxed body. I was collected enough to assume that he had overheard the intruder; had come to investigate, and had been struck down and cunningly thrust into a chair. This inference was followed by a flash of exultation as I remembered that his murderer was known, that the crime could easily be proved against him, that even at the present moment he was safe in Benson's custody.

I moved toward the dead man, fortified by the knowledge of a vast new obligation. It was only after I had examined the face for a second time and seen how death had been caused by a cruelly heavy blow, dealt by some blunt instrument, that the enormity of my own intrusion into that house of horror came home to me. I felt a sudden need for light, for sobering and rationalizing light. Even the ticking from the brazen-faced clock had become something phantasmal and unnerving.

I groped feverishly and blindly about in search of an electric switch-button. Then, of a sudden, I stopped again, my movement arrested by a sound.

I knew, as I stood and listened, that it was only the purr of an automobile, faint and muffled from the street outside. But it suddenly brought home to me the awkwardness of my position. To be found in that house, or even to be seen leaving it, was no longer a desirable thing. My foolhardy caprice, before an actuality so overawing, dwindled into something worse than absurdity. And thought came back at a bound to the porcelain in my pocket. I recalled the old-time rivalry between the dead man and myself for The Flame. I recalled the details of my advent between those walls where I stood. And my blood went cold. It was not a matter of awkwardness; it was a matter of peril. For who, I again asked myself, would believe a story so absurd, or accept an excuse so extravagant?

The clock ticked on accusingly. The sound of the automobile stopped. I had just noted this with relief when the thud of a quietly closed door fell on my startled ears. Then came the murmur of voices. There was no longer any doubt about the matter. A motor had come to the door, and from it certain persons had entered the house.

I crept to the library and listened. Then I tiptoed back and closed the door of the inner room. I felt more secure with even a half-inch panel between me. and what that inner room held.

Then I listened. I began to hear the padded tread of feet. Then came the sound of another opened door, and then the snap of a light-switch. There was nothing secret about the new invasion. I knew, as I shrank back behind one of the high-backed library chairs, that the front of the house was already illuminated.

Then came the sound of a calling voice, apparently from the head of the stairs. It was a cautious and carefully modulated voice; I took it for that of a young man of about twenty.

"Is that you, Caddy?"

Then came a silence.

"I say, is that you, Orrie?" was demanded in a somewhat somnolent stage-whisper. There was something strangely reassuring in that commonplace boyish voice. Anthony Gubtill, I knew, had no immediate family. I vaguely recalled, however, some talk of a Canadian nephew and niece who had at times visited him.

"Sh—s—sh!" said a woman's voice from the lower hall. "Don't wake Uncle Anthony."

It must have been a young woman. Her voice sounded pensive, like that of a girl who might be coming home tired from a dance at Sherry's. Yet, knowing what I did, its girlish weariness took on a pathos indescribably poignant.

"It's an awful hour, isn't it?" asked a second man's voice from the lower hall. There were sounds that seemed to imply that wraps were being removed.

"Almost four," came the answer from above. "Had a good time, Caddy?"

I heard a stifled yawn.

"Rather," answered the girl's voice.

"I say, Orrie, bring up those Egyptian gaspers for a puff or two, will you?" requested the youth from above, still in a stage-whisper. "And, Caddy, be sure the latch is on."

"On what?" demanded Orrie.

"The door, you idiot!" was the sleepily good-natured retort.

Then I suddenly ducked low behind my chair-back, for the young man called Orrie had flung open the library door. He came into the room gropingly, without switching on the electrics. I could see his trim young shoulders, and the white blur of his shirt-front. Behind him, framed in the doorway, stood a young girl of about twenty, a blonde in pale blue, with bare arms and bare shoulders. Her skin looked very soft and baby-like in the strong sidelight. I could not repress something that was almost a shudder at the thought of this careless gaiety and youth so close to the grim tragedy behind me, so unconscious of the awakening that might come to them at almost any moment.

"*Do* hurry!" said the tired girl, as the young man fumbled about the table-end. I realized, as I peeped out at her, that my first duty would be to keep those round young eyes from what might confront them in that inner room.

"I've got 'em!" answered the man. He stood a moment without moving. Then he turned and walked out of the room, quietly closing the door behind him.

I emitted a gasp of relief and stood up once more. Nothing alive or dead, I determined, would now keep me in that house. Yet for all that new-born ecstasy of impatience, I was still compelled to wait, for I could hear the occasional sound of feet and a whisper or two from behind the closed door. Then all sound died away; the gloom and silence again engulfed me.

I took the Yang Lao porcelain from my pocket, unwrapped it, and crept back to the inner room. I groped along the wall in the darkness, circling wide about the green-leather chair in the center. I put the vase back on its cabinet, without so much as flashing my light. Then I circled back along the wall, felt for the library door, and groped cautiously across the perilous breadth of the furniture-crowded chamber. It took me several seconds to find the door that opened into the hallway. Once through it and across the hall, I knew, only a spring-latch stood between me and the street. So I turned the knob quickly and swung back the door.

But I did not pass through it. For, instead of darkness, I found myself confronted by a blaze of light.

In that blaze of light stood three waiting and expectant figures. What most disturbed me was the fact that the man called Orrie held in his hand a revolver that seemed the size of a toy-cannon. This was leveled directly at my blinking eyes. The other youth, in cerise pajamas with orange colored frogs and a dressing-gown tied at the waist with a silk girdle, stood just behind him, holding an extremely wicked-looking Savage of the magazine make. Behind this youth again, close by the newel-post, stood the girl in blue, all the sleepiness gone out of her face.

The sight of that wide-eyed and eager trio irritated me beyond words. There was no longer any thrill in the thing. I had gone through too much; I could not react to this newer emergency. I kept wondering if the idiot with the Colt realized just how delicate a pressure would operate the trigger on which I could see his finger shaking. But that shake, it was plain, was more from excitement than fear.

"We've got him!" cried the youth in the cerise pajamas. I might have been a somewhat obstinate black bass wheedled into his landing-net, from the way he spoke.

"Don't move!" commanded the older of the two, wrinkling his brow into a frown of youthful determination. "Don't you dare move one inch, or I'll put a hole through you."

I had no intention of moving.

"Watch his hands," prompted the younger man. "He ought to put 'em up."

"Yes, Orrie, he ought to put them up," echoed the

girl by the newel-post. She reminded me, with her delicate whites and pinks and blues, of the cabinet of porcelain at which I had so recently stared.

"Back up through the door," cried Orrie. "Come on—back up!"

I wearily obeyed this somewhat equine order. Then he commanded me to hold my hands above my head. I did so without hesitation; I had no wish to argue while that Colt was staring me in the eyes.

They followed me, Indian file, into the room. It was the girl who closed the door as Orrie switched on the lights. She stood with her back to it, studying my face. I could see that I rather interested them all. But in that interest I detected no touch of either friendliness or respect. The only one I seemed to mystify was the girl at the door.

"Have you anything to say?" demanded Orrie, squaring his shoulders.

"Yes, I have a great deal to say," I told him. "But I prefer saying it to you alone."

I could see his movement of disdain.

"Will you listen to that!" commented the youth in the cerise pajamas.

"And if you will be so good as to stop poking that pistol in my face," I continued with some heat, "and then send these children out of the room, I shall say what I have to, and do it very briefly!"

"Children!" came in an indignant gasp from the girl at the door.

"We'll stick by you, old man," assured the youthful hero in cerise, with his heels well apart.

"And just why should I closet myself with a burglar?" inquired the astute Orrie, staring at me with the utmost insolence. Yet I could see that at least the precision of my articulation was puzzling him a bit.

"That's asinine," I retorted. "I'm not a burglar, and you ought to know it."

To my astonishment, a little tripartite ripple of laughter greeted this statement.

"Then what are you?" asked the incredulous Orrie.

I knew there was no further use beating about the bush.

"Yes, who are you?" demanded the other youth.

He still held the magazine-revolver balanced in his right hand. The truth had to come out.

"I'm Witter Kerfoot," I told them, as steadily as I could. "Kerfoot, of Gramercy Park West."

"What number?"

I gave him the number. I could see the trio exchange glances; they were plainly glances of amusement. My young friends, I could see, were enjoying a home melodrama, a melodrama in which I was obviously the most foolish of villains. I began to feel a good deal like a phonograph grinding out a comic record.

"And with that face!" ejaculated the man called Orrie.

The quiet contempt of his glance caused me to shift about, so I could catch a glimpse of myself in the Venetian mirror between the book-shelves. That glimpse was indeed a startling one. I had quite forgotten the transit through the coal-hole. I could not even remember how or when I broke my hat-crown. I had remained as unconscious of the scratch across my cheek as I was of the garret cobwebs that festooned my clothing. I saw as I peeped into the mirror only a sickly-hued and grimy-looking footpad with dirty hands and a broken hat. It was no wonder they laughed. My environment for the last hour had not been one that tended toward consciousness of attire. I was about to remove my disgracefully disfiguring headgear when the younger man swung about on me with the Savage thrust point-blank in my face.

"Don't try any of that!" he gasped. "You keep up those hands."

The whole situation was so beside the mark, was so divorced from the sterner problem confronting both them and myself, that it dispirited and angered me.

"We've had about enough of this tommy-rot!" I protested.

"Yes, we'll cut out the tommy-rot, and get him tied," proclaimed the man with the Colt.

"Then search him first," prompted the young man. "Here, Caddy, take Orrie's Colt while he goes through him," he commanded, in the chest-tones of a newly-acquired savagery, "and if he tries to move, wing him!"

The girl, wide-eyed and reluctant, took the heavy revolver. Then Orrie advanced on me, though in an altogether wary and tight-lipped manner. To continue my protests, I saw, would be only to waste my breath. There was nothing to do but submit to the farce.

I said nothing as he produced the telltale flashlight. I also remained silent as he triumphantly unearthed the jimmy and the damnatory skeleton keys. I could see the interchange of exultant glances as these were tossed out on the polished table-top.

"Get the straps from the golf bags!" suggested the youth with the Savage. I could not help remembering how this scene was paralleling another of the same nature and the same night, when Benson and I had been the masters of the situation.

The man called Orrie seemed a little nonplussed at the fact that he had found no valuables in my outer pockets, but he did not give up. He grimly ignored my protests as he explored still deeper and dug out my monogramed wallet, and then a gold cigarette-case, on which my name was duly inscribed. He turned them over in his hand a couple of times and examined them carefully. Then a great light seemed to come to him. He succumbed, as even his elders have done, to a sudden sense of drama.

I saw him dart to the outer room and catch up a telephone directory. He riffled through the pages with quick and impatient fingers. Then he strode back, and looked me up and down.

"I know what this man's done," he cried, his eyes alight with conviction.

"What?" demanded the younger man.

"He's visited more than this house to-night. He's gone through Witter Kerfoot's, as well. He's taken these things from there. And now *it's up to us to take him back with them!*"

I could see the sheer theatricality of the situation clutch at his two listeners. I could see them surrender to it, although the girl still seemed to hesitate.

"Hadn't I better call Uncle Anthony?" she suggested.

At one breath her words brought me back to both the tragedy that lay so close at hand, and the perilous complexity of my own position.

"No, that's foolish!" cut in Orrie. "The car's still outside. Caddy, I think you'll have to come along. You can sit with Jansen on the driving-seat."

The hero of the maneuver turned back to me. I was thinking mostly of the soft-eyed girl with the baby-white skin, and how I could get her safely away.

"Will you come quietly?" my captor demanded of me.

"Yes," I answered, without looking up, "I'll come quietly."

It was the girl's voice, a little shrill with excitement, that next broke the silence.

"Orrie, he's not a burglar!" she cried out, in her treble-noted conviction.

"Then what is he?"

"He's a gentleman."

"What makes you think so?" demanded the indifferent Orrie as he motioned me, with a curt movement of his Colt-barrel, toward the hall door.

"I know by his nails!" was her inconsequential yet quite definite reply.

Orrie laughed.

"Then you'd give tea and macaroons to every burglarious barber out of Sing Sing," he scoffed. "And our real answer's waiting for us in Gramercy Square."

It seemed to take but a minute or two in the car to swing us from Twelfth Street up to Twentieth, and then eastward into the stillness of the square. My captors had insisted that I should not talk. "Not a word!" commanded Orrie, and I could feel his insolent gun-barrel against my ribs as he gave the command for the second time. They were drunk, I could see, with the intoxication of their exploit. They were preoccupied with inhaling their subtle sense of drama. With the dictatorial self-sufficiency of true inebriety they had enjoined me from every effort at explanation. The bubble, they felt, was far too pretty a one to be pricked.

They alighted, one in front of me and one behind me, still carrying their foolish and murderous-looking firearms. The girl remained in her seat. Then the three of us grimly ascended my steps.

"It's needless to ring the bell," I wearily explained. "My pass-key will admit you."

"But I insist on ringing," said Orrie as I fitted the key to the lock.

"I shall be compelled, in that case, to call the officer who is watching us from the corner," was my quiet response.

"Call and be hanged, then!" was the younger man's ultimatum.

One word over their shoulders brought my old friend McCooey, the patrolman, across the corner and up the steps. I swung open the door as he joined us.

Then I turned on the hall lamps and faced my two captors.

"Officer, I want you to look at me very carefully, and then assure these gentlemen I am Witter Kerfoot, the owner and occupant of this house."

"Sure he's Kerfoot," said the unperturbed McCooey. "But what's the throuble this time?"

"Something more serious than these gentlemen dream of. But if the three of us will go quietly up-stairs, you'll find my man Benson there. You'll also find another man, tied up with half a dozen—"

McCooey, from the doorway, cut me short.

"I'm sorry, sir, but I can't be stayin' to see your joke out."

"But you've got to."

"Fact is, sir," he explained, in a lowered voice, "Creegan, av Headquarthers, has a Sing-Sing lifer bottled up in this block, and I'm holdin' wan end av the p'lice lines—a jail-breaker, sir, and a tricky wan, called Pip Foreman, the Rat!"

"The Rat?" I echoed.

"The same, sir. But I must be off."

"Don't go," I said, closing the door. *"Your man's up-stairs, waiting for you!"*

"Waitin' for me?" he demanded. "What man?"

"The man they call the Rat," I tried to explain to him. "And I'll be greatly obliged to you, McCooey, if you'll make as short work of this situation as you can, for the truth of the matter is, I feel rather tired, and fancy there's five or six hours of good honest sleep awaiting me!"

CHAPTER III

I WAS in for a night of it. I realized that as I lay back in my big green library-chair and closed my eyes. For somewhere just in front of those tightly closed lids of mine I could still see a briskly revolving sort of pin-wheel, glowing like a milk-white orange against a murky violet fog that paled and darkened with every beat of my pulse.

I knew the symptoms only two well. The entire encampment of Consciousness was feverishly awake, was alert, was on the *qui-vive*. That pulsing white pin-wheel was purely a personal matter between me and my imagination. It was something distinctly my own. It was *Me*. And being essentially subjective, it could be neither banished nor controlled.

So I decided to make for the open. To think of a four-poster, in any such era of intensified wakefulness, would be a mockery. For I was the arena of that morbid wakefulness which brought with it an over-crowded mental consciousness of existence far beyond my own physical vision, as though I had been appointed night-watchman for the whole round world, with a searching eye on all its multitudinous activities and aberrations. I seemed able to catch its breathing as it slept its cosmic sleep. I seemed to brood with lunar aloofness above its teeming plains, depressed by its enormous dimensions, confused by its incomprehen-

58

sible tangle and clutter of criss-cross destinies. Its
uncountable midnight voices seemed to merge into a
vague sigh, so pensively remote, so unexpressibly
tragic, that when I stood in my doorway and caught
the sound of a harebrained young Romeo go whistling
down past the Players' Club his shrill re-piping of a
Broadway roof-song seemed more than discordant; it
seemed desecration. The fool was happy, when the
whole world was sitting with its fists clenched, awaiting some undefined doom.

It was long past midnight, I remembered as I closed
the door. For it must have been an hour and more
since I had looked out and seen the twelve ruby
flashes from the topmost peak of the Metropolitan
Tower signaling its dolorous message that another
day had gone. I had watched those twelve winks with
a sinking heart, finding something sardonic in their
brisk levity, for I had been reminded by a telltale neurasthenic twitching of my right eyelid that some angling
Satan known as Insomnia was once more tugging and
jerking at my soul, as a fly-hook tugs and jerks at a
trout's mouth.

I knew, even as I wandered drearily off from my
house-door and paced as drearily round and round the
iron-fence park enclosure, that I was destined for
another sleepless night. And I had no intention of
passing it cooped up between four walls. I had tried
that before, and in that way, I remembered, madness
lay.

So I wandered restlessly on through the deserted
streets, with no active thought of destination and no

immediate sense of direction. All I remembered was that the city lay about me, bathed in a night of exceptional mildness, a night that should have left it beautiful. But it lay about me, in its stillness, as dead and flat and stale as a tumbler of tepid wine.

I flung myself wearily down on a bench in Madison Square, facing the slowly spurting fountain that had so often seemed to me a sort of visible pulse of the sleeping city. I sat peering idly up at the Flatiron Building, where like an eternal plowshare it threw its eternal cross furrows of Fifth Avenue and Broadway along the city's tangled stubble of steel and stone. Then I peered at the sleepers all about me, the happy sleepers huddled and sprawled along the park benches. I envied them, every mortal of that ragged and homeless army! I almost hated them. For they were drinking deep of the one thing I had been denied.

As I lounged there with my hat pulled down over my eyes, I listened to the soothing purr and splash of the ever-pulsing fountain. Then I let my gaze wander disconsolately southward, out past the bronze statue of Seward. I watched the driver of a Twenty-third Street taxicab of the "night-hawk" variety asleep on his seat. He sat there in his faded hat and coat, as motionless as metal, as though he had loomed there through all the ages, like a brazen statue of Slumber under his mellowing *patina* of time.

Then, as I gazed idly northward, I suddenly forgot the fountain and the night-hawk chauffeur and the sleepers. For out of Fifth Avenue, past where the double row of electric globes swung down the gentle slope of Murray Hill like a double pearl-strand down a woman's breast, I caught sight of a figure turning quietly into the quietness of the square. It attracted and held my eye because it seemed the only movement in that place of utter stillness, where even the verdigris-tinted trees stood as motionless as though they had been cut from plates of copper.

I watched the figure as it drew nearer and nearer. The lonely midnight seemed to convert the casual stroller into an emissary of mystery, into something compelling and momentous. I sat indolently back on my park bench, peering at him as he drifted in under the milk-white arc lamps whose scattered globes were so like a scurry of bubbles caught in the tree branches.

I watched the stranger as closely as a traveler in mid-ocean watches the approach of a lonely steamer. I did not move as he stood for a moment beside the fountain. I gave no sign of life as he looked slowly about, hesitated, and then crossed over to the end of the very bench on which I sat. There was something military-like about the slim young figure in its untimely and incongruous cape overcoat. There was also something alert and guardedly observant in the man's movements as he settled himself back in the bench. He sat there listening to the purr and splash of the water. Then, in an incredibly short space of time, he was fast asleep.

I still sat beside him. I was still idly pondering who and what the newcomer could be, when another movement attracted my attention. It was the almost silent approach of a second and larger figure, the figure of a wide-shouldered man in navy blue serge, passing quietly in between the double line of bench sleepers. He circled once about the granite-bowled ring of the fountain. Then he dropped diffidently into the seat next to the man in the cape overcoat, not five feet from where I sat.

Something about him, from the moment he took up that position, challenged my attention. I watched him from under my hat-brim as he looked guardedly about. I did not move as he let his covert eyes dwell for a moment or two on my lounging figure. I still watched him as he bent forward and listened to the deep breathing of the man so close beside him.

Then I saw a hand creep out from his side. There was something quick and reptilious in its movements. I saw it feel and pad about the sleeping man's breast. Then I saw it slip, snake-like, in under the cloth of the coat.

It moved about there, for a second or two, as though busily exploring the recess of every possible pocket.

Then I saw the stealthy hand quietly but quickly withdrawn. As it came away it brought with it a packet that flashed white in the lamplight, plainly a packet of papers. This was thrust hurriedly down into the coat pocket of the newcomer next to me. There was not a sound. There was no more movement.

The wide-shouldered man sat there for what must have been a full minute of time. Then he rose quietly to his feet and started as quietly away.

It wasn't until then that the full reality of what he had done came home to me. He had deliberately robbed a sleeping and unprotected man. He was at that moment actually carrying away the spoils of some predetermined and audacious theft. And I had sat calmly and unprotestingly by and watched a thief, a professional "dip," enact a crime under my very eyes, within five feet of me!

In three quick steps I had crossed to the sleeping man's side and was shaking him. I still kept my eyes on the slowly retreating figure of the thief as he made his apparently diffident way up through the square. I had often heard of those street harpies known as "lush-dips," those professional pickpockets who prey on the wayside inebriate. But never before had I seen one at work.

"Quick! Wake up!" I cried, with a desperate shake at the sleeper's shoulder. "You've been robbed!"

The next move of that little midnight drama was an unexpected and startling one. Instead of being confronted by the disputatious maunderings of a half-wakened sleeper, as I expected, I was suddenly and firmly caught by the arm and jerked bodily into the seat beside him.

"You've been robbed!" I repeated, as I felt that firm grip haul me seatward.

"Shut up!" said a calm and very wide-awake voice, quite close to my ear. I struggled to tear my arm away from the hand that still clung to it.

"But you've been *robbed!*" I expostulated. I noticed that his own gaze was already directed northward, toward where the blue-clad figure still moved aimlessly on under the arc lamps.

"How do you know that?" he demanded. I was struck by his resolute and rather authoritative voice.

"Why, I saw it with my own eyes! And there goes the man who did it!" I told him, pointing northward.

He jerked down my hand and swung around on me.

"Watch that man!" he said, almost fiercely. "But for heaven's sake *keep still!*"

"What does this mean?" I naturally demanded.

He swept me with one quick glance. Yet he looked more at my clothes, I fancy, than at my face. My tailor seemed to be quite satisfactory to him.

"Who are you?" he asked. I took my time in answering, for I was beginning to resent his repeated note of superiority.

"My name, if that's what you mean, happens to be the uneuphonious but highly respectable one of Kerfoot—Witter Kerfoot."

"No, no," he said with quick impatience. *"What are you?"*

"I'm nothing much, except a member of a rather respectable club, and a man who doesn't sleep overly well."

His eyes were still keenly watching the slowly departing figure. My flippancy seemed to have been lost on him. His muscular young hand suddenly tightened on my sleeve.

"By God, sir, you *can* help me!" he cried, under his breath. "You must! I've a right to call on you, as a decent citizen, as—"

"Who are you?" I interrupted, quite myself by this time.

"I'm Lieutenant Palmer," he absently admitted, all
the while eying the moving figure.

"And I've got to get that man, or it'll cost me a
court-martial. I've *got* to get him. Wait! Sit back
here without moving. Now watch what he does!"

I saw the thief drop into an empty bench, glance
down at his time-piece, look carelessly about, and then
lean back with his legs crossed. Nothing more happened.

"Well," I inquired, "what's the game?"

"It's no game," he retorted, in his quick and decisive
tones. "It's damn near a tragedy. But now I've
found him! I've placed him! And *that's* the man
I'm after!"

"I don't doubt it," I languidly admitted. "But
am I to assume that this little bench scene was a sort
of, well, a sort of carefully studied out trap?"

"It was the only way I could clinch the thing," he
admitted.

"Clinch what?" I asked, conscious of his hesitation.

"Oh, you've got to know," he finally conceded, "now
you've seen this much! And I know you're—you're
the right sort. I can't tell you everything. But I'm
off the *Connecticut*. She's the flagship of our Atlantic
fleet's first division, the flagship of Rear-Admiral
Shrodder. I was sent to confer with Admiral Maddox,
the commandant of the Navy Yard. Then I was to
communicate with Rear-Admiral Kellner, the super-
visor of Naval Auxiliaries. It was in connection with
the navy's new Emergency Wheel-Code. I can't explain it to you; there's a lot of navy-department data

I can't go into. But I was ashore here in New York with a list of the new wireless code signals."

"And you let them get away?"

"There was no letting about it. They were stolen from me, stolen in some mysterious way I can't understand. I've only one clue. I'd dined at the Plaza. Then I'd gone to the ballroom and sat through the amateur theatricals for the French Hospital. I'd been carrying the code forms and they'd been worrying me. So I 'split the wheel,' as we say in the service. I mean I'd divided 'em and left one half locked up at my hotel while I still carried the other half. Each part, I knew, would be useless without the other. How or when they got the half I was carrying I can't tell, for the life of me. I remember dancing two or three times in the ballroom after the theatricals. But it couldn't have been any of those women. They weren't that sort."

"Then who was it?" For the first time a sense of his boyishness had crept over me.

"That's just it; I don't know. But I kept feeling that I was being shadowed. I was almost positive I was being trailed. They would be after the second half, I felt. So I made a dummy, and loafed about all day waiting for a sign. I kept it up until to-night. Then, when I actually found I was being followed, every move I made, I—"

His voice trailed off and he caught at my arm again.

"See, he's on the move again! He's going, this time. And *that's* the man! I want you to help me watch him, watch every step and trick. And if there's a second man, I'm going to get you to follow him, while I stick to this one. It's not altogether for myself, remember; it's more for the whole Service!"

We were on our feet by this time, passing northward along the asphalted walks that wound in and out between the trees.

"You mean this man's a sort of agent, a foreign spy, after your naval secrets?" I asked, as we watched the figure in blue circle casually out toward Fifth Avenue.

"That's what I've got to find out. And I'm going to do it, if I have to follow him to hell and back!" was the young officer's answer. Then he suddenly drew up, with a whispered warning.

"You'd better go west, toward Broadway. Then walk north into Fifth Avenue again, toward Brentano's corner. I'll swing up Madison Avenue on the opposite side of him, and walk west on Twenty-sixth Street. Don't speak to me as we pass. But watch him, every moment. And if there's a second man, follow him!"

A moment later I was sauntering westward toward the old Hoffman House corner. As I approached the avenue curb I saw the unperturbed figure in blue stop beside the Farragut Monument on the northwest fringe of Madison Square. I saw him take out a cigar, slowly and deliberately strike a match on the stonework of the exedra, and then as slowly and deliberately light his cigar.

I felt, as I saw it, that it was some sort of a signal. This suspicion grew stronger, when, a moment later, I saw a woman step out of a near-by doorway. She wore a plumed Gainsborough hat and a cream-colored gown. Over her slender young shoulders, I further made out, hung an opera 'cloak of delicate lacework.

She stood for a moment at the carriage step, as though awaiting a car or taxi. Then she quickly crossed the avenue and, turning north, passed the waiting man in blue. She passed him without a spoken word.

But as the cream-colored figure drifted nonchalantly by the broad-shouldered man I caught a fleeting glimpse of something passing between them, a hint of one hand catching a white packet from another. It was a hint, and nothing more. But it was enough.

My first impulse, as I saw that movement, was to circle quickly about and warn Palmer of what had taken place. A moment's thought, however, showed me the danger of this. And the young lieutenant, I could see, had already changed his course, so that his path southward through the center of the square paralleled that of the other man now walking more briskly along the avenue curb.

He had clearly stated that I was to watch any confederate. I had no intention to quibble over side-issues. As I started northward, indeed, after that mysterious figure in the Gainsborough hat and the cream-colored gown, a most pleasurable and purposeful tingle of excitement thrilled up and down my backbone.

I shadowed her as guardedly as I was able, following her block by block as she hurried up the empty thoroughfare that was now as quiet and lonely as a glacial moraine. My one fear was that she would reach the Waldorf, or some equally complex beehive of human life, before I could overtake her. Once there, I knew, she would be as completely lost as a needle in a haystack.

She may have suspected me by this time, I felt, for twice I saw her look back over her shoulder.

Then I suddenly stopped and ducked into a doorway. For a moment after I saw a taxicab come clattering into the avenue out of Thirty-third Street I discovered that, at her repeated gesture, it was pulling up beside the curb.

I stood well back in the shadow until she had climbed into the seat, the door had slammed shut, and the driver had turned his vehicle about and started northward again. Then I skirted along the shop fronts, darted across the street, and made straight for the hotel cabstand and a taxi driver drowsily exhaling cigarette smoke up toward the tepid midnight skies. The bill I thrust into his hand took all the sleep out of his body and ended the incense to the morning stars.

"Up the avenue," I said as I clambered in. "And follow that taxicab two blocks behind until it turns, and then run up on it and wait."

It turned at Forty-second Street and went eastward to Lexington Avenue. Then, doubling on its tracks, it swung southward again. We let it clatter on well ahead of us. But as it turned suddenly westward, at the corner of Twenty-third Street, we broke the speed laws to draw once more up to it. Then, as we crossed

Twenty-third Street, I told the driver to keep on southward toward Gramercy Square. For I had caught sight of the other taxi already drawn up at the curb half-way between Lexington and Fourth Avenues.

A moment after we jolted across the car tracks I slipped away from my cab and ran back to the cross-street on foot. As I reached the corner I caught sight of a figure in a cream-colored gown cross the sidewalk and step quickly into the doorway of a shabby four-storied building.

I had no time to study this building. It might have been an antiquated residence turned into a cluster of artist's studios, or a third-rate domicile of third-rate business firms. My one important discovery was that the door opened as I turned the knob and that I was able quietly and quickly to step into the dark hallway.

I stood there in the gloom, listening intently. I could hear the light and hurried click of shoe heels on the bare tread-boards of the stairs. I waited and listened and carefully counted these clicks. I knew, as I did so, that the woman had climbed to the top floor.

Then I heard the chink of metal, the sound of a key thrust into a lock, and then the cautious closing of a door. Then I found myself surrounded by nothing but darkness and silence again.

I stood there in deep thought for a minute or two. Then I groped my way cautiously to the foot of the stairs, found the heavy old-fashioned balustrade, and slowly and silently climbed the stairway.

I did not stop until I found myself on the top floor

of that quiet and many-odored building. I paused there, at a standstill, peering through the darkness that surrounded me.

My search was rewarded by the discovery of one thin streak of yellow light along what must have been the bottom of a closed door. Just beyond that door, I felt, my pursuit was to come to an end.

I groped my way to the wall and tiptoed quietly forward. When I came to the door, I let my hand close noiselessly about the knob. Then, cushioning it with a firm grasp, I turned it slowly, inch by inch.

The door, I found, was locked. But inside the room I could still hear the occasional click of shoe heels and the indeterminate noises of an occupant moving quietly yet hurriedly about.

I stood there, puzzled, depressed by my first feeling of frustration. Then I made out the vague oblong of what must have been a window in the rear of a narrow hall. I tiptoed back to this window, in the hope that it might lead to something. I found, to my disappointment, that it was barred with half-inch iron rods. And this meant a second defeat.

As I tested these rods I came on one that was not so secure as the others. One quiet and steady wrench brought an end-screw bodily out of the half-rotted wood. Another patient twist or two entirely freed the other end.

I found myself armed with a four-foot bar, sharpened wedge-like at each end for its screw head. So I made my way silently back to the pencil of yellow light and the locked door above it. I stood there listening for a minute or two. All I could hear was the running of tap water and the occasional rustling of a paper. So I quietly forced the edge of my rod in between the door and its jamb, and as quietly levered the end outward.

Something had to give under that strain. I was woefully afraid that it would be the lock bar itself. This I knew would go with a snap, and promptly betray my movement. But as I increased the pressure I could see that it was the socket screws that were slowly yielding in the pinewood jamb.

I stopped and waited for some obliterating noise before venturing the last thrust that would send the bolt free of the loosening socket. It came with the sudden sound of steps and the turning off of the running tap. The door had been forced open and stood an inch or two from the jamb before the steps sounded again.

I waited, with my heart in my mouth, wondering if anything had been overheard, if anything had been discovered. It was only then, too, that the enormity of my offense came home to me. I was a housebreaker. I was playing the part of a midnight burglar. I was facing a situation in which I had no immediate interest. I was being confronted by perils I had no means of comprehending. But I intended to get inside that room, no matter what it cost.

I heard, as I stood there, the sound of a drawer being opened and closed. Then came a heel-click or two on the wooden floor, and then an impatient and quite audible sigh. There was no mistaking that sigh. It was as freighted with femininity as though I had heard a woman's voice. And nothing was to be gained by waiting. So I first leaned my iron rod silently against the door corner. Then, taking a deep breath, I stepped quickly and noiselessly into the lighted room.

I stood there, close beside the partly opened door, blinking a little at the sudden glare of light. There was an appreciable interval before the details of the scene could register themselves on my mind.

What I saw was a large and plainly furnished room. Across one corner stood a rolltop desk, and from the top of this I caught the glimmer of a telephone transmitter. In the rear wall stood two old-fashioned, low-silled windows. Against this wall, and between these two windows, stood a black iron safe.

Before the open door of this safe, with her back turned to me, was the woman in the cream-colored gown. It was quite plain that she was not yet aware of my presence.

She had thrown her hat and cape aside, and was at the moment bending low over the dark maw of the opened safe, reaching into its recesses with one white and rounded arm. I stood there watching her, wondering what move would be most effective. I made no sound; of that I was certain. Yet some sixth sense must have warned her of my presence. For without rhyme or reason she suddenly stood erect, and swinging about in her tracks, confronted me.

Her face, which had been a little flushed from stooping, went white. She stared at me without speaking, her eyes wide with terrified wonder. I could see her lips slowly part, as the shock of what she beheld began to relax the jaw muscles along the olive-white cheek.

I stared back at her with a singularly disengaged mind. I felt, in fact, very much at my ease, very much the master of the situation. As an opponent, I could see, she would be more than mysterious. She would, in fact, be extremely interesting.

Her next move, however, threw a new complexion on the situation. For she unexpectedly let her hand dart out to the wall beside her, just behind the safe top. As she did so, I could hear the snap of a switch button; the next moment the light went out. It left the room in impenetrable darkness.

I stood there, unprepared for any offensive or defensive movement. Yet my enemy, I knew, was not idle. As I stood peering unavailingly through the gloom I could hear the quick thud of the safe door being shut. Then came the distinct sound of a heavy key being thrust and turned in a metal lock—the safe, obviously, was of the old-fashioned key-tumbler make —and then the noise of this key being withdrawn. Then came a click or two of shoe heels, a rustle of clothing, and a moment later the startlingly sharp shattering of a window-pane.

The woman had deliberately locked the safe and flung the key through the window! She had stolen a march on me. She had defeated me in the first movement of our encounter. My hesitation had been a mistake, a costly mistake.

"Be so good as to turn on that light!" I commanded.

Not a sound came from the darkness.

"Turn on that light," I cried. "Turn on that light or I'll fire! I'll rake every foot of this room!" And with that I gave a very significant double click to my cigarette case spring.

The light came on again, as suddenly as it went out. I discreetly pocketed my cigarette case.

The woman was standing beside the safe, as before, studying me with her wide and challenging eyes. But all this time not a word had come from her lips.

"Sit down!" I commanded, as authoritatively and yet as offhandedly as I could. It was then that she spoke for the first time.

"Thank you, I prefer to stand!" was her answer. She spoke calmly and distinctly and almost without accent. Yet I felt the voice was, in some way, a foreign one. Some vague substratum of the exotic in the carefully enunciated tones made me surmise that she was either an Austrian or a Gallicized Hungarian, or if not that, possibly a Polish woman.

"You will be here for some time," I hinted.

"And you?" she asked. I noticed an almost imperceptible shrug of her softly rounded shoulder. Rice powder, I imagined, somewhat increased its general effect of dead-whiteness.

"I'll be here until that safe is opened," was my retort.

"That long?" she mocked.

"That long!" I repeated, exasperated at her slow smile.

"Ah, then I shall sit down," she murmured as she

caught up the lace cape and adjusted it about her shoulders. "For, believe me, that will be a very, very long time, monsieur!"

I watched her carefully as she crossed the room and sank into a chair. She drew her cream-colored train across her knees with frugal and studious deliberateness.

It suddenly flashed over me, as I watched her, that her ruse might have been a double-barreled one. Obliquity such as hers would have unseen convolutions. It was not the key to the safe she had flung through the window! She would never have been so foolish. It was a trick, a subterfuge. She still had that key somewhere about her.

"And now what must I do?" she asked as she drew the cloak closer about her shoulders.

"You can hand me over the key to that safe," was my answer.

She could actually afford to laugh a little.

"That is quite impossible!"

"I want that key!" I insisted.

"*Pardon*, but is this not—dangerous?" she mildly inquired. "Is it not so, to break into houses at midnight, and rob women?"

It was my turn to laugh.

"Not a bit of it," I calmly assured her. "And you can judge if I'm frightened or not. There's something much more dangerous than *that!*"

She was again studying me with her puzzled and ever-narrowing eyes.

"Which means?" she prompted.

"Well, for example, the theft of government naval codes, among other things."

"You are very, very drunk," she retorted with her quietly scoffing smile. "Or you are insane, quite insane. May I not lock my jewels in my own safe? Ah, I begin to see—this is a trick, that you may steal from me!"

"Then why not send for the police?" I challenged, pointing toward the telephone.

A look of guile crept into her studious eyes.

"You will permit that?" she asked.

"I invite it," was my answer.

"Then I shall call for help."

"Only from the police."

"Yes; I shall call for help," she repeated, crossing to the telephone.

I leaned forward as she stood in front of it. I caught her bare arm in my left hand, just below the elbow. As I drew it backward it brought her body against mine, pinning her other arm down close against my side.

The thing was repugnant to me, but it was necessary. As I pinioned her there, writhing and panting, I deliberately thrust my right hand into the open bosom of her gown. I was dimly conscious of a faint aura of perfume, of a sense of warmth behind the soft and lace-fringed *corsage*. But it was the key itself that redeemed the rude assault and brought a gasp of relief to my lips—the huge brass key, as big as an egg beater.

"*Lâche!*" I heard gasped into my ear.

The woman staggered to a chair, white to the lips; and for a moment or two I thought she was going to faint.

"Oh, you *dog!*" she gasped, as she sat there panting and staring at me with blazing eyes. *"Cochon!* Cur!"

But I paid little heed to her, for the wine of victory was already coursing and tingling through my veins.

"You know, you can still call the police," I told her as I faced the heavy black door of the safe. One turn of the wrist, I knew, would bring me face to face with my prize.

A sudden movement from the woman, as I stooped over the safe door, brought me round in a flash. She was on her feet and half-way across the room before I could intercept her. And I was not any too gentle, I'm afraid, for the excitement of the thing had gone to my head.

That earlier assault at my hands seemed to have intimidated her. I could see actual terror in her eyes as I forced her back against the wall. She must have realized her helplessness. She stared up into my face, bewildered, desperate. There was something supple and panther-like about her, something alluring and yet disturbing. I could see what an effective weapon that sheer physical beauty of hers might be, once its tigerish menace had been fully sheathed.

"Wait!" she cried, catching at my arm. "If there is anything you want I will give it to you."

"There are several things I want," was my uncompromising answer.

"But why should you want them?" she asked, still clinging to my arm.

"It's my duty to take them," I replied, unconscious of any mendacity. "That's what I'm sent here for! That's why I've watched the man who gave you the packet!"

"What packet?"

"The packet you took in Madison Square an hour ago; the packet you locked in this safe! And if you like I'll tell you just what that packet is!"

"This is some mistake, some very sad mistake," she had the effrontery to declare. Her arm still clung to me. Her face was very close to mine as she went on. "I can explain everything, if you will only give me the time—everything! I can show you where you are wrong, and how you may suffer through a mistake like this!"

"We can talk all that over later," I promptly told her, for I was beginning to suspect that her object now was merely to kill time, to keep me there, in the hope of some chance discovery. I peered about the room, wondering what would be the quickest way out of my dilemma.

"What are you going to do?" she asked as she watched me shove a chair over against the wall, directly beside the safe.

"I'm going to seat you very comfortably in this very comfortable chair," I informed her, "and in this equally comfortable corner directly behind the safe door. And at the first trick or sign of trouble, I'm afraid I'm going to make a hole right through one of those nice white shoulders of yours!"

She sat down without being forced into the chair. Her alert and ever-moving eyes blazed luminously from her dead-white face. I knew, as I thrust the huge key in the safe lock and turned it back that she would have to be watched, and watched every moment of the time.

I had already counted on the safe door, as it swung back, making a barrier across the corner in which she sat. This I found to be the case. I took a second precaution, however, by shoving a tilted chair-back firmly in under the edge of the safe lock.

I knew, as I stooped before the open strong box, that she could make no sudden move without my being conscious of it. I also knew that time was precious. So I reached into the depths of the almost empty safe and lifted out a number of papers neatly held together by a rubber band.

These I placed on the safe top. Then I snapped off the band and examined the first document. On the back of it, neatly inscribed in French, was the eminently satisfactory legend: "Plans and Specifications; Bs. Lake Torpedo Company, Bridgeport." The next packet was a blue print of war projectiles, and on the back of it was written: "Model Tracings, through Jenner, from the Bliss & Company Works—18—Self-Projectors."

The third packet carried no inscription. But as I opened it I saw at a glance what it was. I knew in a moment that I held before me the governmental wheel-code of wireless signals in active service. It was the code that had been stolen from Lieutenant Palmer. The fourth and last paper, I found, was plainly the dummy which had been taken from the same officer that night in Madison Square. The case was complete. The chase was over and done.

"In the cash drawer, on the right, you will find more," quietly remarked the young woman watching me from the side of the safe.

"It's locked," I said, as I tugged at the drawer knob. I stood erect at her sudden laugh.

"Why not take everything?" she asked, with her scoffing smile.

And I saw no reason why I shouldn't; though a suspicion crossed my mind that this might be still another ruse to kill time. If such it was, I faced it at once, for I sent my boot heel promptly in against the wooden cash drawer, smashing it at one blow.

She had been mistaken, or had deliberately lied, for the drawer was empty. And I told her so, with considerable heat.

"Ah, we all make mistakes, I think," she murmured with her enigmatic shrug.

"What I want to know," I said as I banded the four papers together and thrust them down in my pocket, "is just how you got that first code from my young friend the lieutenant?"

She smiled again, a little wearily, as I swung the safe door shut and locked it. She did not rise from the chair. But as I stood confronting her, something in my attitude, apparently, struck her as distinctly humorous. For she broke into a sudden and deeper ripple of laughter. There was, however, something icy and chilling in it. Her eyes now seemed more veiled. They had lost their earlier look of terror. Her face seemed to have relaxed into softer contours.

"Would you like to know?" she said, lifting her face and looking with that older, half-mocking glance into my own. She was speaking slowly and deliberately, and I could see the slight shrug she gave to one panther-like shoulder. "Would *I* be so out of place in a ballroom? Ah, have not more things than hearts been lost when a man dances with a woman?"

"I see—you mean you stole it, at the Plaza?"

"Not at all, monsieur!" she murmured languidly back. Then she drew a deeper breath, and sat more rigid in her straight-back chair.

Something about her face, at that moment, puzzled me. It seemed to hold some latent note of confidence. The last trace of fear had fled from it. There was something strangely like triumph, muffled triumph, in it.

An arrow of apprehension shot through me, as I stooped peering into her shadowy eyes. It went through my entire body, sharp as an electric shock. It brought me wheeling suddenly about with my back to her and my face to the open room.

Then I understood. I saw through it all, in one tingling second. For there, facing me, stood the figure of a man in navy blue. It was the same figure that I had followed through the square.

But now there was nothing secretive or circuitous

about his attitude. It was quite the other way; for as
he stood there he held a blue-barreled revolver in his
hand. And I could see, only too plainly, that it was
leveled directly at me. The woman's ruse had worked.
I had wasted too much time. The confederate for
whom she was plainly waiting had come to her rescue.

The man took three or four steps farther into the
room. His revolver was still covering me. I heard a
little gasp from the woman as she rose to her feet.
I took it for a gasp of astonishment.

"You are going to kill him?" she cried in German.

"Haven't I got to?" asked back the man. He spoke
in English and without an accent. "Don't you understand *he's a safe-breaker?* He's broken into this
house? So! He's caught in the act—he's shot in self-
defense!"

I watched the gun barrel. The man's calm words
seemed to horrify the woman at my side. But there
was not a trace of pity in her voice as she spoke again.

"Wait!" she cried.

"Why?" asked the man with the gun.

"He has everything—the code, the plans, everything."

"Get them!" commanded the man.

"But he's armed," she explained.

A sneer crossed the other's impassive face.

"What if he is? Take his gun; take everything!"

The woman stepped close to where I stood. Again
I came within the radius of her perfumes. I could
even feel her breath on my face. Her movements
were more than ever panther-like as she went through

my pockets, one by one. Yet her flashing and dextrous hands found no revolver, for the simple reason there was none to find. This puzzled and worried her.

"Hurry up!" commanded the man covering me.

She stepped back and to one side, with the packet in her hand.

"Now close the windows!" ordered the man.

My heart went down in my boots as I heard the thud of that second closed window. There was going to be no waste of time.

I thought of catching the woman and holding her shield-like before me. I thought of the telephone; the light-switch; the window. But they all seemed hopeless.

The woman turned away, holding her hands over her ears. The incongruous thought flashed through me that two hours before I had called the city flat and stale; and here, within a rifle shot of my own door, I was standing face to face with death itself!

"Look here," I cried, much as I hated to, "what do you get out of this?"

"*You!*" said the man.

"And what good will that do?"

"It'll probably shut your mouth, for one thing!"

"But there are other mouths," I cried. "And I'm afraid they'll have a great deal to say."

"I'm ready for them!" was his answer.

I could see his arm raise a little, and straighten out as it raised. The gun barrel was nothing but a black "O" at the end of my line of vision. I felt my heart stop, for I surmised what the movement meant.

Then I laughed outright, aloud, and altogether foolishly and hysterically.

The strain had been too much for me, and the snap
of the release had come too suddenly, too unexpectedly. I could see the man with the gun blink perplexedly, for a second or two, and then I could see the
tightening of his thin-lipped mouth. But that was not
all I had seen.

For through the half-closed door I had caught sight
of the slowly raised iron rod, the very rod I had
wrenched from the outer hall window. I had seen its
descent at the moment I realized the finality in those
quickly tightening lips.

It struck the arm on its downward sweep. But it
was not in time to stop the discharge of the revolver.
The report thundered through the room as the bullet
ripped and splintered into the pine of the floor. At
the same moment the discharged firearm went spinning
across the room, and as the man who held it went down
with the blow, young Palmer himself swung toward
me through the drifting smoke.

As he did so, I turned to the woman with her
hands still pressed to her ears. With one fierce jerk
I tore the rubber-banded packet of papers from her
clutch.

"But the code?" gasped Palmer, as he tugged crazily
at the safe door.

I did not answer him, for a sudden movement from
the woman arrested my attention. She had stooped
and caught up the fallen revolver. The man in blue,

rolling over on his hip, was drawing a second gun from his pocket.

"Quick!" I called to Palmer as I swung him by the armpit and sent him catapulting out through the smoke to the open door. "Quick—and duck low!"

The shots came together as we stumbled against the stairhead.

"Quick!" I repeated, as I pulled him after me.

"But the code?" he cried.

"I've got it!" I called out to him as we went panting and plunging down through that three-tiered well of darkness to the street and liberty. "I've got it— I've got everything!"

CHAPTER IV

"SHALL I call the car, sir?" asked the solicitous-
eyed Benson, covertly watching me as I made
ready for the street.

"No," was my studiously detached retort, "I intend
to walk."

"Latreille was asking, sir, if you would care to have
the car laid up."

The significance of that bland suggestion did not
escape me. And it did not add to my serenity of mind.

"Just what business is that of Latreille's?" I demanded, with a prickle of irritation. My patient-eyed
old butler averted his glance, with a sigh which he
didn't seem quite able to control.

"And at the end of the month," I went on, "I intend to discharge that man. I'm tired of his insolences."

"Yes, sir," Benson softly yet fervently agreed.

My nerves were on edge, I knew, but I wasn't looking for sympathy from my hired help. And when I
swung the door shut behind me I am afraid it was a
movement far from noiseless.

I was glad to get out into the open, glad to get
away from old Benson's commiserative eyes, and have
space about me, and cool air to breathe, and uncounted
miles of pavement to weary my legs on.

I noticed, as I turned into Fifth Avenue, that the

moving finger of light on the Metropolitan clock-dial pointed to an hour past midnight. So I veered about that delta of idleness, where the noontide turbulence of Broadway empties its driftwood into the quietness of the square, and pursued my way up the avenue.

No one can claim to know New York who does not know its avenues in those mystical small hours that fall between the revolving street-sweeper and the robin-call of the first morning paper. Fifth Avenue, above all her sisters, then lies as though tranquillized by Death, as calm as the Coliseum under its Italian moonlight. She seems, under the stars, both medievalized and spiritualized. She speaks then in an intimate whisper foreign to her by day, veiling her earthlier loquacity in a dreaming wonder, softening and sweetening like a woman awaiting her lover. The great steel shafts enclosed in their white marble become turrets crowned with mystery. And the street-floor itself, as clean and polished as a ballroom, seems to undulate off into outer kingdoms of romance. An occasional lonely motor-car, dipping up its gentle slopes like a ship treading a narrow sea-lane buoyed with pearls as huge as pumpkins, only accentuates the midnight solitude.

So up this dustless and odorless and transmuted avenue I wandered, as passively as a policeman on his beat, asking of the quietness when and how I might capture that crown of weariness known as sleep.

I wandered on, mocked at by a thousand drawn blinds, taunted by a thousand somnolently closed doors. I felt, in that city of rest, as homeless as a prairie wolf. The very smugness of those veiled and self-satisfied house-fronts began to get on my nerves. The very taciturnity of the great silent hostelries irritated me; everything about them seemed so eloquent of an interregnum of rest, of relaxed tension, of invisible reservoirs of life being softly and secretly filled.

Yet as I came to the open width of the Plaza, and saw the wooded gloom of Central Park before me, I experienced an even stronger feeling of disquiet. There seemed something repugnant in its autumnal solitudes. That vague *agoraphobia* peculiar to the neurasthenic made me long for the contiguity of my own kind, however unconscious of me and my wandering they might remain. I found myself, almost without thought, veering off eastward into one of the city's side-streets.

Yet along this lateral valley of quietness I wandered as disconsolately as before. What impressed me now was the monotony of the house-fronts which shouldered together, block by block. Each front seemed of the same Indiana limestone, of the same dull gray, as though, indeed, the whole district were a quarry checker-boarded by eroding cross-currents out of the self-same rock. Each tier of windows seemed backed by the same blinds, each street-step barricaded by the same door. I stopped and looked up, wondering if behind those neutral-tinted walls and blinds were lives as bald and monotonous as the materials that screened them. I wondered if an environment so without distinction would not actually evolve a type equally destitute of individuality.

I turned where I stood, and was about to pass diffidently on, when one of the most unexpected things that can come to a man at midnight happened to me.

Out of a clear sky, without a note or movement of warning, there suddenly fell at my feet a heavy bundle.

Where it came from I had no means of telling. The house above me was as silent and dark as a tomb. The street was as empty as a church. Had the thing been a meteor out of a star-lit sky, or a wildcat leaping from a tree-branch, it could not have startled me more.

I stood looking at it, in wonder, as it lay beside the very area-railing on which my hand had rested. Then I stepped back and leaned in over this railing, more clearly to inspect the mystery. Whatever it was, it had fallen with amazingly little noise. There was no open window to explain its source. There had been no wind to blow it from an upper-story sill. There was no movement to show that its loss had been a thing of ponderable import. Yet there it lay, a mystery which only the deep hours of the night, when the more solemnly imaginative faculties come into play, could keep from being ridiculous.

I stood there for several minutes blinking down at it, as though it were a furred beast skulking in a corner. Then I essayed a movement which, if not above the commonplace, was equally related to common sense. I stepped in through the railing and picked up the parcel. I turned it over several times. Then I sat down on the stone steps and deliberately untied the heavy cord that baled it together.

I now saw why I had thought of that falling bundle

as an animal's leap. It was completely wrapped in what I took to be a Russian-squirrel motor-coat. The tightly tied fur had padded the parcel's fall.

Enclosed in that silk-lined garment I found a smaller bundle, swathed about with several lengths of what seemed to be Irish point lace. Inside this again were other fragments of lacework. Through these I thrust my exploring fingers with all the alert curiosity of a child investigating a Christmas-tree cornucopia.

There, in the heart of the parcel, I found a collection which rather startled me. The first thing I examined was a chamois bag filled with women's rings, a dozen or more of them, of all kinds. I next drew out a Florentine *repoussé* hand-bag set with turquoises and seed-pearls, and then a moonstone necklace, plainly of antique Roman workmanship. Next came a black and white Egyptian scarab, and then, of all things, a snuff-box. It was oval and of gold, enameled *en plein* with a pastoral scene swarming with plump pink Cupids. Even in that uncertain light it required no second glance to assure me that I was looking down at a rare and beautiful specimen of Louis XV jeweler's art. Then came a small photograph in an oval gold frame. The remainder of the strange collection was made up of odds and ends of jewelry and a leather-covered traveling-clock stamped with gilt initials.

I did not take the time to look more closely over this odd assortment of valuables, for it now seemed clear that I had stumbled on something as disturbing as it was unexpected. The only explanation of an otherwise inexplicable situation was that a house-breaker was busily operating somewhere behind the gray-stone wall which I faced.

The house behind that wall seemed to take on no new color at this discovery. Its inherent sobriety, its very rectangularity of outline, appeared a contradiction of any claim that it might be harboring a figure either picturesque or picaresque. It was no old mansion stained with time, dark with memories and tears. It carried no atmosphere of romance, no suggestion of old and great adventures, of stately ways and noble idlers, of intrigues and unremembered loves and hates, of silence and gloom touched with the deeper eloquence of unrecorded history. It was nothing more than a new and narrow and extremely modern house, in the very heart of a modern New York, simple in line and as obvious in architecture as the warehouses along an old-world water-front, as bare of heart as it was bald of face, a symbol of shrill materialities, of the day of utility. It could no more have been a harbor for romance, I told myself, than the stone curb in front of it could be translated into a mountain-precipice threaded with brigand-paths.

Yet I went slowly up those unwelcoming stone steps with the bundle under my arm. The thief at work inside the house, I assumed, had simply tied the heavier part of his loot together and dropped it from a quietly opened window, to be gathered as quickly up, once he had effected his escape to the street. The sudden afterthought that it might have been dropped for a confederate caused me to look carefully eastward and then as carefully westward. But not a sign of life met my gaze. My figure standing puzzled before that unknown door was the only figure in the street.

Heaven only knows what prompted me to reach out and try that door. It was, I suppose, little more than the habit of a lifetime, the almost unconscious habit of turning a knob when one finds oneself confronted by a door that is closed. The thing that sent a little thrill of excitement through my body was that the knob turned in my hand, that the door itself stood unlocked.

I stooped down and examined this lock as best I could in the uncertain light. I even ran a caressing finger along the edge of the door. There was no evidence that it had been jimmied open, just as there was nothing to show that the lock itself did not stand intact and uninjured. A second test of the knob, however, showed me that the door was unmistakably open.

My obvious course, at such a time, would have been to wait for a patrolman or to slip quietly away and send word in to police headquarters. But, as I have already said, no man is wholly sane after midnight. Subliminal faculties, ancestral perversions, dormant and wayward tendencies, all come to the surface, emerging like rats about a sleeping mansion. And crowning these, again, was my own neurasthenic craving for activity, my hunger for the narcotizing influence of excitement.

And it has its zest of novelty, this stepping into an unknown and unlighted house at three o'clock in the morning. That novelty takes on a razor-edge when you have fairly good evidence that some one who has no business there has already preceded you into that house.

So as I stepped inside and quietly closed the door after me, I moved forward with the utmost care. Some precautionary sixth sense told me the place was not unoccupied. Yet the darkness that surrounded me was absolute. Not a sound or movement came to my ears as I stood there listening, minute after minute. So I crept deeper into the gloom.

My knowledge of that stereotyped class of residence provided me with a very fair idea of where the stairway ought to stand. Yet it took much prodding and groping and pawing about before I came to it. One flicker of a match, I knew, would have revealed the whole thing to me. But to strike a light, under the circumstances, would be both foolish and dangerous. No house dog, I felt, would interrupt my progress; the mere remembrance of the intruder above me set my mind at rest on this point.

I came to a stop at the head of the first stairway, puzzled by the completeness of the quiet which encompassed me. I directed my attention to each quarter of the compass, point by point.

But I might have been locked and sealed in a cistern, so complete was the silence, so opaque was the blackness. Yet I felt that nothing was to be gained by staying where I was.

So I groped and shuffled my way onward, rounding the banister and advancing step by step up the second stairway. This, I noticed, was both narrower and steeper than the first. I was also not unconscious of the fact that it was leading me into a zone of greater danger, for the floor I was approaching, I knew, would be the sleeping floor.

I was half-way up the stairway when something undefined brought me to a sudden stop. Some nocturnal adeptness of instinct warned me of an imminent presence, of a menace that had not yet disclosed itself.

Once more I came to a stop, straining my eyes through the darkness. Nothing whatever was to be seen. Along the floor of the hallway just above my head, however, passed a small but unmistakable sound. It was the soft *frou-frou* of a skirt, a skirt of silk or satin, faintly rustling as a woman walked the full length of the hall. I had just made a mental register of the deduction that this woman was dressed in street-clothes, and was, accordingly, an intruder from outside, rather than a sleeper suddenly awakened, when a vague suffusion of light filled the space above me and was as quickly quenched again.

I knew the moment I heard the soft thud of wood closing against wood, that a door had been quietly opened and as quietly closed again. The room into which that door led must have been faintly lighted, for it was the flowering of this refracted light that had caught my attention.

I went silently up the stairs, step by step, listening every now and then as I advanced. Once I reached the floor level I kept close to the wall, feeling my way along until I came to the door I wanted.

There was no way whatever of determining what stood on the other side of that door, without opening it. I knew what risks I ran in attempting any such movement. But I decided it was worth the risk.

Now, if a door is opened slowly, if every quarter-inch of movement is measured and guarded, it can, as a rule, be done noiselessly. I felt quite sure there was not one distinguishable sound as I cautiously turned that bronze knob and even more cautiously worked back the door, inch by inch.

I came to a stop when it stood a little more than a 'toot from the jamb. I did not, at first, attempt to sidle in through the aperture; that would have been needlessly reckless. I stood there waiting, anticipating the effect the door-movement might have had on any occupant of the room, had it been seen.

While I waited I also studied that portion of the chamber which fell within my line of vision. I saw enough to convince me that the room was a bedroom. I could also make out that it was large, and from the rose-pink of its walls to the ivory-white of its furnishings it stood distinctly feminine in its note.

There was, I felt, a natural limit to that period of experimental inaction. The silence lengthened. The crisis of tedium approached, arrived, and passed. Audaciousness reconquered me, and I actually advanced a little into the room. Steadying myself with one hand on the door-frame, I thrust my body through the narrow aperture until the whole four walls lay subject to my line of vision.

The first thing I noticed was a green-shaded electric lamp burning on what seemed to be a boudoir writing-table. It left the rest of the room in little more than twilight. But after the utter darkness through which I had groped, this faint illumination was quite adequate for my purposes.

I let my gaze pivot about the room, point by point. Then, if I did not gasp, there was at least a sudden and involuntary cessation of breathing, for standing beside a second door at the farther end of the room was a woman dressed in black. On her head was a black hat, round which a veil was tightly wound, the front of it apparently thrust up hurriedly from her face. But what startled me was the fact that both her attitude and her position seemed such an exact duplication of my own.

With one hand, I noticed, she clung to the frame of the door. With the other hand she held back a heavy portière, which hung across this frame. I could see the white half-oval of her intent face as she stood there. Something about her suggested not the spying intruder so much as the secret listener. Her attention seemed directed toward some object which her eyes were not seeing. It appeared as though she stood waiting to overhear a sound which meant much to her.

As I peered past her through the dim light I could catch a faint glimmer of green and white marble, with here and there the high-lights reflected from polished nickel. I knew then that the room into which she was peering was a bathroom, and this bathroom, I concluded, opened on a second sleeping-chamber which held the *raison d'être* of her motionless apprehension.

I directed my glance once more at the woman. Something almost penitential in her attitude brought the sudden thought to my mind that she had committed a crime at the mere memory of which she was already morally stricken. Unexpected discovery, I began to suspect, had driven her to an extreme which she was already beginning to regret. There was, in fact, something so pregnant and portentous in that unchanging attitude of hers that I began to feel it would be a mean surrender on my part to evade the issue in which I had already risked so much. So I moved silently into the room, crossing it without a sound, until I dropped into a high-backed *fauteuil* upholstered in embossed and pale-green leather.

I sat there studying her, unaccountably at my ease, fortified by the knowledge that I was the observer of an illicit intrusion and that my own presence, if impertinent, might at least be easily explained. I saw her sigh deeply and audibly, and then gently close the door, dropping the curtain as she turned slowly away.

I watched her as she crossed to the dresser, looked over the toilet articles on it, and then turned away. She next skirted a heavy cheval-mirror, crossed to the writing-table with her quick yet quietly restless movements, and from this table caught up what seemed to be a metal paper-knife. She moved on to an ivory and mother-of-pearl desk, which, apparently, she already knew to be locked. For after one short glance toward the curtained door again, she inserted the edge of the knife in a crack of this desk and slowly pried on the lock-bar that held it shut.

I saw her second apprehensive glance toward the curtained door as the lock sprung with a snap. She sank into a chair before it, breathing quickly, obviously waiting a minute or two to make sure she had not been overheard. Then with quick and dextrous fingers she rummaged through the desk. Just what she swept from one of the drawers into her open hand-bag I could not distinguish. But I plainly saw the package of letters which she took up in her hand, turned over and over, then carefully and quietly secreted within the bosom of her dress. She looked deeper into the desk, examined an additional paper or two which appeared not to interest her, and slowly swung back the cover.

Then she slowly rose to her feet, standing beside the desk. She let her gaze, as she stood there, wander about the room. I could distinctly see the look on her face, the hungry and unhappy look of unsatisfied greed. I sat motionless, waiting for that expression to change. I knew that it must change, for it would be but a moment or two before she caught sight of me. But I had seen enough. I felt sure of my position—in fact, I found a wayward relish in it, an almost enjoyable anticipation of the shock which I knew the discovery of my presence there would bring to her. I even exulted a little in that impending dramatic crisis, rejoicing in the slowness with which the inevitable yet epochal moment was approaching.

Her eyes must have dwelt on my figure for several seconds before her mind became convinced of my actual presence there. She did not scream, as I thought she was about to do when I saw one terrified hand go up to her partly open lips. Beyond that single hand-movement there was no motion whatever from her. She simply stood there, white-faced and speechless, staring at me out of wide and vacant eyes.

"Good evening—or, rather, good morning!" I said, with all the calmness at my command.

For one brief second she glanced back toward the curtained door, as though behind it lay a sleeper my words might awaken. Then she stared at me again.

She did not speak. She did not even move. The intent and staring face, white as a half-moon in a misty sky, seemed floating in space. The faint light of the room swallowed up the lines of her black-clad figure, enisling the face in the unbroken gloom of a Rembrandt-like background, making it stand out as though it were luminous.

It was a face well worth studying. What first struck me was its pallor. Across this the arched, faintly interrogative eyebrows gave it a false air of delicacy. The eyes themselves had a spacious clarity which warned me my enemy would not be without a capable enough mind, once she regained possession of her wits. Her mouth, no longer distorted by terror, was the nervous, full-lipped mouth of a once ardent spirit touched with rebellion.

She was, I could see, no every-day thief of the streets, no ordinary offender satisfied with mean and petty offenses. There would, I told myself, always be a largeness about her wrong-doing, a sinister bril-liance in her illicit pursuits. And even while I decided this, I was forced to admit that it was not precisely terror I was beholding on her face. It seemed to merge into something more like a sense of shame, the same speechless horror which I might have met with had I intruded on her bodily nakedness. I could see that she was even beginning to resent my stare of curiosity. Then, for the first time, she spoke.

"Who are you?" she asked. Her voice was low; in it was the quaver of the frightened woman resolutely steeling herself to courage.

"That's a question you're first going to answer for me," was my calmly deliberate retort.

"What are you doing here?" she demanded, still confronting me from the same spot. I remembered the bundle of loot which I had dropped just outside the door.

"I can answer that more easily than you can," I replied, with a slight head-movement toward the broken desk-top.

Once more her glance went back to the curtained door. Then she studied me from head to foot, each sartorial detail and accessory of clothing, hat, gloves, and shoes, as though each must figure in the resolution of some final judgment.

"What do you want?" she demanded.

I preferred to leave that question unanswered.

"What do you intend to do?" she demanded, once more searching my face.

I resented the way in which she anticipated my own questions. I could see, from the first, that she was going to be an extraordinarily adept and circuitous person to handle. I warned myself that I would have to be ready for every trick and turn.

"What do you suppose I'm going to do?" I equivocated, looking for some betraying word to put me on firmer ground. I could see that she was slowly regaining her self-possession.

"You have no right in this house," she had the brazenness to say to me.

"Have *you?*" I quickly retorted. She was silent for a second or two.

"No," she admitted, much as she would like to have claimed the contrary.

"Of course not! And I imagine you realize what your presence here implies, just as what your discovery here entails?"

"Yes," she admitted.

"And I think you have the intelligence to understand that I'm here for motives somewhat more disinterested than your own?"

"What are they?" she demanded, letting her combative eyes meet mine.

"That," I calmly replied, "can wait until you've explained yourself."

"I've nothing to explain."

There was a newer note in her voice again—one of stubbornness. I could see that the calmness with which I pretended to regard the whole affair was a source of bewilderment to her.

"You've *got* to explain," was my equally obdurate retort.

Her next pose was one of frigidity.

"You are quite mistaken. We have nothing whatever to do with each other."

"Oh, yes we have. And I'm going to prove it."

"How?"

"By putting an end to this play-acting."

"That sounds like a threat."

"It was meant for one."

"What right have you to threaten me?"

She looked about as she spoke, almost wearily. Then she sank into the chair that stood beside the ravaged writing-desk. It was all diverting enough, but I was beginning to lose patience with her.

"I'm tired of all this side-stepping," I told her. An answering look of anger flashed from her eyes.

"I object to your presence here," she had the effrontery to exclaim.

"You mean, I suppose, that I'm rather interfering with your night's operations?"

"Those operations," she answered in a fluttering dignity, "are my own affairs."

"Of course they are!" I scoffed. "They *have* to be! But you should have kept them your own affairs. When you drop a bundle of swag out of a window you shouldn't come so perilously near to knocking a man's hat off."

"A bundle of swag?" she echoed, with such a precise imitation of wonder that I could plainly see she was going to be the astutest of liars.

"The loot you intended carrying off," I calmly explained. "The stuff you dropped down beside the house-step, to be ready for your getaway."

"My what?"

"Your escape. And it was rather clever."

"I dropped nothing," she protested, with a fine pretense of bewilderment on her face.

"Nor let it roll quietly off a front window-ledge?" I suggested.

"I was near no window—it would be impossible for me to open a window," she protested. Her words in themselves were a confession.

"You seem to know this house pretty well," I remarked.

"*I ought to—it's my own,*" was her quick retort.

"It's your own?" I repeated, amazed at the woman's mendacity.

"It *was* my own," she corrected.

I peered quickly about the room. It held three doors, one behind the woman, opening into the bathroom, a second opening into the hallway, and a third to the rear, which plainly opened into a clothes-closet. There had been too much of this useless and foolish argument.

"Since your claim to proprietorship is so strong," I said as I crossed to the hall door, and, after locking it, pocketed the key, "there are certain features of it I want you to explain to me."

"What do you mean?" she asked, once more on her feet.

"I want to know," I said, moving toward the curtained door beside her, "just who or what is in that front room?"

The look of terror came back to her white face.

She even stood with her back against the door, as though to keep me from opening it, making an instinctive gesture for silence as I stood facing her.

"I'm going to find out what is in that room," I proclaimed, unmoved by the agony I saw written on her guilty face.

"Oh, believe me," she said, in supplicatory tones, a little above a whisper, "it will do no good. It will only make you sorry you interfered in this."

"But you've made it my duty to interfere."

"No; no; you're only blundering into something where you can do no good, where you have no right."

"Then I intend to blunder into that room!" And I tore the portière from her grasp and flung it to one side.

"Wait," she whispered, white-faced and panting close beside me. "I'll tell you everything. I'll explain it—everything."

The tragic solemnity of that low-toned relinquishment brought me up short. It was my turn to be bewildered by an opponent I could not understand.

"Sit down," she said, with a weary and almost imperious movement of the hand as she advanced into the room and again sank into the chair beside the writing-desk.

"Now what is it you want to know?" she asked, with only too obvious equivocation. Her trick to gain time exasperated me.

"Don't quibble and temporize that way," I cried. "Say what you've got to, and say it quick."

She directed at me a look which I resented, a look

of scorn, of superiority, of resignation in the face of brutalities which I should never have subjected her to. Yet, when she spoke again her voice was so calm as to seem almost colorless.

"I said this was my home—and it's true. This was once my room. Several weeks ago I left it."

"Why?" I inquired, resenting the pause which was plainly giving her a chance to phrase ahead of her words.

"I quarreled with my husband. I went away. I was angry. I—I— There's no use explaining what it was about."

"You've got to explain what it was about," I insisted.

"You couldn't possibly understand. It's impossible to explain," she went quietly on. "I discharged a servant who was not honest. Then he tried to blackmail me. He lied about me. I had been foolish, indiscreet, anything you care to call it. But the lie he told was awful, unbelievable. That my husband should ask me to disprove it was more than I could endure. We quarreled, miserably, hopelessly. I went away. I felt it would be humiliating to stay under the same roof with him."

"Wait," I interposed, knowing the weak link was sure to present itself in time. "Where is your husband now?"

She glanced toward the curtained door.

"He's in that room asleep," she quietly replied.

"And knowing him to be asleep you came to clean out the house?" I prompted.

"No," she answered without anger. "But when service was begun for an interlocutory decree I knew I could never come back openly. There were certain things of my own I wanted very much."

"And just how did you get into the house?"

"The one servant I could trust agreed to throw off the latch after midnight, to leave the door unlocked for me when I knew I would never be seen."

"Then why couldn't that trusted servant have secured the things, these things you came after? Without all this foolish risk of your forcing your way into a house at midnight?"

Her head drooped a little.

"I wanted to see my husband," was the quiet-toned response. Just how, she did not explain. I had to admit to myself that it was very good acting. But it was not quite convincing; and the case against her was too palpably clear.

"This is a fine cock-and-bull story," I calmly declared. "But just how are you going to make me believe it?"

"You don't have to believe it," was her impassive answer. "I'm only telling you what you demanded to know."

"To know, yes—but how am I to know?"

She raised her hand with a movement of listless resignation.

"If you go to the top drawer of that dresser you will see my photograph in a silver frame next to one of my husband. That will show you at a glance."

For just a moment it flashed through me as I

crossed the room that this might be a move to give her time for some attempted escape. But I felt, on second thought, that I was master enough of the situation to run the risk. And here, at least, was a point to which she could be most definitely pinned down.

"The other drawer," she murmured as my hand closed on the fragile ivory-tinted knob. I moved on to the second drawer and opened it. I had thrust an interrogative finger down into its haphazard clutter of knick-knacks, apparently thrown together by a hurried and careless hand, when from the other end of the room came a quick movement which seemed to curdle the blood in my veins. It brought me wheeling about, with a jump that was both grotesque and galvanic.

I was just in time to see the figure that darted out through the suddenly opened door of the clothes-closet.

I found myself confronted by a man, a thin-lipped, heavy-jawed man of about thirty-five, with black pin-point pupils to his eyes. He wore a small-rimmed derby hat and a double-breasted coat of blue cheviot. But it was not his clothes that especially interested me. What caught and held my attention was the ugly, short-barreled revolver which was gripped in the fingers of his right hand. This revolver, I noticed, was unmistakably directed at me as he advanced into the room. I could not decide which was uglier, the blue-metaled gun or the face of the man behind it.

"Get back against that wall," he commanded. "Then throw up your hands. Get 'em up quick!"

I had allowed her to trap me after all! I had even

let myself half-believe that pleasant myth of the slumbering husband in the next room. And all the while she was guarding this unsavory-looking confederate who, ten to one, had been slinking about and working his way into a wall-safe even while I was wasting time with diverting but costly talk.

And with that gun-barrel blinking at me I had no choice in the matter—I was compelled to assume the impotent and undignified attitude of a man supplicating the unanswering heavens. The woman turned and contemplated the newcomer, contemplated him with a fine pretense of surprise.

"*Hobbs,*" she cried, "*how did you get here?*"

"You shut up!" he retorted over his shoulder.

"What are you doing in this house?" she repeated, with a sustained show of amazement.

"Oh, I'll get round to *you*, all right, all right," was his second rejoinder.

Hobbs' left hand, in the meanwhile, had lifted my watch from its pocket and with one quick jerk tore watch and chain away from its waistcoat anchorage.

"You're a sweet pair, you two!" I ejaculated, for that watch was rather a decent one and I hated to see it ill-treated.

"Shut up!" said Hobbs, as his hand went down in my breast-pocket in search of a wallet. I knew, with that gun-barrel pressed close against my body, that it would be nothing short of suicidal to try to have it out with him then and there. I had to submit to that odious pawing and prodding about my body. But if my turn ever came, I told myself, it would be a sorry day for Hobbs—and an equally sorry one for that smooth-tongued confederate of his.

"You're a sweet pair!" I repeated, hot to the bone, as that insolent hand went down into still another pocket.

But it did not stay there. I saw a sudden change creep over the man's face. He looked up with a quick and bird-like side-movement of the head. It was not until he wheeled about that I realized the reason of the movement.

The actual motive behind the thing I could not fathom. The real significance of the tableau was beyond my reach. But as I looked up I saw that the woman had crept noiselessly to the hall door, and with a sudden movement had thrust out her hand and tried to open this door. But as I had already locked it, and still carried the key in my pocket, her effort was a useless one. Just why it should enrage her confederate was more than I could understand. He ignored me for the time being, crossing the room at a run and flinging the woman in black away from the door-knob. She, in turn, was making a pretense to resent that assault. Why she should do this I did not wait to ask. I saw my chance and took it.

Half-a-dozen quick steps brought me to the bathroom door, one turn of the knob threw it open, and another step put me through it and brought the door closed after me. There was, I found, a key in the lock. Another second of time saw that key turned. A quick pad or two about the cool marble wall brought my hand in contact with the light-switch.

The moment the light came on I darted to the inner door and tried it. But this, to my dismay, was locked, although I could catch sight of no key in it. I ran back for the key of the first door, tried it, and found it useless. At any moment, I knew, a shot might come splintering through those thin panels. And at any moment, should they decide on that move, the two of them might have their own door into the hallway forced open and be scampering for the street.

I reached over and wrenched a nickeled towel-bar away from the wall opposite me. One end of this I deliberately jabbed into the white-leaded wood between the frame and the jam of the second door. I was about to pry with all my force, when the sound of yet another voice came from the room before me. It was a disturbed yet sleepy voice, muffled, apparently, by a second portière hung on the outside of the second door.

"Is that you, Simmonds?" demanded this voice.

I continued to pry, for I felt like a rat in a corner, in that bald little bathroom, and I wanted space about me, even though that meant fresh danger. The mysteries were now more than I could decipher. I no longer gave thought to them. The first thing I wanted was liberation, escape. But my rod-end bent under the pressure to which I subjected it, and I had to reverse it and try for a fresh hold.

I could hear, as I did so, the sudden sound of feet crossing a floor, the click of a light-switch, and then the rattle of the portière-rings on the rod above the door at which I stood.

"Who locked this door?" demanded the startled voice on the other side. For answer, I threw my weight on the rod and forced the lock. I still kept the metal rod in my hand, for a possible weapon, as I half-stumbled out into the larger room.

Before me I saw a man in pajamas. He was blond and big and his hair was rumpled—that was all I knew about him, beyond the fact that his pajamas were a rather foolish tint of baby-blue. We stood there, for a second or two, staring at each other. We were each plainly afraid of the other, just as we were each a little reassured, I imagine, at the sight of the other.

"For the love of God," he gasped, wide-eyed, "who are you?"

"Quick," I cried, "is this your house?"

"Of course it's my house," he cried back, retreating as I advanced. He suddenly side-stepped and planted his thumb on a call-bell.

"Good!" I said. "Get your servants here quick. We'll need them!"

"Who'll need them? What's wrong? What's up?"

"I've got two burglars locked in that room."

"Burglars?"

"Yes, and they'll have a nice haul if they get away. Have you got a revolver?"

"Yes," he answered, jerking open a drawer. I saw that his firearm was an automatic.

"Where's the telephone?" I demanded, crossing the room to the door that opened into the hall.

"On the floor below," he answered. He pulled on

a brown blanket dressing-gown, drawing the girdle tight at the waist.

"You can get to it quicker than I can," I told him. "Give me the gun, and throw on the lights as you go down. Then get the police here as soon as you can."

"What'll you do?" he demanded.

"I'll guard the door," I answered as I all but pushed him into that hallway. Then I swung-to the door after me, and locked it from the outside. "Quick, the gun," I said. There was no fear on his face now, yet it was natural enough that he should hesitate.

"What are you? An officer?"

There was no time for an explanation.

"Plain-clothes man," was my glib enough answer, as I caught the pistol from his hand. He switched on the hall lights.

He was half-way to the top of the stairs when a woman's scream, high pitched and horrible, echoed out of the room where I had the two confederates trapped. It was repeated, shrill and sharp. The face of the big blond man went as white as chalk.

"*Who is that?*" he demanded, with staring eyes, facing the locked door of the second room. Then he backed off from the door.

I flung a cry of warning at him, but it did not stop his charge. His great shoulder went against the paneled wood like a battering-ram. Under the weight of that huge body the entire frame-facing gave way; he went lunging and staggering from sight into the dimly-lit inner room.

I waited there, with my gun at half-arm, feeling the room would suddenly erupt its two prisoners. Then, at a cry from the man, I stepped quickly in after him.

I had fortified myself for the unexpected, but the strangeness of the scene took my breath away. For there I beheld the man called Hobbs engaged in the absurd and extraordinary and altogether brutal occupation of trying to beat in his confederate's head with the butt of his heavy revolver. He must have struck her more than once, even before the man in the hairy brown dressing-gown and the blue pajamas could leap for him and catch the uplifted arm as it was about to strike again.

The woman, protected by her hat and veil and a great mass of thick hair, still showed no signs of collapse. But the moment she was free she sat back, white and panting, in the same high-armed *fauteuil* which I myself had occupied a half-hour before. I made a leap for her companion's fallen revolver, before she could get it, though I noticed that she now seemed indifferent to both the loss of it and the outcome of the struggle which was taking place in the center of that pink and white abode of femininity.

And as I kept one eye on the woman and one on the gun in my hand, I, too, caught fleeting glimpses of that strange struggle. It seemed more like a combat between wildcats than a fight between two human beings. It took place on the floor, for neither man was any longer on his feet, and it wavered from one side of the room to the other, leaving a swath of destruction where it went. A table went over, a fragile-limbed chair was crushed, the great cheval-glass was shattered, the writing-desk collapsed with a leg snapped off, a shower of toilet articles littered the rugs, a reading-lamp was overturned and went the way of the other things. But still the fight went on.

I no longer thought of the woman. All my attention went to the two men struggling and panting about the floor. The fury of the man in the shaggy and bear-like dressing-gown was more than I could understand. The madness of his onslaught seemed incomprehensible. This, I felt, was the way a tigress might fight for her brood, the way a cave-man might battle for his threatened mate. Nor did that fight end until the big blond form towered triumphant above the darker clad figure.

Then I looked back at the woman, startled by her stillness through it all. She was leaning forward, white, intent, with parted lips. In her eyes I seemed to see uneasiness and solicitude and desolation, but above them all slowly flowered a newer look, a look of vague exultation as she gazed from the defeated man gasping and choking for breath to the broad back of the shaggy-haired dressing-gown.

I had no chance to dwell on the puzzle of this, for the man enveloped in the shaggy-haired garment was calling out to me.

"Tie him up," he called. "Take the curtain-cords—but tie him tight!"

"Do you know this man?" something in his tone

prompted me to ask, as I struggled with the heavy silk curtain-cords.

"It's Hobbs."

"I know that, but who's Hobbs?"

"A servant dismissed a month ago," was the other's answer.

"Then possibly you know the woman?" I asked, looking up.

"Yes, possibly I know the woman," he repeated, standing before her and staring into her white and desolate face. It took me a moment or two to finish my task of trussing the wrists of the sullen and sodden Hobbs. When I looked up the woman was on her feet, several steps nearer the door.

"Watch that woman!" I cried. "She's got a load of your loot on her!"

My words seemed merely to puzzle him. There was no answering alarm on his face.

"What do you mean?" he inquired. He seemed almost to resent my effort in his behalf. The woman's stare, too, seemed able to throw him into something approaching a comatose state, leaving him pale and helpless, as though her eye had the gift of some hypnotic power. It angered me to think that some mere accidental outward husk of respectability could make things so easy for her. Her very air of false refinement, I felt, would always render her viciousness double-edged in its danger.

"Search her!" I cried. "See what she's got under her waist there!"

He turned his back on me, deliberately, as though

resenting my determination to dog him into an act that was distasteful to him.

"What have you there?" he asked her, without advancing any closer.

There was utter silence for a moment or two.

"Your letters," she at last answered, scarcely above a whisper.

"What are they doing there?" he asked.

"I wanted them," was all she said.

"Why should you want my letters?" was his next question.

She did not answer it. The man in the dressing-gown turned and pointed to the inert figure of Hobbs.

"What about him? How did *he* get here?"

"He must have followed me in from the street when the door was unlocked. Or he may have come in before I did, and kept in hiding somewhere."

"Who left the door unlocked?"

"Simmonds."

"Why?"

"Because he could trust me!"

There was a muffled barb in this retort, a barb which I could not understand. I could see, however, that it had its effect on the other man. He stared at the woman with sudden altered mien, with a foolish drop of the jaw which elongated his face and widened his eyes at the same moment. Then he wheeled on the sullen Hobbs.

"*Hobbs, you lied about her!*" he cried, like a blind man at last facing the light.

He had his hand on the bound and helpless burglar's throat.

"Tell me the truth, or by the living God, I'll kill you! You lied about her?"

"About what?" temporized Hobbs.

"You know what!"

Hobbs, I noticed, was doing his best to shrink back from the throttling fingers.

"It wasn't my fault!" he equivocated.

"But you lied?"

Hobbs did not answer, in words. But the man in the dressing-gown knew the answer, apparently, before he let the inert figure fall away from his grasp. He turned, in a daze, back to the waiting and watching woman, the white-faced woman with her soul in her eyes. His face seemed humbled, suddenly aged with some graying blight of futile contrition.

The two staring figures appeared to sway and waver toward each other. Before I could understand quite what it all meant the man had raised his arms and the woman had crept into them.

"Oh, Jim, I've been such a fool!" I heard her wail. And I could see that she was going to cry.

I knew, too, that that midnight of blunders had left me nothing to be proud of, that I had been an idiot from the first—and to make that idiocy worse, I was now an intruder.

"I'll slip down and look after that phoning," I mumbled, so abashed and humiliated that as I groped wearily out through the door I stumbled over the Russian-squirrel bundle which I had placed there with

my own hands. It was not until I reached the street
that I realized, with a gulp of relief, how yet another
night of threatening misery had been dissembled and
lost in action, very much as the pills of childhood are
dissembled in a spoonful of jelly.

CHAPTER V.

I SAT in that nocturnal sun-parlor of mine, known to the world as Madison Square, demanding of the quiet night why sleep should be denied me, and doing my best to keep from thinking of Mary Lockwood. 1 sat there with my gaze fixed idly on a girl in black, who, in turn, stared idly up at *Sagittarius*.

Then I lost interest in the black-clad and seemingly cataleptic star-gazer. For I was soon busy watching a man in a rather odd-looking velour hat. My eyes followed him from the moment he first turned eastward out of Fifth Avenue. They were still on him as he veered irresolutely southward again into the square where I sat.

The pure aimlessness of his movements arrested my attention. The figure that drifted listlessly in past the Farragut Statue and wandered on under the park trees in some way reminded me of my own. I, too, knew only too well what it was to circle doggedly and sullenly about like a bell-boy paging the corridors of night for that fugitive known as Sleep.

So I continued to watch him, quietly and closely. I had lost my interest in the white-faced girl who sat within twenty paces of me, looking, silent and still, up at the autumn stars.

It was the man's figure, thereafter, that challenged

my attention, for this man marked the only point of movement in what seemed a city of the dead. It was, I remembered, once more long past midnight, the hour of suspended life in the emptied canyons of the lamp-strung streets when the last taxi had hummed the last reveler home, and the first milk-wagons had not yet rattled up from the East River ferries.

So I sat there listlessly watching the listlessly moving figure with the wide hat-brim pulled down over its face. There was something still youthful about the man, for all the despondent droop to the shoulders. I asked myself idly who or what he could be. I wondered if, like myself, he was merely haunted by the curse of wakefulness, if the same bloodhounds of unrest dogged him, too, through the dark hours of the night. I wondered if he, too, was trying to escape from the grinding machinery of thought into some outer passivity.

I saw him thread his indeterminate way along the winding park walks. I saw him glance wearily up at the massive austerity of the Metropolitan Tower, and then turn and gaze at the faded Diana so unconcernedly poised above her stolen Sevillian turrets. I saw him look desolately about the square with its bench-rows filled with huddled and motionless sleepers. These sleepers, with their fallen heads and twisted limbs, with their contorted and moveless bodies, made the half-lit square as horrible as a battlefield. Clouded by the heavy shadows of the park trees, they seemed like the bodies of dead men, like broken and sodden things over which had ground the wheels of carnage. The only murmur or sound of life was the fountain, with its column of slowly rising and slowly falling water, like the tired pulse-beat of the tired city.

The man in the velour hat seemed to find something companionable in this movement, for he slowly drew nearer. He came within three benches of where I sat. Then he flung himself down on an empty seat. I could see his white and haggard face as he watched the splashing fountain. I could see his shadowy and unhappy eyes as he pushed back his hat and mopped his moist forehead. Then I saw him suddenly bury his head in his hands and sit there, minute by minute, without moving.

When he made his next movement, it was a startling one. It sent a tingle of nerves scampering up and down my backbone. For I saw his right hand go down to his pocket, pause there a moment, and then suddenly lift again. As it did so my eye caught the white glimmer of metal. I could see the flash of a revolver as he thrust it up under the hat-brim, and held the nickeled barrel close against his temple, just above the lean jaw-bone.

It was so sudden, so unexpected, that I must have closed my eyes in a sort of involuntary wince. The first coherent thought that came to me was that I could never reach him in time. Some soberer second thought was to the effect that even my interference was useless, that he and his life were his own, that a man once set on self-destruction will not be kept from it by any outside influence.

Yet even as I looked again at his huddled figure, I heard his little gasp of something that must have been between fear and defeat. I saw the arm slowly sink to his side. He was looking straight before him, his unseeing eyes wide with terror and hazy with indecision.

It was then that I decided to interfere. To do so seemed only my plain and decent duty. Yet I hesitated for a moment, pondering just how to phrase my opening speech to him.

Even as I took a sudden, deeper breath of resolution, and was on the point of crossing to his side, I saw him fling the revolver vehemently from him. It went glimmering and tumbling along the coppery-green grass. It lay there, a point of high light against the darkness of the turf.

Then I looked back to the stranger, and saw his empty hands go up to his face. It was a quiet and yet a tragic gesture of utter misery. Each palm was pressed in on the corded cheek-bones, with the finger-ends hard against the eyeballs, as though that futile pressure could crush away all inner and all outer vision.

Then I turned back toward the fallen revolver. As I did so I noticed a figure in black step quietly out and pick up the firearm. It was the white-faced girl who had sat looking up at the stars. Before I fully realized the meaning of her movement, she slipped the weapon out of sight, and passed silently on down the winding asphalt walk, between the rows of sleepers, toward the east. There was something arresting in the thin young figure, something vaguely purposeful and appealing in the poise of the half-veiled head.

I vacillated for a moment, undecided as to which to approach. But a second glance at the man in the velour hat, crouched there in his utter and impassive misery, caused me to cross over to him.

I put a hand on his flaccid shoulder, and shook it. He did not move at first, so I shook him again. Then he directed a slow and resentful glance at me.

"I want to have a talk with you," I began, puzzled as to how to proceed. He did not answer me.

"I want to help you if I can," I explained, as I still let my hand rest on his shoulder.

"Oh, go 'way!" he ejaculated, in utter listlessness, shaking my hand from his shoulder.

"No, I won't!" I quite firmly informed him. He shrank back and moved away. Then he turned on me with a resentment that was volcanic.

"For God's sake leave me alone!" he cried.

A sleeper or two on near-by benches sat up and stared at us with their drowsily indifferent eyes.

"Then why are you making a fool of yourself like this?" I demanded.

"That's my own business," he retorted.

"Then you intend to keep it up?" I inquired.

"No, I don't," he flung back. "*I can't.*"

"Then will you be so good as to talk to me?" His sullen anger seemed strangely removed from that exaltation which tradition imputes to last moments. It even took an effort to be patient with him.

"No, I won't," was his prompt retort. It dampened

all the quixotic fires in my body. Then he rose to
his feet and confronted me. "And if you don't get
out of here, I'll kill you!"

His threat, in some way, struck me as funny. I
laughed out loud.

But I did not waste further time on him.

I was already thinking of the other figure, the equally
mysterious and more appealing figure in black.

I swung round and strode on through the trees just
in time to see that somber and white-faced young
woman cross Madison Avenue, and pass westward between a granite-columned church and the towering
obelisk of a more modern god of commerce. I kept my
eyes on this street-end as it swallowed her up. Then I
passed out through the square and under the clock-
dial and into Twenty-fourth Street.

By the time I had reached Fourth Avenue I again
caught sight of the black-clad figure. It was moving
eastward on the south side of the street, as unhurried
and impassive as a sleep-walker.

When half-way to Lexington Avenue I saw the
woman stop, look slowly round, and then go slowly
up the steps of a red-brick house. She did not ring,
I could see, but let herself in with a pass-key. Once
the door had closed on her, I sauntered toward this
house. To go farther at such an hour was out of
the question. But I made a careful note of the street
number, and also of the fact that a slip of paper pasted
on the sandstone door-post announced the fact of
"Furnished Rooms."

I saw, not only that little was to be gained there,

but also that I 'had faced my second disappointment. So I promptly swung back to Madison Square and the fountain where I had left the man in the velour hat. I ran my eye from bench to bench of sleepers, but he was not among them. I went over the park, walk by walk, but my search was unrewarded. Then I circled about into Broadway, widening my radius of inspection. I shuttled back and forth along the side-streets. I veered up and down the neighboring avenues. But it was useless. The man in the velour hat was gone.

Then, to my surprise, as I paced the midnight streets, a sense of physical weariness crept over me. I realized that I had walked for miles. I had forgotten my own troubles and that most kindly of all narcotics, utter fatigue, crept through me like a drug.

So I went home and went to bed. And for the first time that week I felt the Angel of Sleep stoop over me of her own free will. For the first time that week there was no need of the bitter lash of chloral hydrate to beat back the bloodhounds of wakefulness. I fell into a sound and unbroken slumber, and when I woke up, Benson was waiting to announce that my bath was ready.

Two hours later I was ringing the bell of a certain old-fashioned red-brick apartment-house in East Twenty-fourth Street. I knew little enough about such places, but this was one obviously uninviting, from the rusty hand-rail to the unwashed window draperies. Equally unprepossessing was the corpulent and dead-eyed landlady in her faded blue house-wrapper; and equally depressing did I find the slatternly and bared-armed servant who was delegated to lead me up through the musty-smelling halls. The third-floor front, I was informed, was the only room in the house empty, though its rear neighbor, which was a bargain at two dollars and a half a week, was soon to be vacated.

I took the third-floor front, without so much as one searching look at its hidden beauties. The lady of the faded blue wrapper emitted her first spark of life as I handed over my four dollars. The listless eyes, I could see, were touched with regret at the thought that she had not asked for more. I tried to explain to her, as she exacted a deposit for my passkey, that I was likely to be irregular in my hours and perhaps a bit peculiar in my habits.

These intimations, however, had no ponderable effect upon her. She first abashed me by stowing the money away in the depths of her open corsage, and then perplexed me by declaring that all she set out to do, since her legs went back on her, was to keep her first two floors decent. Above that, apparently, deportment could look after itself, the upper regions beyond her ken could be Olympian in their moral laxities.

As I stood there, smiling over this discovery, a figure in black rustled down the narrow stairway and edged past us in the half-lit hall.

The light fell full on her face as she opened the door to the street. It outlined her figure, as thin as that of a medieval saint from a missal. It was the young woman I had followed from Madison Square.

Of this I was certain—from the moment the light fell on her thin-cheeked face, where anxiety seemed to have pointed the soft oval of the chin into something mask-like in its sharpness. About her, quite beyond the fact that her eyes were the most unhappy eyes I had ever seen, hung a muffled air of tragedy, the air of a spirit both bewildered and baffled. But I could see that she was, or that she had been, a rather beautiful young woman, though still again the slenderness of the figure made me think of a saint from a missal.

I was still thinking of her as I followed the sullen and slatternly servant up the dark stairs. Once in my new quarters, I glanced absently about at the sulphur-yellow wallpaper and the melancholy antiquities that masqueraded as furniture. Then I came back to the issue at hand.

"Who is that young woman in black who happened to pass us in the hall?" I casually inquired.

"*Can* that!" was the apathetic and quite enigmatic retort of the bare-armed girl. I turned to inquire the meaning of this obvious colloquialism.

"Aw, cage the zooin' bug!" said my new-found and cynical young friend. "She ain't that kind."

"What is she?" I asked, as I slipped a bill into the startled and somewhat incredulous hand of toil. The transformation was immediate.

"She ain't nothin'!" was the answer. "She's just a four-flush, an also-ran! And unless she squares wit' the madam by Sat'rday she's goin' to do her washin' in somebody else's bath-tub!"

Through this sordid quartz of callousness ran one silver streak of luck. It was plain that I was to be on the same floor with the girl in black. And that discovery seemed quite enough.

I waited until the maid was lost in the gloom below-stairs and the house was quiet again. Then I calmly and quietly stepped out into the little hall, pushed open the door of the rear room, and slipped inside. I experienced, as I did so, a distinct and quite pleasurable quickening of the pulse.

I found myself in a mere cell of a room, with two dormer windows facing a disorderly vista of chimney-pots and brick walls. On the sill of one window stood an almost empty milk-bottle. Beside the other window was a trunk marked with the initials "H. W." and the pretty-nearly obliterated words "Medicine Hat."

About the little room brooded an almost forlorn air of neatness. On one wall was tacked a picture postcard inscribed "In the Devil's Pool at Banff." On another was a ranch scene, an unmounted photograph which showed a laughing and clear-browed girl on a white-dappled pinto. On the chintz-covered bureau stood a half-filled carton of soda-biscuits. Beside this, again, lay an empty candy-box. From the mirror of this bureau smiled down a face that was familiar to me. It was a magazine-print of Harriet Walter, the young Broadway star who had reached success with the production of *Broken Ties,* the same Harriet Walter who had been duly announced to marry Percy Adams, the son of the Traction Magnate. My own den, I remembered, held an autographed copy of the same picture.

Beyond this, however, the room held little of interest and nothing of surprise. Acting on a sudden and a possibly foolish impulse, after one final look at the room and its record of courageous struggles, I took a bank-note from my waistcoat pocket, folded it, opened the top drawer of the bureau and dropped the bill into it. Then I stood staring down into the still open drawer, for before me lay the revolver which the girl had carried away the night before from Madison Square.

In a few moments I went back to my own room and sat down in the broken-armed rocking-chair, and tried desperately to find some key to the mystery. But no light came to me.

I was still puzzled over it when I heard the sound of steps on the uncarpeted stairway. They were very slow and faltering steps. As I stood at the half-opened door listening, I felt sure I heard the sound of something that was half-way between a sob and a gasp. Then came the steps again, and then the sound of heavy breathing. I heard the rustle of paper as the door of the back room was pushed open, and then the quick slam of the door.

This was followed by a quiet and almost inarticulate cry. It was not a call, and it was not a moan. But what startled me into sudden action was the noise that followed. It was a sort of soft-pedaled thud, as though a body had fallen to the floor.

I no longer hesitated. It was clear that something

was wrong. I ran to the closed door, knocked on it,
and a moment later swung it open.

As I stepped into the room I could see the girl lying
there, her upturned face as white as chalk, with bluish-
gray shadows about the closed eyes. Beside her on
the floor lay a newspaper, a flaring head-lined afternoon edition.

I stood staring stupidly down at the white face for a
moment or two before it came to me that the girl had
merely fallen in a faint. Then, seeing the slow beat
of a pulse in the thin throat, I dropped on one knee
and tore open the neck of her blouse. Then I got
water from the stoneware jug on the wash-stand and
sprinkled the placid and colorless brow. I could see,
as I lifted her up on the narrow white bed, how blood-
less and ill-nurtured her body was. The girl was half
starved; of that there was no shadow of doubt.

She came to very slowly. As I leaned over her,
waiting for the heavy-lidded eyes to open, I let my
glance wander back to the newspaper on the floor. I
there read that Harriet Walter, the young star of the
Broken Ties Company, had met with a serious accident. It had occurred while riding down Morningside
Avenue in a touring-car driven by Percy Alward
Adams, the son of the well-known Traction Magnate. The brake had apparently refused to work on
Cathedral Hill, and the car had collided with a pillar
of the Elevated Railway at the corner of One-hundred-
and-ninth Street. Adams himself had escaped with a
somewhat lacerated arm, but Miss Walter's injuries
were more serious. She had been taken at once to St.

Luke's Hospital, but a few blocks away. She had not, however, regained consciousness, and practically all hope of recovery had been abandoned by the doctors.

I was frenziedly wondering what tie could bind these two strangely diverse young women together when the girl beside me gave signs of returning life. I was still sousing a ridiculous amount of water on her face and neck when her eyes suddenly opened. They looked up at me, dazed and wide with wonder.

"What is it?" she asked, gazing about the room. Then she looked back at me again.

"I think you must have fallen," I tried to explain. "But it's all right; you mustn't worry."

My feeble effort at reassuring her was not effective. I could see the perplexed movement of her hands, the unuttered inquiry still in her eyes. She lay there, staring at me for a long time.

"You see, I'm your new neighbor," I told her, "and I heard you from my room."

She did not speak. But I saw her lips pucker into a little sob that shook her whole body. There seemed something indescribably childlike in the movement. It took a fight to keep up my air of bland optimism.

"And now," I declared, "I'm going to slip out for a minute and get you a little wine."

She made one small hand-gesture of protest, but I ignored it. I dodged in for my hat, descended the stairs to the street, got Benson on the wire; and instructed him to send the motor-hamper and two bottles of Burgundy to me at once. Then I called up St. Luke's Hospital. There, strangely enough, I was re-

fused all information as to Harriet Walter's condition.
It was not even admitted, in fact, that she was at
present a patient at that institution.

The girl, when I got back, was sitting in a rocking-
chair by the window. She seemed neither relieved nor
disturbed by my return. Her eyes were fixed on the
blank wall opposite her. Her colorless face showed
only too plainly that this shock from which she had
suffered had left her indifferent to all other currents of
life, as though every further stroke of fate had been
rendered insignificant. She did not even turn her eyes
when I carried the hamper into the room and opened
it. She did not look up as I poured the wine and held
a glass of it for her to drink.

She sipped at it absently, brokenly, reminding me of
a bird drinking from a saucer-edge. But I made her
take more of it. I persisted, until I could see a faint
and shell-like tinge of color creep into her cheeks.

Then she looked at me, for the first time, with comprehending and strangely grateful eyes. She made a
move, as though to speak. But as she did so I could
see the quick gush of tears that came to her eyes and
her gesture of hopelessness as she looked down at the
newspaper on the floor.

"Oh, I want to die!" she cried brokenly and weakly.
"I want to die!"

Her words both startled and perplexed me. Here,
within a few hours' time, I was encountering the second
young person who seemed tired of life, who was ready
and willing to end it.

"What has happened?" I asked, as I held more of

the Burgundy out for her to drink. Then I picked up the afternoon paper with the flaring head-lines.

She pointed with an unsteady finger to the paper in my hands.

"Do you know her?" she asked.

"Yes, I happen to know her," I admitted.

"Have you known her long?" asked the girl.

"Only a couple of years," I answered. "Since she first went with Frohman."

The possible truth flashed over me. They were sisters. That was the strange tie that bound them together; one the open and flashing and opulent, and the other the broken and hidden and hopeless.

"Do you know Harriet Walter?" I asked.

She laughed a little, forlornly, bitterly. The wine, I imagined, had rather gone to her head.

"I *am* Harriet Walter!" was her somewhat startling declaration.

She was still shaken and ill, I could see. I took the Burgundy glass from her hand. I wanted her mind to remain lucid. There was a great deal for me still to fathom.

"And they say she's going to die?" she half declared, half inquired, as her eyes searched my face.

"But what will it mean to you?" I demanded.

She seemed not to have heard; so I repeated the question.

"It means the end," she sobbed, "the end of everything!"

"But why?" I insisted.

She covered her face with her hands.

"Oh, I can't tell you!" she moaned. "I can't explain."

"But there must be some good and definite reason why this young woman's death should end everything for you."

The girl looked about her, like a life-prisoner facing the four blank walls of a cell. Her face was without hope. Nothing but utter misery, utter despair, was written on it.

Then she spoke, not directly to me, but more as though she were speaking to herself.

"When she dies, I die too!"

I demanded to know what this meant. I tried to burrow down to the root of the mystery. But my efforts were useless. I could wring nothing more out of the unhappy and tragic-eyed girl. And the one thing she preferred just then, I realized, was solitude. So I withdrew.

The entire situation, however, proved rather too much for me. The more I thought it over the more it began to get on my nerves. So I determined on a prompt right-about-face. I decided to begin at the other end of the line.

My first move was to phone for the car. Latreille came promptly enough, but with a look of sophistication about his cynical mouth which I couldn't help resenting.

"St. Luke's Hospital," I told him as I stepped into the car.

At that institution, however, I was again refused all information as to the condition of Harriet Walter.

It was not even admitted, when I became more insistent, that any such person was in the hospital.

"But I'm a friend of this young lady's," I tried to explain. "And I've a right to know of her condition."

The calm-eyed official looked at me quite unmoved.

"This young lady seems to have very many friends. And some of them seem to be very peculiar."

"What do you mean by that?" I demanded. For answer he pointed to a figure pacing up and down in the open street.

"There's another of these friends who've been insisting on seeing her," he explained, with a shrug of extenuation.

The uniformed attendant of that carbolized and white-walled temple of pain must have seen my start as I glanced out at the slowly pacing figure. For it was that of a young man wearing a velour hat. It was the youth I had met the night before in Madison Square.

"Do you happen to know that man's name?" I asked.

"He gave it as Mallory—James Mallory," was the answer.

I wasted no more time inside those depressing walls. I was glad to get out to the street, to the open air and the clear afternoon sunlight. I had already decided on my next step.

Whether the man in the velour hat recognized me or not, I could not say. If he did, he gave no sign of it. Yet I could see that he resented my addressing him, although he showed no surprise as I did so by name. It was not until I point-blank asked if he had been inquiring about Harriet Walter that any trace of interest came into his face.

He replied, with considerable ferocity, that he had. One glimpse of the unsteady fingers and twitching eyelids showed me the tension under which he was struggling. I felt genuinely sorry for him.

"I happen to know Miss Walter," I told him, "and if you'll be so good as to step in my car, I can tell you anything you may want to know."

"Is your name Adams?" the white-faced youth suddenly demanded.

"It is not," I answered, with considerable alacrity, for his face was not pleasant to look at.

"Then why can you tell me what I want to know?" he asked, still eying me with open hostility. I struggled to keep my temper. It was a case where one could afford to be indulgent.

"If we each have a friend in this lady, it's not unreasonable that we should be able to be friends ourselves," I told him. "So let's clear the cobwebs by a spin down-town."

"Gasoline won't wash my particular cobwebs away," he retorted. There was something likable about his audacious young face, even under its cloud of bitterness.

"Then why couldn't you dine with me, at a very quiet club of mine?" I suggested. "Or, better still, on the veranda of the Clairemont, where we can talk together."

He hesitated at first, but under my pressure he yielded, and we both got in the car and swung westward, and then up Riverside to the Clairemont. There I secured a corner piazza-table, overlooking the river. And there I exerted a skill of which I had once been proud, in ordering a dinner which I thought might appeal to the poignantly unhappy young man who sat across the table from me. I could see that he was still looking at me, every now and then, with both revolt and sullen bewilderment written on his lean young face. It would be no easy matter, I knew, to win his confidence.

"I suppose you think I'm crazy, like the rest of them?" he suddenly demanded. I noticed that he had already taken his third drink of wine.

"Why should I think that?"

"I've had enough to make me crazy!" he ejaculated, with that abject self-pity which marks the last milestone on the avenue of hope.

"Perhaps I could help you," I suggested. "Or perhaps I could advise you."

"What good's advice when you're up against what I'm up against?" was his embittered retort.

He was apparently finding relief in the Pommery. I found a compensating relief in merely beholding that look of haunted and abject misery going out of his young eyes.

"Then tell me what the trouble is," I said.

He still shook his head. Then he suddenly looked up.

"How long have you known Harriet Walter?" he asked.

"From the time," I told him, after a moment's

thought, "when she first appeared for the Fresh Air Fund at the Plaza. That was about two years ago—when she first went with Frohman."

"I've known her for twenty years!" was the youth's unexpected exclamation. "We grew up together, out West."

"Where out West?" I asked.

"In Medicine Hat—that's a Canadian prairie town."

"But she's younger than you?"

"Only two years. She's twenty-two; I'm twenty-four. She changed her name from Wilson to Walter when she went on the stage."

"Then you are close friends?" I asked, for I could see the wine had loosened his reticent young tongue.

"Friends!" he scoffed. "I'm the man she promised to marry!"

Here, I told myself, was a pretty kettle of fish. I knew the man before me was not Adams. Yet it was several weeks now since Harriet Walter's engagement to young Adams had been officially announced. And there was nothing unstable or predaceous about the Harriet Walter I had known.

"Would you mind telling me just when she promised to marry you?" I asked. "Remember, this is not prying. I'm only trying to get behind that cobweb."

"She promised me over two years ago," he answered me, quite openly.

"Definitely?" I insisted.

"As definite as pen and ink could make it. Even before she gave in, before she gave the promise, we'd had a sort of understanding. That was before I made my British Columbia strike out West. She'd come East to study for the stage. She always felt she would make a great actress. We all tried to keep her from it, but she said it was her career. She'd been having a hard time of it then, those first six months. So I came through to New York and wanted to take her back, to get her out of all that sort of thing. But she put me off. She wouldn't give in to being defeated in her work. She gave me her promise, but asked for a year's time. When that was up, she'd made her hit. Then, of course, she asked for one year more. And in the meantime I made my own hit—in timber limits."

"But hasn't she justified the time you've given her?" I inquired, remembering the sudden fame that had come to her, the name in electrics over the Broadway theater, the lithographs in the shop windows, the interviews in the Sunday papers.

"Justified!" cried the young man across the table from me. "After I'd waited two years, after she'd given me her promise, she's turned round and promised to marry this man Adams!"

"And has she never explained?"

"Explained? She won't see me. She had me put out of her hotel. She went off to Narragansett. She pretended she doesn't even know me."

This sounded very unlike the Harriet Walter I had known. There had seemed little that was deliberately venal or treacherous in that artless-eyed young lady's nature.

"And what did you do?" I asked.

"What could I do? I waited and tried again. I felt that if I could only see her face to face she'd be able to explain, to make the whole thing seem less like insanity."

"And she wouldn't even see you, meet you?"

"Not once. Something's set her against me; something's changed her. She never used to be that sort—never!"

"And you insist all this is without rhyme or reason?"

"Without one jot of reason. That's what made it so hopeless. And last night when I heard of this accident I put my pride in my pocket, and tried still again. It was the same thing over again. They seemed to take me for a crank, or paranœic of some kind, up there at the hospital. And then I gave up. I felt I'd about reached the end of my rope. I thought it all over, quite calmly, and decided to end everything. I walked the streets half the night, then I sat down and decided to blow my brains out. But I couldn't do it. I was too much of a coward. I hadn't the courage."

"That would have been very foolish," was my inadequate reply, for at a bound my thoughts went back to the night before and the scene in the square.

"Well, what would *you* have done?" was the prompt and bitter challenge of the unhappy youth facing me.

I thought for a moment before attempting to answer him.

"Why," I temporized, "I'd have tried to get down to the root of the mystery. I'd have made some effort to find out the reason for it; for everything seems to have a reason, you know."

Again I heard him emit his listless little scoff of misery.

"There's no reason," he declared.

"There must be," I maintained.

"Then show me where or what it is," he challenged.

"I will," I said, with sudden conviction. "There's a reason for all this, and I'm going to find it out!"

He studied my face with his tired and unhappy young eyes as I sat there trying to fit the edges of the two broken stories together. It was not easy: it was like trying to piece together a shattered vase of cloisonné-work.

"And how will you find it out?" he was listlessly inquiring.

Instead of answering him, I looked up, fixed my eyes on him and asked another question.

"Tell me this: if there is a reason, do you still care for her?"

He resented the question, as I was afraid he would.

"What concern is that of yours?"

"If all this thing's a mistake, it's going to be some concern of yours," I told him.

He sat there in dead silence for a minute or two.

"I've always cared for her," he said, and I knew what his answer was going to be before he spoke. "But it's no use. It's all over. It's over and done with. There's not even a mistake about it."

"There must be. And I'm going to find out where and what it is."

"And how are you going to find that out?" he reiterated.

"Come along with me," I cried a little presumptuous-
ly, a little excitedly, "and by ten o'clock to-night I'll
have your reason for you!"

My flash-in-the-pan enthusiasm was shorter lived
than I had expected. The tingling and wine-like
warmth soon disappeared. A reaction set in, once
we were out in the cool night air. And in that reaction I began to see difficulties, to marshal doubts
and misgivings.

The suspicion crept over me that, after all, I might
have been talking to a man with a slightly unbalanced
mind. Delusions, such as his, I knew, were not uncommon. There were plenty of amiable cranks who
carried about some fixed conviction of their one-time
intimate association with the great, the settled belief
that they are the oppressed and unrecognized friends
of earth's elect.

Yet this did not altogether fill the bill; it could
not explain away everything. There was still the
mystery of the girl in the Twenty-fourth Street rooming-house. There was still the enigma of two persons claiming to be Harriet Walter.

On my way down to that rooming-house an idea
occurred to me. It prompted me to step in at my
club for a minute or two, leaving Mallory in the car.
Then I dodged back to the reading-room, took down
from its shelf a *Who's Who on the Stage,* and
turned up the name of Harriet Walter.

There, to my discomfiture, I read that Harriet
Walter's family name was recorded as "Kellock," and
instead of being a Canadian, and born and brought up

in the western town of Medicine Hat, as young Mallory had claimed, her birthplace was recorded as Lansing, Michigan. She had been educated at the Gilder Seminary in Boston, and had later studied one year at the Wheatley Dramatic School in New York. From there she had gone on the stage, taking small parts, but soon convincing her management that she was capable of better things. In little over a year she had been made a star in the *Broken Ties* production.

The St. Luke's officials, after all, had not been so far wrong. The young man in the velour hat was clearly off his trolley.

It was, however, too late to turn back. And there was still the other end of the mystery to unravel. So I ushered young Mallory up the musty stairs to my third-floor room, and seated him with a cigar and a magazine between those four bald and depressing walls with their sulphur-colored paper. Then I stepped outside, and carefully closed the door after me. Then I crossed the hall to the girl's room and knocked.

There was no answer, so I opened the door and looked in. The room was empty. A sense of frustration, of defeat, of helplessness, swept through me. This was followed by a feeling of alarm, an impression that I might, after all, be too late.

I crossed the room with a sudden premonition of evil. Then I turned on the light and pulled open the top drawer of the chintz-covered bureau. There lay my bank-note. And beside it, I noticed, with a sense of relief, still lay the revolver.

I took the weapon up and looked it over, hesitating whether or not to unload it. I still held it in my hand, staring down at it, when I heard the creak of the door behind me. It was followed by a sudden and quite audible gasp of fright.

It was the owner of the room herself, I saw, the moment I swung around. It was not so much terror in her eyes, by this time, as sheer surprise.

"What are you doing here?" she asked, with a quaver of bewilderment.

"I'll answer that when you answer a question of mine," I temporized, as I held the revolver up before her. "Where did you get this?"

She did not speak for a second or two.

"Why are you spying on me like this?" she suddenly demanded. She sank into a chair, pulling nervously at her pair of worn gloves.

"You insist on knowing?" I asked.

"I've a right to know."

"Because you are not Harriet Walter," was the answer I sent bullet-like at her.

She raised her eyes to mine. There was neither anger nor resentment on her face. All I could see was utter weariness, utter tragedy.

"I know," she said. She spoke very quietly. Something in her voice sent a stab of pity through me.

"I'm only trying to help you," I told her. "I only want to clear up this maddening muddle."

"You can't," she said very simply. "It's too late."

"It's not too late!" I blindly persisted.

"What do you know about it?" was her listless and weary retort.

"I know more about it than you imagine," was my answer. "I know where this revolver came from, just when and where you picked it up, and just how near you came to using it."

She covered her face with her hands. Then she dropped them to her side, with a gesture of hopelessness.

"Oh, they'll all know now!" she moaned. "I knew it would come, some day. And I haven't the strength to face it—I haven't the strength!"

I felt, in some way, that the moment was a climactic one.

"But how did it begin?" I asked more gently, as I gazed down at the fragile and girlish body huddled together in the chair.

"It began two years ago," she went on in her tired and throaty monotone. "It began when I saw I was a failure, when I realized that all was useless, that I'd made a mistake."

"What mistake?" I demanded, still in the dark.

"The mistake I wasn't brave enough to face. I thought it was the life I was made for, that they'd never understood at home. Even *he* couldn't understand, I thought. Then they let me come. I worked, oh, so hard! And when I left the school all I could get was a place in the chorus. I was ashamed to tell them. I pretended I had a part, a real part. He kept arguing that I ought to give it up. He kept asking me to come back. I wasn't brave enough to acknowledge defeat. I still thought my chance would come; I kept asking for more time."

"And then?" I prompted.

"Then I couldn't even stay at the work I had. It became impossible; I can't tell you why. Then I did anything, from extra work with moving pictures to reader in the City Library classes. But I still kept going to the agencies, to the Broadway offices, trying to get a part. And things dragged on and on. And then I did this, this awful thing."

"What awful thing?" I asked, trying to bridge the ever-recurring breaks in her thought. But she ignored the interruption.

"We'd studied together in the same classes at the Wheatley School. And people had said we looked alike. But she was born for that sort of life, for success. As I went down, step by step, she went up. He wrote me that I must be getting famous, for he'd seen my picture on a magazine-cover. It was hers. I pretended it was mine. I pretended I was doing the things she was doing. I let them believe I'd taken a new name, a stage name. I sent them papers that told of her success. I became a cheat, an impostor, a living lie—I *became Harriet Walter!*"

At last the light had come. I saw everything in a flash. I suddenly realized the perplexities and profundities of human life. I felt shaken by a sudden pity for these two bound and unhappy spirits, at that moment so close together, yet groping so foolishly and perversely along their mole-like trails.

I was still thinking of the irony of it all, of the two broken and lonely young lives even at that moment under the same roof, crushed under the weight of their unseeing and uncomprehending misery, when the girl in the chair began to speak again.

"It was terrible," she went on, in her passionate resolve to purge her soul of the whole corroding blight. "I didn't dream what it would lead to, what it would cause. I dreaded every advance she made. It wasn't jealousy, it was more than that; it was fear, terror. She seemed to be feeding on me, day by day, month by month. I knew all the time that the higher she got the lower I had to sink. And now, in a different way, she's taken everything from me. Taken everything, without knowing it!"

"No, you're wrong there," I said. "She hasn't taken everything."

"What is there left?" was her forlorn query.

"Life—all your real life. This has been a sort of nightmare, but now it's over. Now you can go back and begin over again."

"It's too late!" She clasped her thin hands hopelessly together. "And there's no one to go to."

"*There's Mallory,*" I said, waiting for some start as the name fell on her ears. But I saw none.

"No," she cried, "he'd hate and despise me."

"But you still care for him?" I demanded.

"I need him," she sobbingly acknowledged. "Yes— yes, I always cared for him. But he'd never understand. He'd never forgive me. He's grown away from me."

"He's waiting for you," I said.

I stood looking at the bowed figure for a moment. Then I slipped out of the room.

I stepped in through my own door and closed it after me. Young Mallory, with his watch in his hand, swung about from the window and faced me.

"Well, it's ten o'clock—and nothing's settled!"

"It is settled," was my answer.

I led him across the quiet hall to the half-lit back room.

I saw his startled and groping motion. Then I heard his cry of "Harrie!" and her answering cry of "Jamie" as the white face, with its hunger and its happiness, looked up into his.

Then I quietly stepped outside and closed the door, leaving them alone. From that moment I was an outsider, an intruder. My part was over and done. But the sight of those two young people, in each other's arms, made my thoughts turn back to Mary Lockwood and the happiness which had been lost out of my own life. And I didn't sleep so well that night as I had hoped to.

CHAPTER VI

ARE you waiting for some one, sir?"

That question, for all its veneer of respectfulness, was only too patently a message of dismissal. And I resented it, not only because it was an impertinence, but more because it had driven out of my drowsy brain a very beautiful picture of Mary Lockwood as she stooped over an old Italian table-cover embroidered with gold galloon.

"Are you waiting for some one?" repeated that newly arrived all-night waiter, in no way impressed by my silence.

"I am," I announced as I inspected him with open disapproval. I was dreamily wondering why, in the name of common sense, waiters always dressed in such ridiculous and undecorative neckties.

This particular waiter, however, continued to regard me out of a fishy and cynical eye. Then he looked at the clock. Then he looked at my empty wine-cooler, plainly an advertisement of suspended circulation in the only fluid that seemed vital to him.

"Was it a lady?" he had the effrontery to inquire.

I could see his eyes roam about the all but empty room. It was the low-ebb hour when a trolley car is an event along the empty street, the hour when chairs are piled on café tables, the white corpuscles of the

milk wagons begin to move through the city's sleepy
arteries, and those steel nerves known as telegraph
wires keep languidly awake with the sugary thrills of
their night letters.

"Yes, it was a lady," I answered. That wall-eyed
intruder knew nothing of the heavenly supper I had
stumbled on in that wicked French restaurant, or of
the fine and firm *Clos Vougeot* that had been unearthed
from its shabby cellar, or of my own peace of mind as
I sat there studying the empty metal cooler and pondering how the mean and scabby wastes of Champagne
could mother an ichor so rich with singing etherealities.

"Er—just what might she look like, sir?" my tor-
mentor next asked of me, blinking about in a loose
and largely condoning matter-of-factness as though in
placid search of some plumed and impatient demirep
awaiting her chance to cross the bar of acquaintanceship on the careless high tide of inebriacy.

"She moves very, very quietly, and has a star in her
hair," I replied to that fish-eyed waiter. "Her breath
is soft and dewy, and her brow is hooded. And in
her hands she carries a spray of poppies."

The waiter looked down at me with that impersonal
mild pity with which it is man's wont to view the
harmlessly insane.

"Surely," I said with a smothered yawn, "surely
you have met her? Surely you have been conscious
of those soft and shadowy eyes gazing into yours as
you melted into her arms?"

"Quite so, sir," uneasily admitted my wall-eyed
friend. Then I began to realize that he was waking

me up. I grew fearful lest his devastating invasion should frighten away the timorous spirit I had been wooing as assiduously as an angler seeking his first trout. For one long hour, with a full body and an empty head, I had sat there stalking sleep as artfully and as arduously as huntsman ever stalked a deer. And I knew that if I moved from that spot the chase would be over, for that night at least.

"But the odd thing about her," I languidly explained, "is that she evades only those who seek her. She is coy. She denies herself to those who most passionately demand her. Yet something tells me that she is hovering near me at this moment, that she is about to bend over me with those ineffable eyes if only I await the golden moment. And so, my dear sir, if you will take this as a slight reward for your trouble, and cover that exceedingly soiled-looking divan in that exceedingly disreputable-looking alcove with a clean table-cloth, and then draw that curtain which is apparently designed to convert it into a *chambre particuliere,* you will be giving me a chance to consort with an angel of graciousness more lovely than any meretricious head that ever soiled its faded plush. And if I am left uninterrupted until you go off in the morning, your reward will then be doubled."

His puzzled face showed, as he peered down at the bill in his hand, that if this indeed were madness, there was a not repugnant sort of method in it.

So he set about in a half dazed fashion draping that none too clean divan with a table-cloth, making it, in fact, look uncomfortably like a bier. Then he carried

my hat and gloves and overcoat to a chair at the foot
of the divan. Then he took me by the arm, firmly and
solicitously.

His face, as I made my way without one stagger or
reel into that shabby little quietude screened off from
the rest of the world, was a study in astonishment. It
was plain that I puzzled him. He even indulged in a
second wondering glance back at the divan as he drew
the portières. Then, if I mistake not, he uttered the
one explanatory and self-sufficient word—"Needle-
pumper."

I heard him tiptoe in, a few minutes later, and decently cover my legs with the overcoat from the chair.
I did not speak, for bending over me was a rarer and
sweeter Presence, and I wanted no sound or movement
to frighten her away. Just when her hand touched
mine I can not tell. But I fell off into a deep and
natural sleep and dreamed I was being carried through
Sicilian orange groves by a wall-eyed waiter with
wings like a butterfly.

Then the scene changed, as scenes have the habit of
doing in dreams. I seemed to be the center of a sub-
cellar conference of highwaymen, presided over by Latreille himself. Then the voices shifted and changed,
receded and advanced. I seemed to be threading that
buffer-state which lies between the two kingdoms of
Sleep and Wakefulness, the buffer-state that has no
clear-cut outlines and twists like a weevil between ever-
shifting boundaries.

"Where's Sir 'Enery," said a voice from a moun-
tain-top. Then an answering murmur of voices buzzed

about me like bees, only an intelligible word or two seeming to reinforce the fabric of my imaginings as iron rods reinforce concrete-walls. And I continued to lie there in that pleasant borderland torpor, which is neither wakefulness nor slumber. I seemed to doze on, in no ponderable way disturbed by the broken hum of talk that flickered and wavered through my brain.

"Then why can't Sir Henry work on the Belmont job?" one of the voices was asking.

"I told you before, Sir Henry's tied up," another voice answered.

"What doing?" asked the first voice.

"He's fixing his plant for the Van Tuyl coup," was the answer.

"What Van Tuyl?"

"Up in Seventy-third Street. He's got 'em hog tied."

"And what's more," broke in a third voice, "he won't touch a soup case since he got that safe-wedge in the wrist. It kind o' broke his nerve for the nitro work."

"Aw, you couldn't break that guy's nerve!"

"Well, he knows he's marked, anyway."

Then came a lull, followed by the scratch of a match and the mumbling of voices again.

"How'd he get through the ropes up there?" inquired one of these voices.

"Same old way. Butlering. Turk McMeekin doped him up a half-dozen London recommends. That got him started out in Morristown, with the Whippeny Club. Then he did the Herresford job. But he's got

a peach with this Van Tuyl gang. They let him lock
up every night—silver and all—and carry the keys to
bed with him!"

"It's up to Sir 'Enery to make 'em dream he's the
real thing," murmured another of the voices.

"Sure!" answered still another voice that seemed a
great distance away.

Then the mumble became a murmur and the murmur a drone. And the drone became a sighing of
birch tops, and I was stalking Big-Horn across moun-
tain peaks of *café parfait*, where a pompous English
butler served *pêches Melba* on the edge of every second precipice.

When I woke up it was broad daylight, and my
wall-eyed waiter was there waiting for his second bill.
And I remembered that I ought to phone Benson so
he could have the coffee ready by the time I walked
home through the mellow November air.

It was two hours later that the first memory of
those murmuring midnight voices came back to me.
The words I had overheard seemed to have been buried
in my mind like seeds in the ground. Then here and
there a green shoot of suspicion emerged. The more
I thought it over, the more disturbed I became. Yet
I warned myself that I could be sure of nothing. The
one tangibility was the repeated word, "Van Tuyl."
And there at least was something on which I could
focus my attention.

I went to the telephone and called up Beatrice Van
Tuyl. Years before we had played water polo and
catboated on the Sound together. I realized, as I

heard that young matron's cheery voice over the telephone wire, that I would have to pick my steps with care.

"I say, Beatrice, are you possibly in need of a butler?" I began as offhandedly as I was able.

"Out of a place, Witter dear?" was the chuckling inquiry that came to me.

"No, I'm not, but I know of a good man," was my mendacious reply. "And I rather thought—"

"My dear Witter," said the voice over the wire, "we've a *jewel* of a man up here. He's English, you know. And I'm beginning to suspect he's been with royalty. Jim's always wanted to stick pins in his legs to see if he really isn't petrified."

"What's his name?"

"Just what it ought to be—the most appropriate name of Wilkins."

"How long have you had him?"

"Oh, weeks and weeks!" Only a New York householder could understand the tone of triumph in that retort.

"And you're sure of him in every way?"

"Of course we're sure of him. He's been a Gibraltar of dependability."

"Where did you get him from?"

"From Morristown. He was at the Whippeny Club out there before he came to us."

"The Whippeny Club!" I cried, for the name struck like a bullet on the metal of memory.

"Don't you think," the voice over the wire was saying, "that you'd better come up for dinner to-night and inspèct the paragon at close range? And you might talk to us a little, between whiles."

"I'd love to," was my very prompt reply.

"Then do," said Beatrice Van Tuyl. "A little after seven."

And a little after seven I duly rang the Van Tuyls' door-bell and was duly admitted to that orderly and well-appointed Seventy-third Street house, so like a thousand other orderly and well-appointed New York houses hidden behind their unchanging masks of brown and gray.

Yet I could not help feeling the vulnerability of that apparently well-guarded home. For all its walls of stone and brick, for all the steel grills that covered its windows and the heavy scroll work that protected its glass door, it remained a place munificently ripe for plunder. Its solidity, I felt, was only a mockery. It made me think of a fortress that had been secretly mined. Its occupants seemed basking in a false security. The very instruments which went to insure that security were actually a menace. The very machinery of service which made possible its cloistral tranquillity held the factor for its disruption.

As I surrendered my hat and coat and ascended to that second floor where I had known so many sedately happy hours, I for once found myself disquieted by its flower-laden atmosphere. I began to be oppressed by a new and disturbing sense of responsibility. It would be no light matter, I began to see, to explode a bomb of dissension in that principality of almost arrogant aloofness. It would be no joke to confound that smoothly flowing routine with which urban wealth so jealously surrounds itself.

I suddenly remembered there was nothing in which I could be positive, nothing on which I could with certainty rely. And my inward disquiet was increased, if anything, by the calm and blithely contented glance Beatrice Van Tuyl leveled at me.

"And what's all this mystery about our man Wilkins?" she asked me, with the immediacy of her sex.

"Won't you let me answer that question a little later in the evening?"

"But, my dear Witter, that's hardly fair!" she protested, as she held a lighted match for her husband's cigarette. "Do you know, I actually believe you've spotted some one you want to supplant Wilkins with."

"Please—"

"Or did he spill soup on you some time when we didn't see it?"

"I imagine he's spilt a bit of soup in his day," I answered, remembering what I had overheard as to the safe wedge. And as I spoke I realized that my one hope lay in the possibility of getting a glimpse of the mark which that wedge had left—if, indeed, my whole sand-chain of coincidences did not split back into the inconsequentialities of dreamland.

"You can't shake my faith in Wilkins," said the blue-eyed woman in the blue silk dinner gown, as she leaned back in a protecting-armed and softly padded library-chair which suddenly became symbolic of her whole guarded and upholstered life. "Jim, tell Witter what a jewel Wilkins really is."

Jim, whose thought was heavy ordnance beside his wife's flying column of humor, turned the matter solemnly over in his mind.

"He's a remarkably good man," admitted the stolid and levitical Jim, "remarkably good."

"And you've seen him yourself, time and time again," concurred his wife.

"But I've never been particularly interested in servants, you know," was my self-defensive retort.

"Then why, in the face of the Immortal Ironies, are you putting my butler under the microscope?" was the return shot that came from the flying column. The acidulated sweetness of that attack even nettled me into a right-about-face.

"Look here," I suddenly demanded, "have either of you missed anything valuable about here lately?"

The two gazed at each other for a moment in perplexed wonder.

"Of course not," retorted the woman in the dinner gown. "Not a thing!"

"And you know you have everything intact, all your jewelry, your plate, your pocketbooks, the trinkets a sneakthief might call it worth while to round up?"

"Of course we have. And I can't even resent your bracketing my pocketbook in with the trinkets."

"But are you certain of this? Could you verify it at a moment's notice?"

"My dear Witter, we wouldn't need to. I mean we're doing it every day of our lives. It's instinctive; it's as much a habit as keeping moths out of the closets and cobwebs out of the corners."

"What's making you ask all this?" demanded the heavy artillery.

"Yes, what's suddenly making you into a Holmes's watchman?" echoed the flying brigade.

Still again I saw that it was going to be no easy thing to intimate to persons you cared for the possibility of their sleeping on a volcano. Such an intimation has both its dangers and its responsibilities. My earlier sense of delight in a knowledge unparticipated in by others was gradually merging into a consciousness of a disagreeable task that would prove unsavory in both its features and its *finale*.

"I'm asking all this," I replied, "because I have good reason to believe this paragon you call Wilkins is not only a criminal, but has come into this house for criminal purposes."

"For what criminal purposes?"

"For the sake of robbing it."

Beatrice Van Tuyl looked at me with her wide-open azure eyes. Then she suddenly bubbled over with golden and liquid-noted laughter. "Oh, Witter, you're lovely!"

"What proof have you got of that?" demanded Jim.

"Of my loveliness?" I inquired, for Jim Van Tuyl's solidity was as provocative as that of the smithy anvil which the idler can not pass without at least a hammer-tap or two. Yet it was this same solidity, I knew, that made him the safest of financiers and the shrewdest of investors.

"No," he retorted, "proofs of the fact that Wilkins is here for other than honest purposes."

"I've no proof," I had to confess.

"Then what evidence have you?"

"I've not even any evidence as yet. But I'm not stirring up this sort of thing without good reason."

"Let's hope not!" retorted Jim.

"My dear Witter, you're actually getting fussy in your old age," said the laughing woman. It was only the solemnity of her husband's face that seemed to sober her. "Can't you see it's absurd? We're all here, safe and sound, and we haven't been robbed."

"But what I want to know," went on the heavier artillery, "is what your reasons are. It seems only right we should inquire what you've got in the shape of evidence."

"What I have wouldn't be admitted as evidence," I confessed.

He threw down his cigarette. It meant as much as throwing up his hands.

"Then what do you expect us to do?"

"I don't expect you to do anything. All I ask is that you let me try to justify this course I've taken, that the three of us dine quietly together. And unless I'm greatly mistaken, before that dinner is over I think I can show you that this man—"

I saw Beatrice Van Tuyl suddenly lift a forefinger to her lip. The motion for silence brought me up short. A moment later I heard the snap of a light-switch in the hallway outside and then the click of jade curtain-rings on their pole. Into the doorway stepped a figure in black, a calm and slow-moving and altogether self-assured figure.

"Dinner is served," intoned this sober personage, with a curate-like solemnity all his own.

I had no wish to gape at the man, but that first glimpse of mine was a sharp one, for I knew that it was Wilkins himself that I was confronting. As I beheld him there in all the glory of his magisterial assurance I felt an involuntary and ridiculous sinking in the diaphragm. I asked myself in the name of all the Lares and Penates of Manhattan, why I had suddenly gone off on a wild-goose chase to bag an inoffensive butler about whom I had had a midnight nightmare?

Then I looked at the man more closely. He wore the conventional dress livery of twilled worsted, with an extremely high-winged collar and an extremely small lawn tie. He seemed a remarkably solid figure of a man, and his height was not insignificant. Any impression of fragility, of sedentary bloodlessness, which might have been given out by his quite pallid face, was sharply contradicted by the muscular heaviness of his limbs. His hair, a Kyrle-Bellewish gray over the temples, was cut short. The well-powdered and close-shaven face was bluish white along the jowls, like a priest's. The poise of the figure, whether natural or simulated, was one marked for servitude.

Yet I had to admit to myself, as we filed out and down to the dining-room, that the man was not without his pretended sense of dignity. He seemed neither arrogant nor obsequious. He hovered midway between the Scylla of hauteur and the Charybdis of considerate patience. About the immobile and mask-like face hung that veil of impersonality which marked him as a but-

ler—as a butler to the finger-tips. When not actually
in movement he was as aloofly detached as a totem-
pole. He stood as unobtrusive as a newel-post, as impassive as some shielding piece of furniture, beside
which youth might whisper its weightiest secret or con-
spiracy weave its darkest web.

I had to confess, as I watched his deft movements
about that china-strewn oblong of damask which
seemed his fit and rightful domain, that he was in no
way wanting in the part—the only thing that puzzled
me was the futility of that part. There was authority,
too, in his merest finger-movement and eye-shift, as
from time to time he signaled to the footman who
helped him in his duties. There was grave solicitude
on his face as he awaited the minutest semaphoric nod
of the woman in the blue silk dinner gown. And this
was the man, with his stolid air of exactitude, with his
quick-handed movements and his alert and yet unparticipating eyes, whom I had come into that quiet house-
hold to proclaim a thief!

I watched his hands every course as I sat there
talking against time—and Heaven knows what I talked
of! But about those hands there was nothing to discover. In the first thing of importance I had met
with disappointment. For the cuffs that projected
from the edges of the livery sleeves covered each large-
boned wrist. In the actual deportment of the man
there was nothing on which to base a decent suspicion.
And in the meanwhile the dinner progressed, as all
such dinners do, smoothly and quietly, and, to outward
appearances, harmoniously and happily.

But as it progressed I grew more and more perplexed. There was another nauseating moment or two
when the thought flashed over me that the whole thing
was indeed a mistake, that what I had seemed to hear
in my restless moments of the night before was only
a dream projected into a period of wakefulness.
Equipped with nothing more than an echo from this
dream, I had started off on this mad chase, to run
down a man who had proved and was proving himself
the acme of decorous respectability.

But if this thought was a sickening one, it was also
a sickly one. Like all sickly things, too, it tended to
die young. It went down before the crowding actuali-
ties of other circumstances which I could not overlook.
Coincidence, repeated often enough, became more than
fortuity. The thing was more than a nightmare. I
had heard what I had heard. There was still some
method by which I could verify or contradict my suspicion. My problem was to find a plan. And the
gravity of my dilemma, I suppose, was in some way
reflected in my face.

"Well, what are you going to do about it?" asked
Van Tuyl, with his heavy matter-of-factness, at a moment when the room happened to be empty.

"Don't you see it's a mistake?" added his wife, with
a self-assuring glance about the rose-shaded table and
then a wider glance about the room itself.

"Wait," I suddenly said. "What were his refer-
ences?"

"He gave us a splendid one from the Whippeny
Club. We verified that. Then he had letters, six of

them from some very decent people in London.   One
of them was a bishop."

"Did you verify those?"

"Across the Atlantic, Witter?   It really didn't seem
worth while!"

"And it's lucky for him you didn't!"

"Why?"

"Because they're forgeries, every one of them!"

"What ground have you for thinking that?" asked
the solemn Van Tuyl.

"I don't think it—I know it.   And, I imagine, I can
tell you the name of the man who forged them for
him."

"Well, what is it?"

"A worthy by the name of Turk McMeekin."

Van Tuyl sat up with a heavy purpose on his honest
and unimaginative face.

"We've had a nice lot of this mystery, Witter, but
we've got to get to the end of it.   Tell me what you
know, everything, and I'll have him in here and face
him with it.   Now, what is there beside the Turk Mc-
Meekin item?"

"Not yet!" murmured Beatrice Van Tuyl warningly, as Wilkins and his mask-like face advanced into
the room.

I had the feeling, as he served us with one of those
delectable ices which make even the epicureanism of
the Cyrenaics tame in retrospect, that we were deliberately conspiring against our own well-being, that
we were dethroning our own peace of mind.   We were
sitting there scheming to undo the agency whose sole

function was to minister to our delights. And I could not help wondering why, if the man was indeed what I suspected, he chose to follow the most precarious and the most ill-paid of all professions. I found it hard to persuade myself that behind that stolid blue-white mask of a face could flicker any wayward spirit of adventure—and yet without that spirit my whole case was a card house of absurdities.

I noticed that for the first time Beatrice Van Tuyl's own eyes dwelt with a quick and searching look on her servant's immobile face. Then I felt her equally searching gaze directed at me. I knew that my failure to make good would meet with scant forgiveness. She would demand knowledge, even though it led to the discovery of the volcano's imminence. And after so much smoke it was plainly my duty to show where the fire lay.

I seized the conversation by the tail, as it were, and dragged it back into the avenues of inconsequentiality. We sat there, the three of us, actually making talk for the sake of a putty-faced servant. I noticed, though, that as he rounded the table he repeatedly fell under the quickly questioning gaze of both his master and mistress. I began to feel like an Iago who had willfully polluted a dovecote of hitherto unshaken trust. It became harder and harder to keep up my pretense of artless good humor. Time was flying, and nothing had as yet been found out.

"Now," demanded Van Tuyl, when the room was once more empty, "what are you sure of?"

"I'm sure of nothing," I had to confess.

"Then what do you propose doing?" was the somewhat arctic inquiry.

I glanced up at the wall where Ezekiah Van Tuyl, the worthy founder of the American branch of the family, frowned reprovingly down at me over his swathing black stock.

"I propose," was my answer, "having your great grandfather up there let us know whether I am right or whether I am wrong."

And as Wilkins stepped into the room I rose from the table, walked over to the heavy-framed portrait, and lifted it from its hook. I held it there, with a pretense of studying the face for a moment or two. Then I placed my table napkin on a chair, mounted it, and made an unsuccessful effort to rehang the portrait.

"If you please, Wilkins," I said, still holding the picture flat against the wall.

"A little higher," I told him, as I strained to loop the cord back over its hook. I was not especially successful at this, because at the time my eyes were directed toward the hands of the man holding up the picture.

His position was such that the sleeves of his black service coat were drawn away from the white and heavy-boned wrists. And there, before my eyes, across the flexor cords of the right wrist was a wide and ragged scar at least three inches in length.

I returned to my place at the dinner table. Van Tuyl, by this time, was gazing at me with both resentment and wonder.

"Shall we have coffee up-stairs?" his wife asked

with unruffled composure. I could see her eye meet her husband's.

"Here, please," I interpolated.

"We'll have coffee served here," Beatrice Van Tuyl said to her butler.

"Very good, madam," he answered.

I wondered, as I watched him cross the room, if he suspected anything. I also wondered how hare-brained the man and woman seated at the table thought me.

"Listen," I said, the moment we were alone; "have you a servant here you can trust, one you can trust implicitly?"

"Of course," answered my hostess.

"Who is it?"

"Wilkins," was the answer.

"Not counting Wilkins?"

"Well, I think I can also trust my maid Felice—unless you know her better than I do."

I could afford to ignore the thrust.

"Then I'd advise you to send her up to look over your things at once."

"Why do you say that?"

"Because now I know this man Wilkins is a criminal of the worst type!"

"You know it?"

"Yes, I know it as well as I know I'm sitting at this table. And I can prove it."

"How?" demanded Van Tuyl.

"I'll show you how in a very few moments. And, on second thoughts, I'd have that maid Felice bring

what you regard as valuable right to this dining-room
—I mean your jewels and things."

"But this sounds so silly," demurred my still reluctant hostess.

"It won't sound half so silly as a Tiffany advertisement of a reward and no questions asked."

Beatrice Van Tuyl intercepted a footman and sent
him off for the maid Felice. A moment later Wilkins
was at our side quietly serving the *café noir* in tiny
gold-lined cups.

"This method of mine for identifying the real pearl,
as you will see," I blandly went on, "is a very simple
one. You merely take a match end and dip it in clear
water. Then you let a drop of water fall on the pearl.
If the stone is an imitation one the water-drop will
spread and lie close to the surface. If the stone is
genuine the drop will stand high and rounded, like a
globe of quicksilver, and will shake with the minute
vibrations which pass through any body not in perfect
equilibrium."

Before I had completed that speech the maid Felice
had stepped into the room. She was a woman of about
thirty, white-skinned, slender of figure, and decidedly
foreign-looking. Her face was a clever one, though I
promptly disliked an affectation of languor with which
she strove to hide a spirit which was only too plainly
alert.

"I want you to fetch my jewel case from the boudoir
safe," her mistress told her. "Bring everything in the
box."

I could not see the maid's face, for at that moment

I was busy watching Wilkins. From that worthy, however, came no slightest sign of disturbance or wonder.

"Here, madam?" the maid was asking.

"Yes, here and at once, please," answered Beatrice Van Tuyl. Then she turned to me. "And since you're such a jewel expert you'll be able to tell me what's darkening those turquoises of mine."

I dropped a lump of sugar into my coffee and sipped it. Wilkins opened a dark-wooded buffet humidor before me, and I picked out a slender-waisted Havana corseted in a band of gold. I suddenly looked up at the man as he stood at my side holding the blue-flamed little alcohol lamp for the contact of my waiting cigar end.

"Wilkins, how did you get that scar?" I asked him, out of a clear sky. The wrist itself was covered by its cuff and sleeve end, but under them, I knew, was the telltale mark.

"What scar, sir?" he asked, his politeness touched with an indulgent patience which seemed to imply that he was not altogether unused to facing gentlemen in unaccountably high spirits.

"This one!" I said, catching his hand in mine and running the cuff back along the white forearm. Not one trace of either alarm or resentment could I see on that indecipherable countenance. I almost began to admire the man. In his way he was superb.

"Oh, that, sir!" he exclaimed, with an almost offensively condoning glance at the Van Tuyls, as though inquiring whether or not he should reply to a question at once so personal and at the same time so out of place.

"Tell him where you got it, Wilkins," said Beatrice Van Tuyl, so sharply that it practically amounted to a command.

"I got it stopping Lord Entristle's brougham, madam, in London, seven years ago," was the quiet and unhesitating answer.

"How?" sharply asked the woman.

"I was footman for his lordship then, madam," went on the quiet and patient-noted voice. "I had just taken cards in when the horses were frightened by a tandem bicycle going past. They threw Siddons, the coachman, off the box as they jumped, and overturned the vehicle. His lordship was inside. I got the reins as one of the horses went down. But he kicked me against the broken glass and I threw out one hand, I fancy, to save myself."

"And the coach glass cut your wrist?" asked Van Tuyl.

"Yes, sir," replied the servant, moving with methodic slowness on his way about the table. His figure, in its somber badge of livery, seemed almost a pathetic one. There was no anxiety on his face, no shadow of fear about the mild and unparticipating eyes. I was suddenly conscious of my unjust superiority over him —a superiority of station, of birth, of momentary knowledge.

The silence that ensued was not a pleasant one. I felt almost grateful for the timely entrance of the maid Felice. In her hands she carried a japanned tin box, about the size of a theatrical makeup box. This she placed on the table beside her mistress.

"Is there anything else, madam?" she asked.

"That is all," answered Beatrice Van Tuyl as she threw back the lid of the japanned box. I noticed that although the key stood in it, it was unlocked. Then my hostess looked up at the waiting butler. "And, Wilkins, you can leave the cigars and liqueur on the table. I'll ring if I want anything."

The carefully coiffured blonde head was bent low over the box as the servants stepped out of the room. The delicate fingers probed through the array of leather-covered cases. I could see by her face, even before she spoke, that the box's contents were intact.

"You see," she said, ladling handful after handful of glittering jewelry out on the white table-cloth between her coffee-cup and mine, "everything is here. Those are my rings. There's the dog collar. There's angel Jim's sunburst. Here's the ordinary family junk."

I sat for a moment studying that Oriental array of feminine adornment. It was plainly an array of evidence to discountenance me. I felt a distinct sense of relief when the woman in blue suddenly dropped her eyes from my face to her jewel box again. It was Van Tuyl's persistent stare that roweled me into final activity.

"Then so far, we're in luck! And as from now on I want to be responsible for what happens," I said, as I reached over and gathered the glittering mass up in a table napkin, "I think it will simplify things if you, Van Tuyl, take possession of these."

I tied the napkin securely together and handed it to my wondering host. Then I dropped a silver bon-bon dish and a bunch of hothouse grapes into the emptied box, locking it and handing the key back to Beatrice Van Tuyl.

That lady looked neither at me nor the key. Instead, she sat staring meditatively into space, apparently weighing some question in which the rest of that company could claim no interest. It was only after her husband had spoken her name, sharply, that she came back to her immediate surroundings.

"And now what must I do?" she asked, with a new note of seriousness.

"Have the maid take the box back to where it came from," I told her. "But be so good as to retain the key."

"And then what?" mocked Van Tuyl.

"Then," cut in his wife, with a sudden note of antagonism which I could not account for, "*the sooner we send for the police the better.*"

An answering note of antagonism showed on Van Tuyl's face.

"I tell you, Kerfoot, I can't do it," he objected, even as his wife rang the bell. "You've got to *show* me!"

"Please be still, Jim," she said, as Wilkins stepped into the room. She turned an impassive face to the waiting servant. "Will you ask Felice to come here."

None of us spoke until Felice entered the room. Wilkins, I noticed, followed her in, but passed across the room's full length and went out by the door in the rear.

"Felice," said the woman beside me, very calmly and coolly, "I want you to take this box back to the safe."

"Yes, madam."

"Then go to the telephone in the study and ring up police headquarters. Tell them who you are. Then explain that I want them to send an officer here, at once."

"Yes, madam," answered the attentive-faced maid.

"Felice, you had better ask them to send two men, two—"

"Two plain-clothes men," I prompted.

"Yes, two plain-clothes men. And explain to them that they are to arrest the man-servant who opens the door for them—at once, and without any fuss. Is that quite clear?"

"Yes, madam, quite clear," answered the maid.

"Then please hurry."

"Yes, madam."

I looked up at Van Tuyl's audible splutter of indignation.

"Excuse *me*," he cried, "but isn't all this getting just a little highhanded? Aren't we making things into a nice mess for ourselves? Aren't we moving just a little too fast in this game, calling out the reserves because you happen to spot a scar on my butler's wrist?"

"I tell you, Jim," I cried with all the earnestness at my command, "the man's a thief, a criminal with a criminal's record!"

"Then prove it!" demanded Jim.

"Call him in and I will."

Van Tuyl made a motion for his wife to touch the bell.

Her slippered toe was still on the rug-covered button when Wilkins entered, the same austere and self-assured figure.

"Wilkins," said Van Tuyl, and there was an outspoken and deliberate savagery in his voice even as his wife motioned to him in what seemed a signal for moderation, "Wilkins, I regard you as an especially good servant. Mr. Kerfoot, on the other hand, says he knows you and says you are not."

"Yes, sir," said Wilkins with his totem-pole abstraction.

There was something especially maddening in that sustained calmness of his.

"And what's more," I suddenly cried, exasperated by that play-acting rôle and rising and confronting him as he stood there, "your name's not Wilkins, and you never got that wrist scar from a coach door."

"Why not, sir?" he gently but most respectfully inquired.

"Because," I cried, stepping still nearer and watching the immobile blue-white face, "in the gang you work with you're known as Sir Henry, and you got that cut on the wrist from a wedge when you tried to blow open a safe door, and the letters of introduction which you brought to the Whippeny Club were forged by an expert named Turk McMeekin; and I know what brought you into this house and what your plans for robbing it are!"

There was not one move of his body as he stood there. There was not one twitch of his mask-like face. But on that face, point by point, came a slow suffusion of something akin to expression. It was not fear. To call it fear would be doing the man an injustice. It began with the eyes, and spread from feature to feature, very much, I imagine, as sentient life must have spread across the countenance of Pygmalion's slowly awakening marble.

For one fraction of a moment the almost pitiful eyes looked at me with a quick and imploring glance. Then the mask once more descended over them. He was himself again. And I felt almost sure that in the mellowed light about us the other two figures at the table had not seen that face as I did.

There was, in fact, something almost like shame on Van Tuyl's heavy face as the calm-voiced servant, utterly ignoring me and my words, turned to him and asked if he should remove the things.

"You haven't answered the gentleman," said Beatrice Van Tuyl, in a voice a little shrill with excitement.

"What is there to answer, madam?" he mildly asked. "It's all the young gentleman's foolishness, some foolishness which I can't understand."

"But the thing can't stand like this," protested the ponderous Van Tuyl.

There must have been something reassuring to them both in the methodic calmness with which this calumniated factor in their domestic Eden moved about once more performing his petty domestic duties.

"Then you deny everything he says?" insisted the woman.

The servant stopped and looked up in mild reproof.

"Of course, madam," he replied, as he slowly removed the liqueur glasses. I saw my hostess look after him with one of her long and abstracted glances. She was still peering into his face as he stepped back to the table. She was, indeed, still gazing at him when the muffled shrill of an electric bell announced there was a caller at the street door.

"Wilkins," she said, almost ruminatively, "I want you to answer the door—the street door."

"Yes, madam," he answered, without hesitation.

The three of us sat in silence, as the slow and methodic steps crossed the room, stepped out into the hall, and advanced to what at least one of us knew to be his doom. It was Van Tuyl himself who spoke up out of the silence.

"What's up?" he asked. "What's he gone for?"

"The police are there," answered his wife.

"Good God!" exclaimed the astounded husband, now on his feet. "You don't mean you've sprung that trap on the poor devil? You—"

"Sit down, Jim," broke in his wife with enforced calmness. "Sit down and wait."

"But I won't be made a fool of!"

"You're not being made a fool of!"

"But who's arresting this man? Who's got the evidence to justify what's being done here?"

"I have," was the woman's answer.

"What do you mean?"

She was very calm about it.

"I mean that Witter was right. *My Baroda pearls and the emerald pendant were not in the safe. They're gone.*"

"They're gone?" echoed the incredulous husband.

"Listen," I suddenly cried, as Van Tuyl sat digesting his discovery. We heard the sound of steps, the slam of a door, and the departing hum of a motor-car. Before I realized what she was doing Beatrice Van Tuyl's foot was once more on the call bell. A footman answered the summons.

"Go to the street door," she commanded, "and see who's there."

We waited, listening. The silence lengthened. Something about that silence impressed me as ominous. We were still intently listening as the footman stepped back into the room.

"It's the chauffeur, sir," he explained.

"And what does he want?"

"He said Felice telephoned for the car a quarter of an hour ago."

"Send Felice to me," commanded my hostess.

"I don't think I can, ma'am. *She's gone in the car with Wilkins.*"

"With Wilkins?"

"Yes, ma'am. Markson says he can't make it out, ma'am, Wilkins driving off that way without so much as a by-your-leave, ma'am."

The three of us rose as one from the table. For a second or two we stood staring at one another.

Then Van Tuyl suddenly dived for the stairs, with

the napkin full of jewelry in his hand. I, in turn, dived for the street door. But before I opened it I knew it was too late.

I suddenly stepped back into the hallway, to confront Beatrice Van Tuyl.

"How long have you had Felice?" I asked, groping impotently about the hall closet for my hat and coat.

"She came two weeks before Wilkins," was the answer.

"Then you see what this means?" I asked, still groping about for my overcoat.

"What *can* it mean?"

"They were working together—they were confederates."

Van Tuyl descended the stairs still carrying the table napkin full of jewelry. His eyes were wide with indignant wonder.

"It's gone!" he gasped. "He's taken your box!"

I emerged from the hall closet both a little startled and a little humiliated.

"Yes, and he's taken my hat and coat," I sadly confessed.

CHAPTER VII

THE PANAMA GOLD CHESTS

IT is one of life's little ironies, I suppose, that man's surest escape from misery should be through the contemplation of people more miserable than himself. Such, however, happens to be the case. And prompted by this genial cross between a stoic and a cynic philosophy, I had formed the habit of periodically submerging myself in a bath of cleansing depravity.

The hopelessness of my fellow-beings, I found, seemed to give me something to live for. Collision with lives so putrescently abominable that my own by contrast seemed enviable, had a tendency to make me forget my troubles. And this developed me into a sort of calamity chaser. It still carried me, on those nights when sleep seemed beyond my reach, to many devious and astounding corners of the city, to unsavory cellars where lemon-steerers and slough-beaters foregathered, to ill-lit rooms where anarchists nightly ate the fire of their own ineffectual oratory, to heavy-fumed drinking-places where pocket-slashers and till-tappers and dummy-chuckers and dips forgot their more arduous hours.

But more and more often I found my steps unconsciously directed toward that particular den of subterranean iniquities known as *The Café of Failures*. For it was in this new-world *Cabaret du Neant* that

I had first heard of that engaging butler known to his confederates as "Sir Henry." And I still had hopes of recovering my stolen great-coat.

Night by night I went back to that dimly lit den of life's discards, the same as a bewildered beagle goes back to its last trace of aniseed. I grew inured to its bad air, unobservant of its scorbutic waiters, undisturbed by its ominous-looking warren of private rooms, and apathetic before its meretricious blondes.

Yet at no time was I one of the circle about me. At no time was I anything more than a spectator of their ever-shifting and ever-mystifying dramas. And this not unnatural secretiveness on their part, combined with a not unnatural curiosity of my own, finally compelled me to a method of espionage in which I grew to take some little pride.

This method, for all its ingenuity, was simple enough to any one of even ordinary scientific attainments. When I found, for example, that the more select of those underworld conferences invariably took place in one of that tier of wood-partitioned drinking-rooms which lined the café's east side, I perceived that if I could not invade those rooms in body I might at least be there in another form. So with the help of my friend Durkin, the reformed wire-tapper, I acquired a piece of machinery for the projection of the spirit into unwelcome corners.

This instrument, in fact, was little more than an enlargement of the ordinary telephone transmitter. It was made by attaching to an oblong of glass, constituting of course, an insulated base, two carbon supports, with cavities, and four cross-pieces, also of carbon, with pointed ends, fitting loosely into the cavities placed along the side of the two supports. The result was, this carbon being what electricians call "a high resistance" and the loose contact-points where the laterals rested making resistance still higher, that all vibration, however minute, jarred the points against their supports and varied resistance in proportion to the vibration itself. This, of course, produced a changing current in the "primary" of the induction coil, and was in turn reproduced, greatly magnified, in the "secondary" where with the help of a small watch-case receiver it could be easily heard.

In other words, I acquired a mechanical sound-magnifier, a microphone, an instrument, of late called the dictaphone, which translates the lightest tap of a pencil-end into something which reached the ear with the force of a hammer-blow. And the whole thing, battery, coil, insulated wire, carbon bars and glass base, could be carried in its leather case or thrust under my coat as easily as a folded opera hat.

It was equally easy, I found, to let it hang flat against the side wall of that rancid little *chambre particuliere* which stood next to the room where most of those star-chamber conspiracies seemed to take place. My method of adjusting the microphone was quite simple.

From the painted wooden partition I lifted down the gilt-framed picture of a bacchanalian lady whose semi-nudity disseminated the virtues of a champagne which I knew to be made from the refuse of the humble apple-evaporator. At the top-most edge of the square of dust where this picture had stood, I carefully screwed two L-hooks and on these hooks hung my microphone-base. Then I rehung the picture, leaving it there to screen my apparatus. My cloth-covered wires, which ran from this picture to the back of the worn leather couch against the wall, I very nicely concealed by pinning close under a stretch of gas pipe and poking in under the edge of the tattered brown linoleum.

Yet it was only on the third evening of my mildly exhilarating occupation in that stuffy little *camera obscura* that certain things occurred to rob my espionage of its impersonal and half-hearted excitement. I had ordered a bottle of *Chianti* and gone into that room to all intents and purposes a diffident and maundering *bon-vivant* looking for nothing more than a quiet corner wherein to doze.

Yet for one long hour I had sat in that secret auditorium, with my watch-case receiver at my ear, while a garrulous quartette of strike-breakers enlarged on the beatitude of beating up a "cop" who had ill-used one of their number.

It must have been a full half hour after they had gone before I again lifted the phone to my ear. What I heard this time was another man's voice, alert, eager, a little high-pitched with excitement.

"I tell you, Chuck," this thin eager voice was declaring, "the thing's a pipe! I got it worked out like a game o' checkers. But Redney 'nd me can't do a thing unless you stake us to a boat and a batch o' tools!"

"What kind o' tools?" asked a deep and cavernous bass voice. In that voice I could feel caution and stolidity, even an overtone of autocratic indifference.

"Ten bones'd get the whole outfit," was the other's answer.

"But what kind o' tools?" insisted the unperturbed bass voice.

There was a second or two of silence.

"That's spielin' the whole song," demurred the other.

"Well, the whole song's what I want to know," was the calm and cavernous answer. "You'll recall that three weeks ago I staked you boys for that express-wagon job—and I ain't seen nothing from it yet!"

"Aw, that was a frame-up," protested the first speaker. "Some squealer was layin' for us!"

It was a new voice that spoke next, a husky and quavering voice, as though it came from an alkaline throat not infrequently irrigated with fusel-oil whisky.

"Tony, we got to let Chuck in on this. We got to!"

"Why've we got to?"

"Two men can't work it alone," complained the latest speaker. "You know that. We can't take chances—and Gawd knows there's enough for three in this haul!"

Again there was a brief silence.

"You make me sick!" suddenly exploded the treble-voiced youth who had first spoken. "You'd think it was *me* who's been singin' about keepin' this thing so quiet!"

"What're you boys beefin' about, anyway?" interposed the placid bass voice.

"I ain't beefin' about you. I ain't kickin' against lettin' you in. But what I want to know is how're we goin' to split when you *are* in? Who follied this thing up from the first? Who did the dirty work on it? Who nosed round that pier and measured her off, and got a bead on the whole lay-out?"

"Then what'd you take *me* in for?" demanded the worthy called Redney. "Why didn't you go ahead and hog the whole thing, without havin' me trailin' round?"

"Cut that out. You know I've got to have help," was the treble-noted retort. "You know it's too big for one guy to handle."

"And it's so big you've got to have a boat and out-fit," suggested the bass-voiced man. "And I'll bet you and Redney can't raise two bits between you."

"But *you* get me a tub with a kicker in, and two or three tools, and then you've got the nerve to hold me up for a third rakeoff!"

"I don't see as I'm holdin' anybody up," retorted the deep-voiced man. "You came to me, and I told you I was ready to talk business. You said you wanted help. Well, if you want help you've got to pay for it, same as I pay for those cigars."

"I'm willin' to pay for it," answered the high-voiced youth, with a quietness not altogether divorced from sulkiness.

"Then what're we wastin' good time over?" inquired the man known as Redney. "This ain't a case o' milk-in' coffee-bags from a slip-lighter. This haul's big enough for three."

"Well, what *is* your haul?" demanded the bass voice.

Again there was a silence of several seconds.

"Cough it up," prompted Redney. The silence that ensued seemed to imply that the younger man was slowly and reluctantly arriving at a change of front. There was a sound of a chair being pushed back, of a match being struck, of a glass being put down on a table-top.

"Chuck," said the treble-voiced youth, with a slow and impressive solemnity that was strangely in contrast to his earlier speech, "Chuck, we're up against the biggest stunt that was ever pulled off in this burg of two-bone pikers!"

"So you've been insinuatin'," was the answer that came out of the silence. "But I've been sittin' here half an hour waitin' to get a line on what you're chewin' about."

"Chuck," said the treble voice, "you read the papers, don't you?"

"Now and then," acknowledged the diffident bass voice.

"Well, did you see yesterday morning where the steamer *Finance* was rammed by the White Star *Georgic?* Where she went down in the Lower Bay before she got started on her way south?"

"I sure did."

"Well, did you read about her carryin' six hundred and ten thousand dollars in gold—in gold taken from the Sub-Treasury here and done up in wooden boxes and consigned for that Panama Construction Com-p'ny."

"I sure did."

"And did your eye fall on the item that all day yesterday the divers from the wreckin' comp'ny were workin' on that steamer, workin' like niggers gettin' that gold out of her strong room?"

"Sure!"

"And do you happen to know where that gold is now?" was the oratorical challenge flung at the other man.

"Just wait a minute," remarked that other man in his heavy guttural. "Is *that* your coup?"

"That's my coup!" was the confident retort.

"Well, you've picked a lemon," the big man calmly announced. "There's nothin' doin', kiddo, nothin' doin'!"

"Not on your life," was the tense retort. "I know what I'm talkin' about. And Redney knows."

"And *I* know that gold went south on the steamer *'Advance*," proclaimed the bass voice. "I happen to know they re-shipped the whole bunch o' metal on their second steamer."

"Where'd you find that out?" demanded the scoffing treble voice.

"Not bein' in the Sub-Treasury this season, I had to fall back on the papers for the news."

"And that's where you and the papers is in dead wrong! That's how they're foolin' you and ev'ry other guy not in the know. I'll tell you where that gold is. I'll tell you where it lies, to the foot, at this minute!"

"Well?"

"She's lyin' in the store-room in a pile o' wooden

boxes, on that Panama Comp'ny's pier down at the foot o' Twenty-eight' Street!"

"You're dreamin', Tony, dreamin'. No sane folks leave gold lyin' round loose that way. No, sir; that's what they've got a nice stone Sub-Treasury for."

"Look a' here, Chuck," went on the tense treble voice. "Jus' figure out what day this is. And find out when them wreckers got that gold out o' the *Finance's* strong room. And what d'you get? They lightered them boxes up the North River at one o'clock Saturday afternoon. They swung in next to the *Advance* and put a half-a-dozen cases o' lead paint aboard. Then they tarpaulined them boxes o' gold and swung into the Panama Comp'ny's slip and unloaded that cargo *at two o'clock Saturday afternoon!*"

"'Well, s'pose they did?'"

"Don't you tumble? Saturday afternoon there's no Sub-Treasury open. And to-day's Sunday, ain't it? And they won't get into that Sub-Treasury until to-morrow morning. And as sure as I know I'm sittin' in this chair I know that gold's lyin' out there on that Twenty-eight' Street pier!"

No one in that little room seemed to stir. They seemed to be sitting in silent tableau. Then I could hear the man with the bass voice slowly and meditatively intone his low-life expletive.

"Well, I'll be damned!"

The youngest of the trio spoke again, in a lowered but none the less tense voice.

"In gold, Chuck, pure gold! In fine yellow gold lyin' there waitin' to be rolled over and looked after!

Talk about treasure-huntin'! Talk about Spanish Mains and pirate ships! My Gawd, Chuck, we don't need to travel down to no Mosquito Coast to dig up our doubloons! We got 'em right here at our back door!"

Some one struck a match.

"But how're we goin' to pick 'em?" placidly inquired the man called Chuck. It was as apparent that he already counted himself one of the party as it was that their intention had not quite carried him off his feet.

"Look here," broke in the more fiery-minded youth known as Tony, and from the sound and the short interludes of silence he seemed to be drawing a map on a slip of paper. "Here's your pier. And here's your store-room. And here's where your gold lies. And here's the first door. And here's the second. We don't need to count on the doors. They've got a watchman somewhere about here. And they've put two of their special guards here at the land end of the pier. The store-room itself is empty. They've got it double-locked, and a closed-circuit alarm system to cinch the thing. But what t'ell use is all that when we can eat right straight up into the bowels o' that room without touchin' a lock or a burglar alarm, without makin' a sound!"

"How?" inquired the bass voice.

"Here's your pier bottom. Here's the river slip. We row into that slip without showin' a light, and with the kicker shut off, naturally. We slide in under without makin' a sound. Then we get our measurements. Then we make fast to this pile, and throw out a line to this one, and a second to this one, to hold us steady against the tide and the ferry wash. Then we find our right plank. We can do that by pokin' a flashlight up against 'em where it'll never be seen. Then we take a brace and bit and run a row of holes across that plank, the two rows about thirty inches apart, each hole touchin' the other. Don't you see, with a good sharp extension bit we can cut out that square in half an hour or so, without makin' any more noise than you'd make scratchin' a match on your pants leg!"

"And when you get your square?"

"Then Redney and me climbs through. Redney'll be the stall. He watches the door from the inside. You stay in the boat, with an eye peeled below. I pass you the gold. We cut loose and slip off with the tide. When we're out o' hearin' we throw on the kicker and go kitin' down to that Bath Beach joint o' yours where we'll have that six hundred and ten thousand in gold melted down and weighed out before they get that store-room door unlocked in the morning!"

"Not so loud, Tony; not so loud!" cautioned the conspirator called Redney. There was a moment of silence.

In that silence, and without the aid of my microphone, I heard the sound of steps as they approached my door and came to a stop.

"Listen!" suddenly whispered one of the men in the other room.

As I sat there, listening as intently as my neighbors,

the knob of my door turned. Then the door itself was impatiently shaken.

That sound brought me to my feet with a start of alarm. Accident had enmeshed me in a movement that was too gigantic to be overlooked. The one thing I could not afford, at such a time, was discovery.

Three silent steps took me across the room to my microphone. One movement lifted that telltale instrument from its hooks, and a second movement jerked free the wires pinned in close along the gas pipe. Another movement or two saw my apparatus slipped into its case and the case dropped down behind the worn leather-couch back. Then I sank into the chair beside the table, knowing there was nothing to betray me. Yet as I lounged there over my bottle of *Chianti* I could feel the excitement of the moment accelerate my pulse. I made an effort to get my feelings under control as second by second slipped away and nothing of importance took place. It was, I decided, my wall-eyed waiter friend, doubtlessly bearing a message that more lucrative patrons were desiring my fetid-aired cubby-hole.

Then, of a sudden, I became aware of the fact that voices were whispering close outside my door. The next moment I heard the crunch of wood subjected to pressure, and before I could move or realize the full meaning of that sound, the door had been forced open and three men were staring in at me.

I looked up at them with a start—with a start, however, which I had the inspired foresight to translate into a hiccough. That hiccough, in turn, reminded me that I had a rôle to sustain, a rôle of care-free and irresponsible intoxication.

So, opprobrious as the whole farce seemed to me, I pushed my hat back on my head and blinkingly stared at the three intruders as they sauntered nonchalantly into the room. Yet as I winked up at them, with all the sleepy unconcern at my command, I could plainly enough see that each one of that trio was very much on the alert. It was the youngest of the three who turned to me.

"Kiddo," he said, and he spoke with an oily suavity not at all to my liking, "I kind o' thought I smelt gas leakin' in here."

He had the effrontery to turn and stare about at the four walls of the room. Then he moved easily across the floor to where the champagne picture hung. What he saw, or did not see there, I had no means of determining. For to turn and look after him would be to betray my part.

"That leak ain't in this room," admitted the second of the trio, a swarthy and loose-lipped land pirate with a sweep of carroty bang which covered his left eyebrow. I knew, even before he spoke, that he was the man called Redney, just as I knew the first speaker was the youth they had addressed as Tony. About the third man, who towered above the other two in his giant-like stature, there was a sense of calm and solidity that seemed almost pachydermatous. Yet this same solidity in some way warned me that he might be the most dangerous of them all.

" 'Sssh all righ'!" I loosely condoned, with a sleepy

lurch of the body. How much my acting was convincing to them was a matter of vast concern to me. The
man named Tony, who had continued to study the
wooden partition against which my microphone had
hung, turned back to the table and calmly seated himself beside me. My heart went down like an elevator
with a broken cable when I noticed the nervous sweat
which had come out on his forehead.

"Say, Sister, this puts the drinks on us," he declared, with an airiness which I felt to be as unreal as
my own inebriacy. I saw him motion for the other
two to seat themselves.

They did so, a little mystified, each man keeping his
eyes fixed on the youth called Tony. The latter
laughed, for no reason that I could understand, and
over his shoulder bawled out the one word, "Shimmey!"

Shimmey, I remembered, was my friend the wall-
eyed waiter. And this waiter it was who stepped trail-
ingly into the room.

"Shimmey," said the voluble youth at my side. "We
introoded on this gen'lmun. And we got to square
ourselves. So what's it goin' to be?"

"Nothin'!" I protested, with a repugnant wave of
the hand.

"You mean we ain't good enough for you to drink
with?" demanded the youth called Tony. I could see
what he wanted. I could feel what was coming. He
was looking for some reason, however tenuous, to
start trouble. Without fail he would find it in time.
But my one desire was to defer that outcome as long

as possible. So I grinned back at him, rather idiotically, I'm afraid.

"All righ'," I weakly agreed, blinking about at my tormentors. "Bring me a bran'y an' soda."

The other three men looked at the waiter. The waiter, in turn, looked at them. Then he studied my face. There was something decidedly unpleasant in his coldly speculative eyes.

"Shimmey, d'you understand? This gen'lmun wants a brandy and soda."

The waiter, still studying me, said "Sure!" Then he turned on his heel and walked out of the room.

I knew, in my prophetic bones, that there was some form of trouble brewing in that odoriferous little room. But I was determined to side-step it, to avoid it, to the last extremity. And I was still nodding amiably about when the waiter returned with his tray of glasses.

"Well, here's how," said the youth, and we all lifted our glasses.

That brandy and soda, I knew, would not be the best of its kind. I also clearly saw that it would be unwise to decline it. So I swallowed the stuff as a child swallows medicine.

I downed it in a gulp or two, and put the glass back on the table. Then I proceeded to wipe my mouth with the back of my hand, after the approved fashion of my environment.

It was fortunate, at that moment, that my hand was well up in front of my face. For as the truth of the whole thing came home to me, as sharp and quick as an electric spark, there must have been a second or two when my rôle slipped away from me.

I had, it is true, inwardly fortified myself against a draught that would prove highly unpalatable. But the taste which I now detected, the acrid, unmistakable, over-familiar taste, was too much for my startled nerves. I hid my sudden body-movement only by means of a simulated hiccough. The thing I had unmistakably tasted was chloral hydrate. They had given me knock-out drops.

The idea, of a sudden, struck me as being so ludicrous that I laughed. The mere thought of any such maneuver was too much for me—the foolish hope that a homeopathic little pill of chloral would put me under the table, like any shopgirl lured from a dance-hall! They were trying to drug me. Drug *me*, who had taken double and triple doses night after night as I fought for sleep!

They were trying to drug me, me who on my bad nights had, even known the narcotic to be forcibly wrested from my clutch by those who stood appalled at the quantities that my too-immured system demanded, and knew only too well that in time it meant madness!

But I remembered, as I saw the three men staring at me, that I still had a rôle to sustain. I knew it would be unwise to let those sweet worthies know just how the land lay. I enjoyed an advantage much too exceptional and much too valuable to be lightly surrendered.

So to all outward signs and appearances I let the

drug do its work. I carefully acted out my pretended lapse into somnolent indifference. I lost the power to coordinate; my speech grew inarticulate; my shoulders drooped forward across the table edge. I wilted down like a cut dock-weed, until my face lay flat against the beer-stained wood.

"He's off," murmured the man called Chuck. He rose to his feet as he spoke.

"Then we got to beat it," declared the youth named Tony, already on his feet. I could hear him take a deep breath as he stood there. "And the next long nose who gives me heart disease like this is goin' to get five inches o' cold steel!"

He knelt before me as he spoke, pulled back my feet, and ran a knife edge along the shoe laces. Then he promptly pulled the shoes from my feet. These shoes, apparently, he kept in his hand. "That'll help anchor 'im, I guess," I heard him remark.

"Let's get on the job," suggested the big man, obviously impatient at the delay. "If there's nothin' but five inches o' plank between us and that gold, let's get busy!"

I sat there, with my head on that table top so redolent of the soured beverages of other days, and listened to them as they moved across the room. I listened as they passed out and swung the door shut behind them. I waited there for another minute or two, without moving, knowing only too well what a second discovery would entail.

My head was still bent over that unclean table top when I heard the broken-latched door once more pushed slowly open, and steps slowly cross the floor to where I sat.

Some one, I knew, was staring down at me. I felt four distended finger-tips push inquisitively at my head, rolling it a little to one side. Then the figure bending above me shifted its position. A hand felt cautiously about my body. It strayed lower, until it reached my watch pocket.

I could see nothing of my enemy's face, and nothing of his figure. All I got a glimpse of was a patch of extremely soiled linen. But that glimpse was sufficient. It was my friend, the wall-eyed waiter, resolutely deciding to make hay while the sun shone. And that decided me.

With one movement I rose from the chair and wheeled about so as to face him. That quick body-twist spun his own figure half-way around.

My fist caught him on the foreward side of the relaxed jawbone. He struck the worn leather couch as he fell, and then rolled completely over, as inert as a sack of bran.

I looked down at him for a moment or two as he lay face upward on the floor. Then I dropped on one knee beside him, unlaced his well-worn and square-toed shoes, and calmly but quietly adjusted them to my own feet.

Once out in the street I quickened my steps and rounded the first corner. Then I hurried on, turning still another, and still another, making doubly sure I was leaving no chance to be trailed. Then I swung aboard a cross-town car, alighting again at a corner flashing with the vulgar brilliance of an all-night drug store.

I went straight to the telephone booth of that drug store, and there I promptly called up police headquarters. I felt, as I asked for Lieutenant Belton, a person of some importance. Then I waited while the precious moments flew by.

Lieutenant Belton, I was finally informed, was at his room in the Hotel York, on Seventh Avenue. So I rang up the Hotel York, only to be informed that the lieutenant was not in.

I slammed the receiver down on its hook and ended that foolish colloquy. I first thought of Patrolman McCooey. Then I thought of Doyle, and then of Creegan, my old detective friend. Then with a jaw-grip of determination I caught that receiver up again, ordered a taxicab, paid for my calls, consulted my watch, and paced up and down like a caged hyena, waiting for my cab.

Another precious ten minutes slipped away before I got to Creegan's door in Forty-third Street. Then I punched the bell-button above the mail-box, and stood there with my finger on it for exactly a minute and a half.

I suddenly remembered that the clicking door latch beside me implied that my entrance was being automatically solicited. I stepped into the dimly lighted hall and made my way determinedly up the narrow carpeted stairs, knowing I would get face to face with Creegan if I had to crawl through a fanlight and pound in his bedroom door.

But it was Creegan himself who confronted me as I swung about the banister turn of that shadowy second landing.

"You wake those kids up," he solemnly informed me, "and I'll kill you!"

"Creegan," I cried, and it seemed foolish that I should have to inveigle and coax him into a crusade which meant infinitely more to him than to me, "I'm going to make you famous!"

"How soon?" he diffidently inquired.

"Inside of two hours' time," was my answer.

"Don't *wake* those *kids!*" he commanded, looking back over his shoulder.

I caught him by the sleeve, and held him there, for some vague premonition of a sudden withdrawal and a bolted door made me desperate. And time, I knew, was getting short.

"For heaven's sake, listen to me," I said as I held him. And as he stood there under the singing gas-jet, with his hurriedly lit and skeptically tilted stogie in one corner of his mouth, I told him in as few words as I could what had happened that night.

"Come in while I get me boots on," he quietly remarked, leading me into an unlighted hallway and from that into a bedroom about the size of a ship's cabin. "And speak low," he said, with a nod toward the rear end of the hall. Then as he sat on the edge of the bed pulling on his shoes he made me recount everything for the second time, stopping me with an occasional question, fixing me occasionally with a cogitative eye.

"But we haven't a minute to lose," I warned him,

for the second time, as he slipped away into a remoter cubby-hole of a room to see, as he put it, "if the kids were keeping covered."

He rejoined me at the stairhead, with the softest of Irish smiles still on his face. By the time we had reached the street and stepped into the waiting taxi, that smile had disappeared. He merely smoked another stogie as we made our way toward the end of Twenty-eighth Street.

At Tenth Avenue, he suddenly decided it was better for us to go on foot. So he threw away his stogie end, a little ruefully, and led me down a street as narrow and empty as a river bed. He led me into a part of New York that I had never before known. It was a district of bald brick walls, of rough flag and cobblestone underfoot, of lonely street lamps, of shipping platforms and unbroken warehouse sides, of storage yards and milk depots, with railway tracks bisecting streets as empty as though they were the streets of a dead city. No one appeared before us. Nothing gave signs of being alive in that area of desolate ugliness which seemed like the back yard of all the world concentrated in a few huddled squares.

We were almost on West Street itself before I was conscious of the periodic sound of boat whistles complaining through the night. The air, I noticed, took on a fresher and cleaner smell. Creegan, without speaking, drew me in close to a wall-end, at the corner, and together we stood staring out toward the Hudson.

Directly in front of us, beyond a forest of barrels which stippled the asphalt, a veritable city of barrels

that looked like the stumpage of a burned-over Doug-
las-pine woodland, stood the façade of the Panama
Company's pier structure. It looked substantial and
solemn enough, under its sober sheeting of corru-
gated iron. And two equally solemn figures, somber
and silent in their dark overcoats, stood impassively
on guard before its closed doors.

"Come on," Creegan finally whispered, walking
quickly south to the end of Twenty-seventh Street.
He suddenly stopped and caught at my arm to arrest
my own steps. We stood there, listening. Out of the
silence, apparently from mid-river, sounded the quick
staccato coughing of a gasoline motor. It sounded
for a moment or two, and then it grew silent.

We stood there without moving. Then the figure
at my side seemed stung into sudden madness. Without a word of warning or explanation, my companion
ducked down and went dodging in and out between
the huddled clumps of barrels, threading a circuitous
path toward the slip edge. I saw him drop down on
all fours and peer over the string-piece. Then I saw
him draw back, rise to his feet, and run northward
toward the pier door where the two watchmen stood.

What he said to those watchmen I had no means of
knowing. One of them, however, swung about and
tattooed on the door with a night-stick before Creegan
could catch at his arm and stop him. Before I could
join them, some one from within had thrown open the
door. I saw Creegan and the first man dive into the
chill-aired, high-vaulted building, with its exotic odors
of spice and coffee and mysterious tropical bales. I

heard somebody call out to turn on the lights, and then Creegan's disgustedly warning voice call back for him to shut up. Then somewhere in the gloom inside a further colloquy took place, a tangle of voices, a call for quietness, followed by a sibilant hiss of caution.

Creegan appeared in the doorway again. I could see that he was motioning for me.

"Come on," he whispered. And I tiptoed in after him, under that echoing vaulted roof where the outline of a wheeled gangway looked oddly like the skeleton of some great dinosaur, and the pungent spicy odors took me at one breath two thousand miles southward into the Tropics.

"Take off those shoes," quietly commanded Creegan. And I dropped beside him on the bare pier planks and slipped my feet out of Shimmey's ungainly toed shoes.

A man moved aside from a door as we stepped silently up to it. Creegan turned to whisper a word or two in his ear. Then he opened the door and led me by the sleeve into the utter darkness within, closing and locking the door after him.

I was startled by the sudden contact of Creegan's groping fingers. I realized that he was thrusting a short cylindrical object up against my body.

"Take this," he whispered.

"What is it?" I demanded in an answering whisper.

"It's a flashlight. Press here—see! And throw it on when I say so!"

I took the flashlight, pressed as he told me, and saw a feeble glow of light from its glass-globed end. About this end he had swathed a cotton pocket handkerchief

More actual illumination would have come from a tallow candle. But it seemed sufficient for Creegan's purpose. I could see him peer about, step across to a pile of stout wooden boxes, count them, test one as to its weight, squint once more searchingly about the room, and then drop full length on the plank flooring and press his ear to the wood.

He writhed and crawled about there, from one quarter of the room to another, every minute or so pressing an ear against the boards under him, for all the world like a physician sounding a patient's lungs. He kept returning, I noticed, to one area in the center of the room, not more than a yard away from the pile of wooden boxes. Then he leaned forward on his knees, his hands supporting his body in a grotesque bear-like posture. He continued to kneel there, intently watching the oak plank directly in front of him.

I saw one hand suddenly move forward and feel along an inch or two of this plank, come to a stop, and then suddenly raise and wave in the air. I did not realize, at that moment, that the signal was for me.

"Put her out," he whispered. And as I lifted my thumb from the contact point the room was again plunged into utter darkness. Yet through that darkness I could hear a distinct sound, a minute yet unmistakable noise of splintering wood, followed by an even louder sound, as though an auger were being withdrawn from a hole in the planking at my feet.

Then up from the floor on which Creegan knelt a thin ray of light flickered and wavered and disappeared. A rumble of guarded voices crept to my ears, and again I could detect that faint yet pregnant gnawing sound as the busy auger once more ate into the oak planking on which we stood.

I suddenly felt Creegan's hand grope against my knee. He rose to his feet beside me.

"It's all right," he whispered, with a calmness which left me a little ashamed of my own excitement. "You stay here until I come back."

I stood there listening to the slight noise of the door as he opened it and closed it after him. I stood there as I once more heard the telltale splintering of wood, indicating that the auger had completed its second hole through the planking. Then came the sound of its withdrawal, and again the wavering pencil of light as the men under the pier examined their work and adjusted their auger-end for its next perforation.

A new anxiety began to weigh on me. I began to wonder what could be keeping Creegan so long. I grew terrified at the thought that he might be too late. Vague contingencies on which I had failed to reckon began to present themselves to me. I realized that those three desperate men, once they saw I was again coming between them and their ends, would be satisfied with no half measure.

Then occurred a movement which nearly brought a cry from my startled lips. A hand, reaching slowly out through the darkness, came in contact with my knee, and clutched it. That contact, coming as it did without warning, without reason, sent a horripilating chill through all my body. The wonder was that I did not kick out, like a frightened colt, or start to flail about me with my flashlight. All I did, however, was to twist and swing away. Yet before I could get to my feet, the hand had clutched the side of my coat. And as those clutching fingers held there, I heard a voice whisper out of the darkness:

"Here, take this," and the moment I heard it I was able to breathe again, for I knew it was Creegan. "You may need it."

He was holding what I took to be a policeman's night-stick up in front of me. I took it from him, marveling how he could have re-entered that room without my hearing him.

"There's a light-switch against the wall there, they say," was his next whispered message to me. "Find it. Keep back there and throw it on if I give the word."

I felt and pawed and padded about the wall for an uncertain moment or two. "Got it?" came Creegan's whispering voice across the darkness.

"Yes," I whispered back.

He did not speak again, for a newer sound fell on both his ears and mine. It was a sound of prodding and prying, as though the men below were jimmying at their loosened square of planking.

I leaned forward, listening, for I could hear the squeak and grate of the shifting timber block. I did not hear it actually fall away. But I was suddenly conscious of a breath of cooler air in the room where I stood and the persistent ripple of water against pile-sides.

Then I heard a treble voice say, "A little higher."

The speaker seemed so close that I felt I could have stooped down and touched his body. I knew, even before I saw the spurt of flame where he struck a match along the floor, that the man was already half-way up through the hole. I could see the dirt-covered, claw-like hand as it held the match, nursing the tiny flame, patiently waiting for it to grow. It was not until this hand held the flaring match up before his very face that Creegan moved.

That movement was as simple as it was unexpected. I had no distinct vision of it, but I knew what it meant. I knew, the moment I heard the dull and sickening impact of seasoned wood against a human skull-bone.

There was just one blow. But it was so well placed that a second seemed unnecessary. Then, as far as I could judge, Creegan took hold of the stunned man and drew him bodily up through the hole in the floor.

A moment later a voice was saying, "Here, pull!" And I knew that the second man was on his way up into the room.

What prevented Creegan from repeating his maneuver with the night-stick I could not tell. But I knew the second attack was not the clean-cut job of the first, for even as Creegan seized the body half-way up through the opening, the struggle must have begun.

The consciousness that that struggle was not to be promptly decided, that a third factor might at any moment appear in the fight, stung me into the necessity of some sort of blind action on my own part. I remembered the first man, and that he would surely be armed. I ran out toward the center of the room, stumbled over the boxes of gold, and fell sprawling along the floor. Without so much as getting on my feet again I groped about until I found the prostrate body. It took me only a moment to feel about that limp mass, discover the revolver, and draw it from its pocket. I was still on my knees when I heard Creégan call out through the darkness.

"The light!" he gasped. "Turn on the light!"

I swung recklessly about at the note of alarm in his voice and tried to grope my way toward him. Only some last extremity could have wrung that call from him. It was only too plain that his position was now a perilous one. But what that peril was I could not decipher.

"Where are you?" I gasped, feeling that wherever he lay he needed help, that the quickest service I could render him would be to reach his side.

"The light, you fool!" he cried out. "The light!"

I dodged and groped back to the wall where I felt the light-switch to be. I had my fingers actually on the switch when an arm like the arm of a derrick itself swung about through the darkness, and at one stroke knocked the breath out of my body and flattened me against the wall. Before I could recover my breath, a second movement spun me half around and lifted me clear off my feet. By this time the great arm was close about me, pinning my hands down to my side.

Before I could cry out or make an effort to escape, the great hulk holding me had shifted his grip, bringing me about directly in front of him and holding me there with such a powerful grasp that it made breathing a thing of torture. And as he held me there, he reached out and turned on the light with his own hand. I knew, even before I actually saw him, that it was the third man.

I also knew, even before that light came on, what his purpose was. He was holding me there as a shield in front of him. This much I realized even before I saw the revolver with which he was menacing the enemy in front of him. What held my blinking and bewildered eyes was the fact that Creegan himself, on the far side of the room, was holding the struggling and twisting body of the man called Redney in precisely the same position.

But what disheartened me was the discovery that Creegan held nothing but a night-stick in his left hand. All the strength of his right hand, I could see, was needed to hold his man. And his revolver was still in his pocket.

I had the presence of mind to remember my own revolver. And my predicament made me desperate. That gang had sown their dragon teeth, I decided, and now they could reap their harvest.

I made a pretense of struggling away from my captor's clutch, but all the while I was working one elbow back, farther and farther back, so that a hand could be thrust into my coat pocket. I reached the pocket without being noticed. My fingers closed about the butt of the revolver. And still my purpose had not been discovered.

As I lifted that firearm from my pocket I was no

longer a reasoning human being. At the same time I felt this red flash of rage through my body, I also felt the clutch about my waist relax. The big man behind me was ejaculating a single word. It was *"Creegan!"*

Why that one shout should have the debilitating effect on Creegan which it did, I had no means of knowing. But I saw the sweat-stained and blood-marked face of my colleague suddenly change. His eyes stared stupidly, his jaw fell, and he stood there, panting and open-mouthed, as though the last drop of courage had been driven out of his body.

I felt that he was giving up, that he was surrendering, even before I saw him let the man he had been holding fall away from him. But I remembered the revolver in my hand and the ignominies I had suffered. And again I felt that wave of something stronger than my own will, and I knew that my moment had come.

I had the revolver at half-arm, with its muzzle in against the body crushing mine, when Creegan's voice, sharp and short as a bark, arrested that impending finger-twitch.

"Stop!" he cried, and the horror of his voice puzzled me.

"Why?" I demanded in a new and terrible calm. But I did not lower my revolver.

"Stop that!" he shouted, and his newer note, more of anger than fear, bewildered me a bit.

"Why?"

But Creegan, as he caught at the coat collar of the

man called Redney, did not answer my repeated question. Instead, he stared at the man beside me.

"Well, I'll be damned!" he finally murmured.

"What t' hell are *you* doin' here?" cut in the big man as he pushed my revolver-end away and dropped his own gun into his pocket. "I've been trailin' these guys for five weeks—and I want to know why you're queerin' my job!"

Creegan, who had been feeling his front teeth between an investigatory thumb and forefinger, blinked up at the big man. Then he turned angrily on me.

"Put down that gun!" he howled. He took a deep breath. Then he laughed, mirthlessly, disgustedly. "You can't shoot *him!*"

"Why can't I?"

"He's a stool pigeon! A singed cat!"

"And what's a stool pigeon?" I demanded. "And what's a singed cat?"

Creegan laughed for the second time as he wiped his mouth with the back of his hand.

"He's a Headquarters gink who stays on the fence, and tries to hunt with the hounds the same time he's runnin' with the hares—and gener'ly goes round queerin' an honest officer's work. And I guess he's queered ours. So about the only thing for us to do, 's far as I can see, is for us to crawl off home and go to bed!"

CHAPTER VIII

THE DUMMY-CHUCKER

IT WAS unquestionably a momentous night, that night I discharged Latreille. I had felt the thing coming, for weeks. But I had apparently been afraid to face it. I had temporized and dallied along, dreading the ordeal. Twice I had even bowed to tacit blackmail, suavely disguised as mere advances of salary. Almost daily, too, I had been subjected to vague insolences which were all the more humiliating because they remained inarticulate and incontestable. And I realized that the thing had to come to an end.

I saw that end when Benson reported to me that Latreille had none too quietly entertained a friend of his in my study, during my absence. I could have forgiven the loss of the cigars, and the disappearance of the *cognac,* but the foot-marks on my treasured old San Domingoan mahogany console-table and the overturning of my Ch'ien-lung lapis bottle were things which could not be overlooked.

I saw red, at that, and promptly and unquaveringly sent for Latreille. And I think I rather surprised that cool-eyed scoundrel, for I had grown to know life a little better, of late. I had learned to stand less timorous before its darker sides and its rougher seams. I could show that designing chauffeur I was no longer in his power by showing that I was no longer afraid of him. And this latter I sought to demonstrate by promptly and calmly and unequivocally announcing that he was from that day and that hour discharged from my service.

"You can't do it!" he said, staring at me with surprised yet none the less insolent eyes.

"I have done it," I explained. "You're discharged, now. And the sooner you get out the better it will suit me."

"And you're ready to take that risk?" he demanded, studying me from under his lowered brows.

"Any risks I care to assume in this existence of mine," I coolly informed him, "are matters which concern me alone. Turn your keys and service-clothes and things in to Benson. And if there's one item missing, you'll pay for it."

"How?" he demanded, with a sneer.

"By being put where you belong," I told him.

"And where's that?"

"Behind bars."

He laughed at this. But he stopped short as he saw me go out to the door and fling it open. Then he turned and faced me.

"I'll make things interesting for you!" he announced, slowly and pregnantly, and with an ugly forward-thrust of his ugly pointed chin.

It was my turn to laugh.

"You *have* made them interesting," I acknowledged. "But now they are getting monotonous."

"They won't stay that way," he averred.

I met his eye, without a wince. I could feel my fighting blood getting hotter and hotter.

"You understand English, don't you?" I told him. "You heard me say get out, didn't you?"

He stared at me, with that black scowl of his, for a full half minute. Then he turned on his heel and stalked out of the room.

I wasn't sorry to see him go, but I knew, as he went, that he was carrying away with him something precious. He was carrying away with him my peace of mind for that whole blessed night.

Sleep, I knew, was out of the question. It would be foolish even to attempt to court it. I felt the familiar neurasthenic call for open spaces, the necessity for physical freedom and fresh air. And it was that, I suppose, which took me wandering off toward the water-front, where I sat on a string-piece smoking my seventh cigarette and thinking of Creegan and his singed cat as I watched the light-spangled Hudson.

I had squatted there for a full half-hour, I think, before I became even vaguely conscious of the other presence so near me. I had no clear-cut memory of that figure's advent. I had no impression of its movement about my immediate neighborhood, I feel sure, until my self-absorbed meditations were broken into by the discovery that the stranger on the same wharf where I loitered had quietly and deliberately risen to an erect position. It startled me a little, in fact, to find that he was standing at one end of the same string-piece where I sat.

Then something about the figure brought a slow perplexity into my mind, as I lounged there inhaling the musky harbor-odors, under a sky that seemed

Italian in its serenity, and a soft and silvery moon that made the shuttling ferries into shadows scaled with Roman gold. This perplexity grew into bewilderment, for as I studied the lean figure with its loose-fitting paddock-coat flapping in the wharf-end breeze I was reminded of something disturbing, of something awesome. The gaunt form so voluminously draped, the cadaverous face with the startlingly sunken cheeks, the touch of tragedy in the entire attitude, brought sharply and suddenly to my mind the thought of a shrouded and hollow-eyed symbol of Death, needing only the scythe of honored tradition to translate it into the finished picture.

He stood there for some time, without moving, studying the water that ran like seamless black velvet under the wharf-end. Then he slowly took off his coat, folded it and placed it on the string-piece, and on top of this again placed his hat. Then he laughed audibly. I looked away, dreading that some spoken triviality might spoil a picture so appealingly mysterious. When I next peered up at him he seemed engaged in the absurd occupation of slowly turning inside out the quite empty pockets of his clothing. Then he once more looked down at the black water.

Those oily velvet eddies, apparently, were too much for him. I saw him cover his face with his hands and sway back with a tragically helpless mutter of "I can't do it!" And both the gesture and the words made my mind go back to the man from Medicine Hat.

A thousand crawling little tendrils of curiosity overran resentment at being thus disturbed in my quest for solitude. I continued my overt watch of the incredibly thin stranger who was still peering down at the slip-water. I was startled, a minute or two later, to hear him emit a throat-chuckle that was as defiant as it was disagreeable. Then with an oddly nervous gesture of repudiation he caught up his hat and coat, turned on his heel, and passed like a shadow down the quietness of the deserted wharf.

I turned and followed him. The tragedy recorded on that pallid face was above all pretense. He could never be taken for a "dummy-chucker"; the thing was genuine. Any man who could squeeze life so dry that he thought of tossing it away like an orange-skin was worth following. He seemed a contradiction to everything in the city that surrounded us, in that mad city where every mortal appeared so intent on living, where the forlornest wrecks clung so feverishly to life, and where life itself, on that murmurous and moonlit night, seemed so full of whispered promises.

I followed him back to the city, speculating, as idle minds will, on who and what he was and by what mischance he had been cast into this lowest pit of indifferency. More things than his mere apparel assured me he was not a "crust-thrower." I kept close at his heels until we came to Broadway, startling myself with the sudden wonder if he, too, were a victim of those relentless hounds of wakefulness that turn night into a never-ending inquisition.

Then all speculation suddenly ended, for I saw that he had come to a stop and was gazing perplexedly up and down the light-strewn channel of Broadway. I noticed his eye waver on a passing figure or two, whom he seemed about to accost. Then, as though from that passing throng he beheld something kindred and common in my face, he touched me lightly on the arm.

I came to a stop, looking him full in the face. There seemed almost a touch of the supernatural in that encounter, as though two wondering ghosts stood gazing at each other on the loneliest edges of a No-man's Land.

He did not speak, as I was afraid he might, and send a mallet of banality crashing down on that crystal of wonderment. He merely waved one thin hand toward the façade of a mirrored and pillared caravansary wherein, I knew, it was the wont of the homeless New Yorker to purchase a three-hour lease on three feet of damask and thereby dream he was probing the innermost depths of life. His gesture, I saw, was an invitation. It was also a challenge.

And both the invitation and the challenge I accepted, in silence, yet by a gesture which could not be mistaken. It was in silence, too, that I followed him in through the wide doorway and seated myself opposite him at one of the rose-shaded parallelograms of white linen that lay about us in lines as thick and straight as tombstones in an abbey-floor.

I did not look at him, for a moment or two, dreading as I did the approaching return to actuality. I let my gaze wander about the riotous-colored room into which the flood-tide of the after-theater crowds was now eddying. It held nothing either new or appealing to me. It was not the first time I had witnessed the stars of stageland sitting in perigean torpor through their seven-coursed suppers, just as it was not the first time I had meekly endured the assaulting vulgarities of onyx pillars and pornographic art for the sake of what I had found to be the most matchless cooking in America.

It seemed an equally old story to my new friend across the table, for as I turned away from the surrounding flurry of bare shoulders, as white and soft as a flurry of gull-wings, I saw that he had already ordered a meal that was as mysteriously sumptuous as it was startlingly expensive. He, too, was apparently no stranger to Lobster Square.

I still saw no necessity for breaking the silence, although he had begun to drink his wine with a febrile recklessness rather amazing to me. Yet I felt that with each breath of time the bubble of mystery was growing bigger and bigger. The whole thing was something more than the dare-devil adventure of a man at the end of his tether. It was more than the extravagance of sheer hopelessness. It was something which made me turn for the second time and study his face.

It was a remarkable enough face, remarkable for its thinness, for its none too appealing pallor, and for a certain tragic furtiveness which showed its owner to be not altogether at peace with his own soul. About his figure I had already detected a certain note of distinction, of nervous briskness, which at once lifted him above the place of the anemic street-adventurer. There was something almost Heraclitean in the thin-lipped and satyric mouth. The skin on the sunken cheeks seemed as tight as the vellum across a snare-drum. From the corner of his eyes, which were shadowed by a smooth and pallid frontal-bone, radiated a network of minutely small wrinkles. His hands, I could see, were almost femininely white, as womanish in their fragility as they were disquieting in their never-ending restless movements. In actual years, I concluded, he might have been anywhere between twenty-five and thirty-five. He was at least younger than I first thought him. Then I looked once more about the crowded room, for I had no wish to make my inspection seem inquisitorial. He, too, let his eyes follow mine in their orbit of exploration. Then, for the first time, he spoke.

"They'll suffer for this some day!" he suddenly declared, with the vehemence of a Socialist confronted by the voluptuosities of a Gomorrah. "They'll suffer for it!"

"For what particular reason?" I inquired, following his gaze about that quite unapprehensive roomful of decorous revelers.

"Because one-half of them," he avowed, "are harpies, and the other half are thieves!"

"Are you a New Yorker?" I mildly asked him. I had been wondering if, under the circumstances, even a voluminous paddock-coat would be reckoned as adequate payment for a repast so princely. The man had already proved to me that his pockets were empty.

"No, I'm not," he retorted. "I'm from God's country."

That doubtlessly irreproachable yet vaguely denominated territory left me so much in doubt that I had to ask for the second time the place of his origin.

"I come from Virginia," he answered, "and if I'd stayed there I wouldn't be where I am to-night."

As this was an axiom which seemed to transcend criticism I merely turned back to him and asked: "And where are you to-night?"

He lifted his glass and emptied it. Then he leaned forward across the table, staring me in the eyes as he spoke. "Do you know the town of Hanover, down in Virginia?"

I had to confess that I did not. As he sat looking at me, with a shadow of disappointment on his lean face, I again asked him to particularize his present whereabouts.

"I'm on the last inch of the last rope-end," was his answer.

"It seems to have its ameliorating condition," I remarked, glancing about the table.

He emitted a sharp cackle of a laugh.

"You'll have to leave me before I order the liqueur. This," with a hand-sweep about the cluster of dishes, "is some music I'll have to face alone. But what's that, when you're on the last inch of the last rope-end?"

"Your position," I ventured, "sounds almost like a desperate one."

"Desperate!" he echoed. "It's more than that. It's hopeless!"

"You have doubtless been visiting Wall Street or possibly buying mining-stock?" was my flippant suggestion. His manner of speech, I was beginning to feel, was not markedly southern.

"No," he cried with quick solemnity. "I've been *selling* it."

"But such activities, I assumed, were far removed from the avenues of remorse."

He stared at me, absently, for a moment or two. Then he moved restlessly in his chair.

"Did you ever hear of a wire-tapper?" he demanded.

"Quite often," I answered.

"Did you ever fall for one of their yarns? Did you ever walk into one of their nice, gold-plated traps and have them shake you down for everything you owned—and even for things you didn't own?"

Here was a misfortune, I had to confess, which had not yet knocked at my door.

"I came up to this town with thirty thousand dollars, and not quite a third of it my own. Twenty of it was for a marble quarry we were going to open up on the Potomac. They sent me north to put through the deal. It was new to me, all right. I wasn't used to a town where they have to chain the door-mats down and you daren't speak to your neighbor without a police-permit. And when a prosperous-looking traveler at my hotel got talking about horses and races and the string that Keene sent south last winter, he struck something that was pretty close to me, for that's what we go in for down home—horse-breeding and stock-farming. Then he told me how the assistant superintendent of the Western Union, the man who managed their racing department, was an old friend of his. He also allowed this friend of his was ready to phone him some early track-returns, for what he called a big rakeoff. He even took me down to the Western Union Building, on the corner of Dey and Broadway, and introduced me to a man he called the assistant superintendent. We met him in one of the halls—he was in his shirt-sleeves, and looked like a pretty busy man. He was to hold back the returns until our bets could be laid. He explained that he himself couldn't figure in the thing, but that his sister-in-law might possibly handle the returns over her own private wire."

"That sounds very familiar," I sadly commented.

"He seemed to lose interest when he found I had only a few thousand dollars of my own. He said the killing would be a quarter of a million, and the risk for holding up the company's despatches would be too great for him to bother with small bets. But he said he'd try out the plan that afternoon. So my traveler friend took me up to a pool-room with racing-sheets and blackboards and half a dozen telegraph keys and twice as many telephones. It looked like the real thing to me. When the returns started to come in and we got our flash, our private tip from the Western Union office, I tried fifty dollars on a three-to-one shot."

"And of course you won," was my sympathetic rejoinder, as I sat listening to the old, sad tale. "You always do."

"Then I met the woman I spoke about, the woman who called herself the sister-in-law of the racing-wire manager."

"And what was *she* like?" I inquired.

"She looked a good deal like any of these women around here," he said with an eye-sweep over the flurry of gull-wing backs and the garden of finery that surrounded us. *"She looked good enough to get my thirty thousand and put me down and out."*

At which he laughed his mirthless and mummy-like laugh.

"You see, I had sense enough to get cold feet, over-night. But when I talked it over with her next day, and I saw her calling up a few of her Wall Street friends, I kind of forgot my scruples. She got me thinking crooked again. And that's all. That's where the story ends."

His docility, as I sat thinking of that odious and flamboyant type of she-harpy, began to irritate me.

"But why should it end here?" I demanded.

"Because I put twenty thousand dollars of other people's money into a phony game, and lost it."

"Well, what of it?"

"Do you suppose I could go home with that hanging over me?"

"Supposing you can't. Is that any reason why you should lie down at this stage of the game?"

"But I've lost," he averred. "Everything's gone!"

" 'All is not lost,' " I quoted, feeling very much like

Francis the First after the Battle of Pavia, " 'till honor's self is gone!' "

"But even *that's* gone," was his listless retort. He looked up, almost angrily, at my movement of impatience. "Well, what would *you* do about it?" he challenged.

"I'd get that money back or I'd get that gang behind the bars," was the answer I flung out at him. "I'd fight them to a finish."

"But there's nothing to fight. There's nobody to get hold of. That Western Union man was only a capper, a come-on. Their poolroom's one of those dirigible kind that move on when the police appear. Then they'd claim I was as bad as they were, trying to trick an honest bookmaker out of his money. And besides, there's nothing left to show I ever handed them over anything."

"Then I'd keep at it until I found something," I declared. "How about the woman?'

"She'd be too clever to get caught. And I don't suppose she'd know me from a piece of cheese."

"Do you suppose you could in any way get me in touch with her?" I asked.

"But she's got police protection. I tried to have her arrested myself. The officer told me to be on my way, or he'd run me in."

"Then you know where she lives?" I quickly inquired.

He hesitated for a moment, as though my question had caught him unawares. Then he mentioned one of the smaller apartment-hotels of upper Broadway.

"And what's her name?"

Again he hesitated before answering.

"Oh, she's got a dozen, I suppose. The only one I know is Brunelle, Vinnie Brunelle. That's the name she answered to up there. But look here—you're not going to try to see her, are you?"

"That I can't tell until to-morrow."

"I don't think there'll be any to-morrow, for me," he rejoined, as his earlier listless look returned to his face. He even peered up a little startled, as I rose to my feet.

"That's nonsense," was my answer. "We're going to meet here to-morrow night to talk things over."

"But why?" he protested.

"Because it strikes me you've got a duty to perform, a very serious duty. And if I can be of any service to you it will be a very great pleasure to me. And in the meantime, I might add that I am paying for this little supper."

There is no activity more explosive than that of the chronic idler. Once out on Broadway, accordingly, I did not let the grass grow under my feet. Two minutes at the telephone and ten more in a taxicab brought me in touch with my old friend Doyle who was "working" a mulatto shooting case in lower Seventh Avenue as quietly as a gardener working his cabbage-patch.

"What do you know about a woman named Vinnie Brunelle?" I demanded.

He studied the pavement. Then he shook his head. The name clearly meant nothing to him.

"Give me something more to work on!"

"She's a young woman who lives by her wits. She keeps up a very good front, and now and then does a variety of the wire-tapping game."

"I wonder if that wouldn't be the Cassal woman Andrus used as a come-on for his Mexican mine game? But *she* claimed Andrus had fooled her."

"And what else?" I inquired.

Doyle stood silent, wrapt in thought for a moment or two.

"Oh, that's about all. I've heard she's an uncommonly clever woman, about the cleverest woman in the world. But what are you after?"

"I want her record—all of it."

"That sort of woman never has a record. That's what cleverness is, my boy, maintaining your reputation at the expense of your character."

"You've given birth to an epigram," I complained, "but you haven't helped me out of my dilemma." Whereupon he asked me for a card.

"I'm going to give you a line to Sherman—Camera-Eye Sherman we used to call him down at Headquarters. He's with the Bankers' Association now, but he was with our Identification Bureau so long he knows 'em all like his own family."

And on the bottom of my card I saw Doyle write: "Please tell him what you can of Vinnie Brunelle."

"Of course I couldn't see him to-night?"

Doyle looked at his watch.

"Yes, you can. You'll get him up at his apartment on Riverside. And I'll give you odds you'll

find the old night-owl playing bezique with his sister-
in-law!"

That, in fact, was precisely what I found the man
with the camera-eye doing. He sat there dealing out
the cards, at one o'clock in the morning, with a face
as mild and bland as a Venetian cardinal feeding his
pigeons.

My host looked at the card in his fingers, looked at
me, and then looked at the card again.

"She got you in trouble?" was his laconic query.

"I have never met the lady. But a friend of mine
has, I'm sorry to say. And I want to do what I can
to help him out."

"How much did he lose?"

"About thirty thousand dollars, he claims."

"What was the game?"

"It appears to have been one of those so-called wire-
tapping coups."

"Funny how that always gets 'em!" ruminated that
verger of long-immured faces. "Well, here's what I
know about Vinnie. Seven or eight years ago she was
an artist's model. Then a sculptor called Delisle took
her over to Paris—she was still in her teens then. But
she was too brainy to stick to the studio-rat arrange-
ment. She soon came to the end of her rope there.
Then she came home—I've an idea she tried the stage
and couldn't make it go. Then she was a pearl-agent
in London. Then she played a variation of the 'lost-
heir' game in what was called the Southam case, working under an English confidence-man called Adams.
Then she got disgusted with Adams and came back to

America. She had to take what she could get, and for a few weeks was a capper for a high-grade woman's bucket-shop. When Headquarters closed up the shop she went south and was in some way involved in the Parra uprising in the eastern end of Cuba."

My apathetic chronicler paused for a moment or two, studying his lacerated cigar-end.

"Then she married a Haytian half-cast Jew in the Brazilian coffee business who'd bought a Spanish title. Then she threw the title and the coffee-man over and came back to Washington, where she worked the ropes as a lobbyist for a winter or two. Then she took to going to Europe every month or so. I won't say she was a steamship gambler. I don't think she was. But she made friends—and she could play a game of bridge that'd bring your back hair up on end. Then she worked with a mining share manipulator named Andrus. She was wise enough to slip from under before he was sent up the river. And since then they tell me, she's been doing a more or less respectable game or two with Coke Whelan, the wire-tapper. And that, I guess, is about all."

"Has she ever been arrested that you know of? Would they have her picture, for instance, down at Headquarters?"

The man who had grown old in the study of crime smiled a little.

"You can't arrest a woman until you get evidence against her."

"Yet you're positive she was involved in a number of crooked enterprises?"

"I never called her a crook," protested my host, with an impersonality that suddenly became as Olympian as it was exasperating. "No one ever proved to me she was a crook."

"Well, I'm going to prove it. And I rather imagine I'm going to have her arrested. Why," I demanded, nettled by his satiric smile, "you don't mean to say that a woman like that's immune?"

"No, I wouldn't say she was immune, exactly. On the other hand, I guess she's helped our people in a case or two, when it paid her."

"You mean she's really an informer, what they call a welcher?"

"By no means. She's just clever, that's all. The only time she ever turned on her own people was when they threw her down, threw her flat. Then she did a bit of secret service work for Wilkie's office in Washington that gave her more pull than all your Tammany 'politics' east of Broadway."

"Am I to understand that what you call politics and pull, then, will let a woman rob a man of thirty thousand dollars and go scot free?"

"My dear fellow, that type of woman never *robs* a man. She doesn't need to. They just blink and hand it over. Then they think of home and mother, about ten hours after."

"But that doesn't sound quite reasonable," I contended.

The older man looked solemnly at his cigar-end before asking his next question.

"Have you seen her yet?"

"No, I haven't," I replied as I rose to go. "But I intend to."

He moved his heavy shoulder in a quick half-circular forward thrust. It might have meant anything. But I did not linger to find out. I was too impressed with the need of prompt and personal action on my part to care much for the advice of outsiders.

But as each wakeful hour went by I found myself possessed of an ever widening curiosity to see this odd and interesting woman who, as Doyle expressed it, had retained reputation at the expense of character.

It was extremely early the next morning that I presented myself at Vinnie Brunelle's apartment-hotel. I had not only slept badly; I had also dreamed of myself as a flagellant monk sent across scorching sands to beg a barbaric and green-eyed Thais to desist from tapping telegraph-wires leading into the camp of Alexander the Great.

The absurdity of that opianic nightmare seemed to project itself into my actual movements of the morning. The exacting white light of day withered the last tendril of romance from my quixotic crusade. It was only by assuring myself, not so much that I was espousing the cause of the fallen, but that I was about to meet a type of woman quite new to my experience, that I was able to face Miss Brunelle's unbetrayingly sober door.

This door was duly answered by a maid, by a surprisingly decorous maid in white cap and apron. I was conscious of her veiled yet inquisitorial eye resting on my abashed person for the smallest fraction of a second. I almost suspected that in that eye might be detected a trace of something strangely like contempt. But, a little to my astonishment, I was admitted quite without question.

"Miss Brunelle is just back from her morning ride in the park," this maid explained.

I entered what was plainly a dining-room, a small but well-lighted chamber. Striped awnings still kept the tempered autumn sun from the opened windows, where a double row of scarlet geranium-tops stood nodding in the breeze. At one end of the table in the center of the room sat a woman, eating her breakfast.

She was younger looking, much younger looking, than I had thought she would be. Had she not sat there already inundated by the corroding acids of an earlier prejudice, I would even have admitted that she was an extremely beautiful woman.

She was in a rose-colored dressing-gown which showed a satin-like smoothness of skin at the throat and arms. Her eyes, I could see, were something between a hazel and a green, set wide apart under a Pallas Athena brow, that might have been called serene, but for some spirit of rebellion vaguely refracted from the lower part of the face. The vividness of her color, which even the flaming sweep of her gown could not altogether discount, made me think of material buoyancies, of living flesh and blood and a body freshly bathed.

Her gaze was direct, disconcertingly direct. It even made me question whether or not she was reading my thought as I noted that her hands were large and white, that her mouth, for all its brooding discontent, was not without humor, and, strangely enough, that her fingers, ears, and throat were without a touch of that jewelry which I had thought peculiar to her kind.

That she possessed some vague yet menacing gift of intimacy I could only too plainly feel, not so much from the undisturbed ease of her pose and the negligently open throat and arms as from the direct gaze of those searching and limpid eyes, which proclaimed that few of the poppied illusions of life could flower in their neighborhood. This discomforting sense of mental clarity, in fact, forced me into the consciousness not so much of being in the presence of a soft and luxurious body as of standing face to face with a spirit that in its incongruous way was as austere as it was alert.

"You wish to see me?" she said, over her coffee-cup. My second glance showed me that she was eating a breakfast of iced grape-fruit and chops and scrambled eggs and buttered toast.

"Very much," I answered.

"About what?" she inquired, breaking a square of toast.

"About the unfortunate position of a young gentleman who has just parted company with thirty thousand dollars!"

She bent her head, with its loose and heavy coils of dark hair, and glanced at my card before she spoke again.

"And what could I possibly do for him?"

There was something neither soothing nor encouraging in her unruffled calmness. But I did not intend to be disarmed by any theatrical parade of tranquillity.

"You might," I suggested, "return the thirty thousand."

There was more languor than active challenge in her glance as she turned and looked at me.

"And I don't think I even know who you are," she murmured.

"But I happen to know just who you are," was my prompt and none too gentle rejoinder.

She pushed back her hair—it seemed very thick and heavy—and laughed a little.

"Who am I?" she asked, licking the toast-crumbs from her white finger-tips.

"I'll tell you who you are," I retorted with some heat. "You're a figure-model that a sculptor named Delisle took to Paris. You're the old running-mate of Adams in the Southam heir case. You're the wife of a Haytian half-caste Jew with a Spanish title. You're the woman who worked with Andrus, the wild-cat mine-swindler who is now doing time in Sing Sing. And just at present you're the accomplice of a gang headed by a certain Coke Whelan, a wire-tapper well known to the police."

Her face showed no anger and no resentment as I unburdened myself of this unsavory pedigree. Her studious eyes, in fact, became almost contemplative.

"And supposing that's all true?" she finally asked. "What of it?"

She sat and looked at me, as cool as a cucumber.

I could no longer deny that as a type she interested me. Her untamed audacities were something new to my experience. She seemed still in the feral state. Her mere presence, as she sat there in the lucid morning light, exerted over me that same spell which keeps children rooted before a circus-animal's cage.

"What of it?" she quietly repeated.

"I'm afraid there's nothing of it," I admitted, "except in the one point where it impinges on my personal interests. I intend to get that thirty thousand dollars back."

The resolution of my tone seemed only to amuse her.

"But why come to me?" she asked, turning back to her breakfast. "Supposing I really was a cog in some such machinery as you speak of, how much would be left on one small cog when so many wheels had to be oiled?"

"I have no great interest in your gang and its methods. All I know is a tremendous wrong's been done, and I want to see it righted."

"From what motive?" she asked, with that barbaric immediacy of approach peculiar to her.

"From the most disinterested of motives—I mean from the standpoint of that rather uncommon thing known as common honesty."

She looked at me, long and intently, before she spoke again. I had the feeling of being taken up and turned over and inspected through a lens of implacable clarity.

"Do you know this young man who lost his money on what he took for a fixed race?"

"I have met him," I answered, a little discomfited at the recollection of how tenuous that acquaintanceship was.

"And have you known him long?"

I was compelled to confess to the contrary.

"And you understand the case, through and through?"

"I think I do," was my curt retort.

She turned on me quickly, as though about to break into an answering flash of anger. But on second thoughts she remained silent.

"If life were only as simple as you sentimental charity-workers try to make it!" she complained, studying me with a pitying look which I began most keenly to resent. She swept the room with a glance of contempt. "If all those hay-tossers who come to this town and have their money taken away from them were only as lamb-like as you people imagine they are!"

"Is this an effort toward the justification of theft?" I inquired. For the first time I saw a touch of deeper color mark her cheek. I had been conscious of a certain duality in her mental equipment, just as I could detect a higher and lower plane in her manner of speech.

"Not at all," she retorted. "I'm not talking of theft. And we may as well keep to cases. I don't think very much is ever gained by being impolite, do you?"

I was compelled to agree with her, though I could not shake off the feeling that she had in some dim way scored against me. And this was the woman I had once feared would try to toy with my coat-buttons.

"I'm afraid," she went on with her grave abstraction of tone, "that you'll find me very matter-of-fact. A woman can't see as much of the world as I have and then—oh! and then beat it back to the Elsie Books."

I resented the drop to the lower plane, as though she had concluded the upper one to be incomprehensible to me.

"Pardon me, madam; it's not my windmills I'm trying to be true to; it's one of my promises."

"The promise was a very foolish one," she mildly protested. "Yet for all that," she added, as an afterthought, "you're intelligent. And I like intelligence."

Still again her deep and searching eyes rested on my face. Her next words seemed more a soliloquy than a speech.

"Yet you *are* doing this just to be true to your windmills. You're doing it out of nothing more than blind and quixotic generosity."

The fact that my allusion had not been lost on her pleased me a little more, I think, than did her stare of perplexed commiseration.

"Isn't is odd," she said, "how we go wrong about things, how we jump at conclusions and misjudge people? You think, at this very moment, that I'm the one who sees crooked, that I'm the one who's lost my perspective on things. And now I'm going to do something I hadn't the remotest intention of doing when you came into this room."

"And what is that?"

"I'm going to show you how wrong you've been, how wrong you are."

"In what?" I inquired as she again sat in silence before me.

"In everything," she finally answered, as she rose to her feet. I was at once more conscious of her physical appeal, of her inalienable bodily buoyancy, as I saw her standing there at her full height. The deep flow of color in her loosely draped gown gave her an almost pontifical stateliness. Instinctively I rose as she did. And I could see by her eyes that the courtesy was neither negligible nor distasteful to her. She was about to say something; then she stopped and looked at me for a hesitating moment or two.

One would have thought, from the solemnity of that stare, that she faced the very Rubicon of her life. But a moment later she laughed aloud, and with a multitudinous rustling of skirts crossed the room and opened an inner door.

Through this door, for a moment or two, she completely left my sight. Then she returned, holding a cabinet photograph in her hand.

"Do you know it?" she quietly asked as she passed it over to me.

It took but a glance to show me that it was a picture of the man whose cause I was at that moment espousing, the man I had followed from the North River pier-end the night before. A second glance showed me that the photograph had been taken in London; it bore the stamped inscription: "Garet Childs, Regent's Park, N. W."

The woman's sustained attitude of anticipation, of

expectation unfulfilled, puzzled me. I saw nothing remarkable about the picture or her possession of it.

"This, I believe, is the man you're trying to save
from the clutches of a wire-tapper named Whelan,
Coke Whelan, as you call him?"

I acknowledged that it was.

"Now look at the signature written across it," she
prompted.

I did as she suggested. Inscribed there I read:
"Sincerely and more, Duncan Cory Whelan."

"Have I now made the situation comparatively clear
to you?" she asked, watching my face as I looked from
her to the photograph and then back to her again.

"I must confess, I don't quite grasp it," I admitted,
thinking at the moment how her face in the strong
side-light from the windows had taken on a quite accidental touch of pathos.

"It's simply that the man you are trying to save
from Coke Whelan *is Coke Whelan himself.*"

"That's impossible!" was my exclamation.

"It's not impossible," she said a little wearily, "because the whole thing's nothing more than a plant, a
frame-up. And you may as well know it. It can't
go on. The whole thing *was a plan to trap you.*"

"A plan to trap me?"

"Yes, a carefully worked-out plan to gather you in.
And now, you see, the machinery is slipping a cog
where it wasn't expected to!"

I stood there incredulous, dazed, trying to digest the
shock.

"You mean that the man I met and talked to last night is actually an accomplice of yours?"

"Yes," she answered, "if you care to put it that way."

"But I can't believe it. I *won't* believe it until you bring him here and prove it."

She sank into her chair, with a half-listless motion for me to be seated.

"Do you know why he's called Coke Whelan?" she demanded.

I did not.

"That, too, you've got to know. It's because he's a heroin and cocaine fiend. He's killing himself with the use of drugs. He's making everything impossible. It's left him irresponsible, as dangerous as any lunatic would be at large."

She turned and looked at a tiny jeweled watch.

"He will be here himself by ten o'clock. And if he heard me saying what I am at this moment, he would kill me as calmly as he'd sit at a café table and lie to you."

"But what's the good of those lies?"

"Don't you suppose he knew you were Witter Kerfoot, that among other things you owned a house, and a car, that you were worth making a try for? Don't you suppose he found all that out before he laid his ropes for this wire-tapping story? Can't you see the part *I* was to play, to follow his lead and show you how we could never bring his money back, but that we could face the gang with their own fire. I was to weaken and show you how we could tap the tapper's own wire, choose the race that promised the best odds, and induce you to plunge against the house on what seemed a sure thing?"

I sat there doing my best to Fletcherize what seemed a remarkably big bite of information.

"But why are you telling me all this?" I still parried, pushing back from the flattering consciousness that we had a secret in common, that I had proved worthy an intimacy denied others.

"Because I've just decided it's the easiest way out."

"For whom?"

"For me!"

"What made you decide that?"

"I've done a lot of thinking since you came into this room. And for a long time I've been doing a lot of thinking. I don't do things Coke Whelan's way. I took pity on him, once. But I'm getting tired of trying to keep him up when he insists on dropping lower, lower and lower every day. Don't imagine, because you've got certain ideas of me and my life, that I haven't common sense, that I can't see what this other sort of thing leads to. I've seen too many of them, and how they all ended. I may have been mixed up with some strange company in my day, but I want you to know that I've kept my hands clean!"

She had risen by this time and was moving restlessly about the room.

"Do you suppose I'd ever be satisfied to be one of those painted Broadway dolls and let my brain dry up like a lemon on a pantry shelf? I couldn't if I wanted to. I couldn't, although I can see how easy it makes everything. I tell you, a woman with a reputation like mine has got to pay, and keep on paying. She's got to pay twice over for the decencies of life. She's got to pay twice over for protection. Unless you're respectable you can't have respectable people about you. You've got to watch every one in your circle, watch them always, like a hawk. You've got to watch every step you take, and every man you meet—and sometimes you get tired of it all."

She sat down, in the midst of her febrile torrent of words, and looked at me out of clouded and questioning eyes. I knew, as I met that troubled gaze, so touched with weariness and rebellion, that she was speaking the truth. I could see truth written on her face. I tried to imagine myself in her place, I tried to see life as she had seen it during those past years, which no charity could translate into anything approaching the beautiful. And much as I might have wished it, I could utter no emptiest phrase of consolation. Our worlds seemed too hopelessly wide apart for any common view-point.

"What are you going to do?" I asked, humiliated by the inadequacy of the question even as I uttered it.

"I'm going to get away from it. I'm going to get away where I can breathe in peace. Oh, believe me, I can be irreproachable without even an effort. I want to be. I prefer it. I've found how much easier it makes life. It's not my past I've been afraid of. It's that one drug-soaked maniac, that poor helpless thing who knows that if I step away from him he daren't round a street-corner without being arrested."

She stopped suddenly and the color ebbed out of her face. Then I saw her slowly rise to her feet and look undecidedly about the four corners of the room. Then she turned to me. Her eyes seemed ridiculously terrified.

"*He's come!*" she said, in little more than a whisper. "He's here now!"

The door opened before I could speak. But even before the mummy-faced man I had left at the café table the night before could stride into the room, the woman in front of me sank back into her chair. Over her face came a change, a veil, a quickly coerced and smiling-lipped blankness that reminded me of a pastoral stage-drop shutting out some grim and moving tragedy.

The change in the bearing and attitude of the intruder was equally prompt as his startled eyes fell on me calmly seated within those four walls. He was not as quick as the woman in catching his cue.

I could plainly detect the interrogative look he flashed at her, the look which demanded as plain as words: "What is this man doing here?"

"This," said the woman at the table, in her most dulcet and equable tones, "is the altruistic gentleman who objects to your losing thirty thousand dollars in a race which I had no earthly way of controlling."

Here, I saw, was histrionism without a flaw. Her fellow-actor, I could also see, was taking more time to adjust himself to his rôle. He was less finished in his assumption of accusatory indignation. But he did his best to rise to the occasion.

"I've got to get that money back," he cried, leveling a shaking finger at her. "And I'm going to do it without dragging my friends into it!"

She walked over to the windows and closed them before she spoke.

"What's the use of going over all that?" she continued, and I had the impression of sitting before a row of foot-lights and watching an acted drama. "You took your risk and lost. I didn't get it. It's not my fault. You know as well as I do that McGowan and Noyes will never open up unless you're in a position to make them. It's a case of dog eat dog, of fighting fire with fire. And I've just been telling it all to your friend Mr. Kerfoot, who seems to think he's going to have some one arrested if we don't suddenly do the right thing."

"I want my money!" cried the man named Whelan. I could see, even as he delivered his lines, that his mind was floundering and groping wildly about for solid ground.

"And Mr. Kerfoot," continued the tranquil-voiced woman at the table, "says he has a house in Gramercy Square where we can go and have a conference. I've phoned for a telegraph operator called Downey to be there, so we can decide on a plan for tapping McGowan's wire."

"And what good does that do me?" demanded the mummy-faced youth.

"Why, that gives Mr. Kerfoot his chance to bet as much as he likes, to get as much back from McGowan as he wants to, without any risk of losing."

"But who handles the money?" demanded the wary Whelan.

"That's quite immaterial. *You* can, if you're his friend, or he can handle it himself. The important thing is to get your plan settled and your wire tapped. And if Mr. Kerfoot will be so good as to telephone to his butler I'll dress and be ready in ten minutes."

She leaned forward and swung an equipoise phone-bracket round to my elbow.

But I did not lift the receiver from its hook. For at that moment the door abruptly opened. The maid in the white cap and apron stood trembling on its threshold.

"That's a lie!" she was crying, in her shrill and sudden abandon, and the twin badges of servitude made doubly incongruous her attitude of fierce revolt. "It's a lie, Tony! She's welched on you!"

She took three quick steps into the room.

"She's only playing you against this guy. I've heard every word of it. She never phoned for an operator. That's a lie. She's throwing you down, for good. She's told him who you are and what your game is!"

I looked at the other woman. She was now on her feet.

"Don't let her fool you this time, Tony," was the passionate cry from the quivering breast under the incongruous white apron-straps. "Look at how she's treated you! Look at your picture there, that she cinched her talk with! She never did half what I did for you! And now you're letting her throw you flat! You're standing there and letting—"

The woman stopped, and put her hands over her ears. For she saw, even as I did, the hollow-eyed, mummy-faced youth reach a shaking hand back to his hip.

"You liar!" he said, as his hand swung up with the revolver in it. "You lying welcher!" he cried, in a thin and throaty voice that was little more than a cackle.

He took one step toward the woman in the rose-colored dressing-gown. She was, I could see, much the taller of the two. And she was standing, now, with her back flat against the wall. She made no attempt to escape. She was still staring at him out of wide and bewildered eyes when he fired.

I saw the spit of the plaster and the little shower of mortar that rained on her bare shoulder from the bullet-hole in the wall.

Then I did a very ordinary and commonplace thing. I stooped quickly forward to the end of the table and caught up the nickeled coffee-pot by its ebony handle. The lunatic with the smoking revolver saw my sudden movement, for as I swung the metal instrument upward he turned on me and fired for the second time.

I could feel the sting of the powder smoke on my up-thrust wrist. I knew then that it was useless to try to reach him. I simply brought my arm forward and let the metal pot fly from my hand. I let it fly forward, targeting on his white and distorted face.

Where or how it struck I could not tell. All I knew was that he went down under a scattering geyser of black coffee. He did not fire again. He did not even move. But as he fell the woman in the cap and apron dropped on her knees beside him. She knelt there with an inarticulate cry like that of an animal over its fallen mate, a ludicrous, mouse-like sound that was almost a squeak. Then she suddenly edged about and reached out for the fallen revolver.

I saw her through the smoke, but she had the gun in her hand before I could stop her. She fought over it like a wildcat. The peril of that combat made me desperate. Her arm was quite thin, and not overly strong. I first twisted it so the gun-barrel pointed outward. The pain, as I continued to twist, must have been intense. But I knew it was no time for half-measures. Just how intense that pain was came home to me a moment later, when the woman fell forward on her face, in a dead faint.

The other woman had calmly thrown open the windows. She watched me, almost apathetically, as I got to my feet and stooped in alarm over the unconscious man in his ridiculous welter of black coffee. Then she stepped closer to me.

"Have you killed him?" she asked, with more a touch of childlike wonder than any actual fear.

"No; he's only stunned."

"But how?"

"It caught him here on the forehead. He'll be around in a minute or two."

Once more I could hear the multitudinous rustle as she crossed the room.

"Put him here on my bed," she called from an open door. And as I carried him in and dropped him in a sodden heap on the white coverlet, I saw the woman unsheathe her writhing body of its rose-colored wrapping. From that flurry of warmth her twisting body emerged almost sepulchrally white. Then she came to a pause, bare-shouldered and thoughtful before me.

"Wait!" she said as she crossed the room. "I must telephone McCausland."

"Who's McCausland?" I asked as she stepped out into the dining-room.

"He's a man I know at Headquarters," was her impersonal-noted reply.

For the second time, as she stepped hurriedly back into the room with me, I was conscious of the satin-like smoothness of her skin, the baby-like whiteness of her rounded bare arms. Then wholly unabashed by my presence, she flung open a closet door and tossed a cascade of perfumed apparel out beside the bed where I stood.

"What are you going to do?" I demanded, as I saw her white-clad figure writhe itself into a street dress. There was something primordial and Adamitic in the very calmness with which she swept through the flimsy reservations of sex. She was as unconscious of my predicament as a cave woman might have been. And the next moment she was crushing lingerie and narrow-toed shoes and toilet articles and undecipherable garments of folded silk into an English club-bag. Then she turned to glance at her watch on the dresser.

"I'm going!" she said at last, as she caught up a second hand-bag of alligator skin and crammed into it jewel boxes of dark plush and cases of different colored kid, and still more clothing and lingerie. "I'm going to catch the *Nieuw Amsterdam*."

"For where?"

"For Europe!"

Her quick and dextrous hands had pinned on a hat and veil as I stood in wonder watching her.

"Call a taxi, please," she said, as she struggled into her coat. "And a boy for my bags."

I was still at the receiver when she came into the room and looked down for a moment at the woman moaning and whimpering on the coffee-stained floor. Then she began resolutely and calmly drawing on her gloves.

"Couldn't we do something for them?" I said as I stepped back into the bedroom for her hand-bag.

"What?" she demanded, as she leaned over the bed where Whelan's reviving body twitched and moved.

"There must be something."

"There's nothing. Oh, believe me, you can't help him. I can't help him. He's got his own way to go. And it's a terribly short way!"

She flung open a bureau drawer and crammed a further article or two down in her still open chatelaine bag.

Then she opened the outer door for the boy who had come for the bags. Then she looked at her watch again.

"You must not come back," she said to me. "They may be here any time."

"Who may?" I asked.

"The police," she answered as she closed the door.

She did not speak again until we were at the side of the taxicab.

"To the Holland American Wharf," she said.

Nor did she speak all the while we purred and hummed and dodged our way across the city. She did not move until we jolted aboard the ferry-boat, and the clanging of the landing-float's pawl-and-rachet told us we were no longer on that shrill and narrow island where the fever of life burns to the edge of its three laving rivers. It was then and only then that I noticed the convulsive shaking of her shoulders.

"What is it?" I asked, helplessly, oppressed by the worlds that seemed to stand between us.

"It's nothing," she said, with her teeth against her lip. But the next minute she was crying as forlornly and openly as a child.

"What is it?" I repeated, as inadequately as before, knowing the uselessness of any debilitating touch of sympathy.

"It's so hard," she said, struggling to control her voice.

"What is?"

"It's so hard to begin over."

"But they say you're the cleverest woman in the world!" was the only consolation I could offer her.

CHAPTER IX

I LIFTED my face to the sudden pelt of the rain-shower, feeling very much like a second edition of King Lear as I did so. Not that I had lost a kingdom, or that I'd ever been turned out of an ungrateful home circle! But something quite as disturbing, in its own small way, had overtaken me.

I had been snubbed by Mary Lockwood. While I stood watching that sudden shower empty upper Broadway as quickly as a fusillade of bullets might have emptied it, I encountered something which quite as promptly emptied my own heart. It was the cut direct. For as I crouched back under my dripping portico, like a toad under a rhubarb-leaf, I caught sight of the only too familiar wine-colored landaulet as it swung about into Longacre Square. I must have started forward a little, without being quite conscious of the movement. And through the sheltering plate-glass of the dripping hood I caught sight of Mary Lockwood herself.

She saw me, at the same time that I saw her. In fact, she turned and stared at me. I couldn't have escaped her, as I stood there under the street-lamp. But no slightest sign of recognition came from that coldly inquiring face. She neither smiled nor bowed nor looked back. And the wine-colored landaulet swept on, leaving me standing there with my sodden hat in my hand and a great ache of desolation in my heart.

She must have seen me, I repeated as I turned disconsolately back and stood watching men and women still ducking under doorways and dodging into side-streets and elbowing into theater-lobbies. It seemed during the next few moments as though that territory once known as the Rialto were a gopher-village and some lupine hunger had invaded it. Before the searching nuzzles of those rain-guests all pleasure-seekers promptly vanished. Gaily cloaked and slippered women stampeded away as though they were made of sugar and they and their gracious curves might melt into nothing at the first touch of water. Above the sidewalk, twenty paces from the empty doorway where I loitered, an awning appeared, springing up like a mushroom from a wet meadow. In toward one end of this awning circled a chain of limousines and taxicabs, controlled by an impassive Hercules in dripping oil-skins. And as a carrier-belt empties grain into a mill-bin, so this unbroken chain ejected hurrying men and women across the wet curb into the light-spangled hopper of the theater-foyer. And the thought of that theater, with its companionable crush of humanity, began to appeal to my rain-swept spirit.

Yet I stood there, undecided, watching the last of the scattering crowd, watching the street that still seemed an elongated bull-ring where a matador or two still dodged the taurine charges of vehicles. I watched the electric display-signs that ran like liquid ivy about the shop fronts, and then climbed and flut-

tered above the roofs, misty and softened by rain. I
watched the ironic heavens pour their unabating floods
down on that congested and overripe core of a city
that no water could wash clean.

Then the desolation of the empty streets seemed to
grow unbearable. The spray that blew in across my
dampened knees made me think of shelter. I saw the
lights of the theater no more than twenty paces away.
It was already a warren of crowded life. The thought
of even what diluted companionship it might offer me
continued to carry an appeal that became more and
more clamorous.

A moment later I stood before its box-office window,
no wider than a medieval leper-squint, from which
cramped and hungry souls buy access to their modern
temples of wónder.

"Standing room only," announced the autocrat of
the wicket. And I meekly purchased my admission-
ticket, remembering that the head usher of that particular theater had in the past done me more than one
slight service.

Yet the face of this haughtily obsequious head
usher, as his hand met mine in that free-masonry
which is perpetuated by certain silk-threaded scraps of
oblong paper, was troubled.

"I haven't a thing left," he whispered.

I peered disconsolately about that sea of heads seeking life through the clumsy lattice of polite melodrama.

"Unless," added the usher at my elbow, "you'll take
a seat in that second lower box?"

Even through the baize doors behind me I could

hear the beat and patter of the rain. It was a case of any port in a storm.

"That will do nicely," I told him and a moment later he was leading me down a side aisle into the curtained recess of the box entrance.

Yet it was not ordained that I should occupy that box in lonely and unrivaled splendor. One of its chairs, set close to the brass rail and plush-covered parapet that barred it off from the more protuberant stage box, was already occupied by a man in full evening dress. He, like myself, perhaps, had never before shared a box with other than his own acquaintances. At any rate, before favoring me with the somewhat limited breadth of his back, he turned on me one sidelong and unmistakably resentful stare.

Yet I looked at this neighbor of mine, as I seated myself, with more interest than I looked at the play-actors across the foot-lights, for I rather preferred life in the raw to life in the sirups of stage emotionalism.

It startled me a little to find that the man, at the moment, was equally oblivious of anything taking place on the stage. His eyes, in fact, seemed fixed on the snowy shoulders of the woman who sat at the back of the stage box, directly in front of him. As I followed the direction of his gaze I was further surprised to discover the object on which it was focused. He was staring, not at the woman herself, but at a pigeon-blood ruby set in the clasp of some pendant or necklace encircling her throat.

There was, indeed, some excuse for his staring at it. In the first place it was an extraordinarily large and vivid stone. But against the background where it lay, against the snow-white column of the neck (whitened, perhaps, by a prudent application of rice powder) it stood out in limpid ruddiness, the most vivid of fire against the purest of snow. It was a challenge to attention. It caught and held the eye. It stood there, just below where the hair billowed into its crown of Venetian gold, as semaphoric as a yard-lamp to a night traveler. And I wondered, as I sat looking at it, what element beyond curiosity could coerce the man at my side into studying it so indolently and yet so intently.

About the man himself there seemed little that was exceptional. Beyond a certain quick and shrewd alertness in his eye-movements as he looked about at me from time to time with muffled resentment which I found not at all to my liking, he seemed medium in everything, in coloring, in stature, in apparel. His face was of the neutral sallowness of the sedentary New Yorker. His intelligence seemed that of the preoccupied office-worker who could worm his way into an ill-fitting dress suit and placidly approve of second-rate melodrama. He seemed so without interest, in fact, that I was not averse to directing my glance once more toward the pigeon-blood ruby which glowed like a live coal against the marble whiteness of the neck in front of me.

It may have been mere accident, or it may have been that out of our united gaze arose some vague psychic force which disturbed this young woman. For as I sat there staring at the shimmering jewel, its wearer suddenly turned her head and glanced back at me. The

next moment I was conscious of her nod and smile, unmistakably in my direction.

Then I saw who it was. I had been uncouthly staring at the shoulder-blades of Alice Churchill—they
were the Park Avenue Churchills—and farther back
in the box I caught a glimpse of her brother Benny,
who had come north, I knew, from the Nicaraguan
coast to recuperate from an attack of fever.

Yet I gave little thought to either of them, I must
confess. At the same time that I had seen that momentarily flashing smile I had also discovered that the
jeweled clasp on the girl's neck was holding in place
a single string of graduated pearls, of very lovely
pearls, the kind about which the frayed-cuff garret-
author and the Sunday "yellows" forever love to romance. I was also not unconscious of the quick and
covert glance of the man who sat so close to me.

Then I let my glance wander back to the ruby, apparently content to study its perfect cutting and its un-
matchable coloring. And I knew that the man beside
me was also sharing in that spectacle. I was, in fact,
still staring at it, so unconscious of the movement of
the play on the stage that the "dark scene," when
every light in the house went out for a second or two,
came to me with a distinct sense of shock.

A murmur of approval went through the house as
the returning light revealed to them a completely meta-
morphosed stage-setting. What this setting was I did
not know, nor did I look up to see. For as my idly
inquisitive glance once more focused itself on the col-
umnar white neck that towered above the chair-back

a second and greater shock came to me. Had that neck stood there without a head I could have been scarcely more startled.

The pigeon-blood ruby was gone. There was no longer any necklace there. The column of snow was without its touch of ruddy light. It was left as disturbingly bare as a target without its bull's-eye. It reminded me of a marble grate without its central point of fire.

My first definite thought was that I was the witness of a crime as audacious as it was bewildering. Yet, on second thought, it was simple enough. The problem of proximity had already been solved. With the utter darkness had come the opportunity, the opportunity that obviously had been watched for. With one movement of the hand the necklace had been quietly and cunningly removed.

My next quick thought was that the thief sat there in my immediate neighborhood. There could be no other. There was no room for doubt. By some mysterious and dextrous movement the man beside me had reached forward and with that delicacy of touch doubtless born of much experience had unclasped the jewels, all the time shrouded by the utter darkness. The audacity of the thing was astounding, yet the completeness with which it had succeeded was even more astounding.

I sat there compelling myself to a calmness which was not easy to achieve. I struggled to make my scrutiny of this strange companion of mine as quiet and leisured as possible.

Yet he seemed to feel that he was still under my eye. He seemed to chafe at that continued survey; for even as I studied him I could see a fine sweat of embarrassment come out on his face. He did not turn and look at me directly, but it was plain that he was only too conscious of my presence. And even before I quite realized what he was about, he reached quietly over, and taking up his hat and coat, rose to his feet and slipped out of the box.

That movement on his part swept away my last shred of hesitation. The sheer precipitancy of his flight was proof enough of his offense. His obvious effort to escape made me more than ever determined to keep on his trail.

And keep on his trail I did, from the moment he sidled guiltily out of that lighted theater foyer into the still drizzling rain of Broadway. Stronger and ever stronger waves of indignation kept sweeping through me as I watched him skulk northward, with a furtive glance over his shoulder as he fled.

He was a good two hundred feet ahead of me when I saw him suddenly turn and at the risk of a visit to the hospital or the morgue, cross the street in the middle of the block, dodge desperately between the surface cars and automobiles, and beat it straight for the Times Building. I promptly threw decorum away and ran, ran like a rabbit, until I came to the Forty-second Street entrance to the drug store through whose revolving doors I had seen my man disappear. I felt reasonably certain he wouldn't stop to drink an ice-cream soda and he didn't, for as I hurried past the

fountain I caught sight of him turning into the stairway that leads to the subway station. I dashed ahead
but he was through the gate before I could catch up
with him. I had no time for a ticket as the guards
were already slamming shut the doors of a south-
bound "local."

"Buy me a ticket," I called to the astonished "chop-
per" as I tossed a dollar bill over the arm which he
thrust out to stop me. I did not wait to argue it out,
for the car door in front of me was already beginning
to close. I had just time to catapult my body in between that sliding door and its steel frame. I knew,
as I caught my breath again, that I was on the platform of the car behind the jewel thief.

And I stood there, carefully scrutinizing the line of
car doors as we pulled into the Grand Central Station.
I did the same as we passed Thirty-third Street, and
the same again at Twenty-eighth Street. The man
had given no sign that he actually knew I was on his
track. He might or might not have seen me. As to
that I had no means of being certain. But I was certain of the fact that he was making off in a panic of
indeterminate fear, that he was doing his utmost to
evade pursuit.

This came doubly home to me as the train stopped
at Twenty-third Street and I saw him step quickly
out of the far end of the car, look about him, and dart
across the station platform and up the stairway two
steps at a time.

I was after him, even more hurriedly. By the time
I reached the street he was swinging up on the step

of a cross-town surface car. To catch that car was out of the question, but I waited a moment and swung aboard the one that followed it, thirty yards in the rear. Peering ahead, I could plainly see him as he dropped from his car on the northeast corner of Sixth Avenue. I could see him as he hurried up the steps of the Elevated, crossed the platform, and without so much as buying a ticket, hurried down the southeast flight of steps.

I had closed in on him by this time, so that we were within a biscuit toss of each other. Yet never once did he look about. He was now doubling on his tracks, walking rapidly eastward along Twenty-third Street. I was close behind him as he crossed Broadway, turning south, and then suddenly tacking about, entered the hallway of the building that was once the Hotel Bartholdi and promptly directed his steps toward the side entrance on Twenty-third Street.

Even as he emerged into the open again he must have seen the antediluvian night-hawk cab waiting there at the curb. What his directions to the driver were I had no means of knowing. But as that dripping and water-proofed individual brought his whip lash down on his steaming horse a door slammed shut in my face. Once more I so far forgot my dignity as to dodge and run like a rabbit, this time to the other side of the cab as it swung briskly northward. One twist and pull threw the cab door open and I tumbled in—tumbled in to see my white-faced and frightened jewel thief determinedly and frenziedly holding down the handle of the opposite door.

His face went ashen as I came sprawling and lurching against him. He would have leaped bodily from the carriage, which was now swinging up an all but deserted Fifth Avenue, had I not caught and held him there with a grimness born of repeated exasperation.

He showed no intention of meekly submitting to that detaining grasp. Seeing that he was finally cornered, he turned on me and fought like a rat. His strength, for one of his weight, was surprising. Much more surprising, however, was his ferocity. And it was a strange struggle, there in the half light of that musty and many-odored night-hawk cab. There seemed something subterranean about it, as though it were a battle at the bottom of a well. And but for one thing, I imagine, it would not, for me, have been a pleasant encounter. It's a marvelous thing, however, to know that you have Right on your side. The panoply of Justice is as fortifying as any chain armor ever made.

And I knew, as we fought like two wharf-rats under a pier-end, that I was right. I knew that my cause was the cause of law and order. That knowledge gave me both strength and a boldness which carried me through even when I saw my writhing and desperate thief groping and grasping for his hip pocket, even when I saw him draw from it a magazine-revolver that looked quite ugly enough to stampede a regiment. And as that sodden-leathered night-hawk went placidly rolling up Fifth Avenue we twisted and panted and grunted on its floor as though it were a mail-coach in

the Sierras of sixty years ago, fighting for the possession of that ugly firearm.

How I got it away from him I never quite knew.
But when I came to my senses I had him on the cab
floor and my knee on his chest, with his body bent
up like a letter U. I held him there while I went
through his pockets, quietly, deliberately, one by one,
with all the care of a customs inspector going through
a suspected smuggler.

I had no time to look over his wallet (which I remembered as being as big as a brief-bag) or his papers,
nor had I time to make sure how much of the jewelry
he wore might be his own. The one thing I wanted
was the pearl necklace with the pigeon-blood ruby.
And this necklace I found, carefully wrapped in a silk
handkerchief tucked down in his right-hand waistcoat
pocket—which, by the way, was provided with a buttoned flap to make it doubly secure.

I looked over the necklace to make sure there could
be no mistake. Then I again wrapped it up in the silk
handkerchief and thrust it well down in my own waistcoat pocket.

"Get up!" I told the man on the cab floor.

I noticed, as I removed my knee from his chest,
what a sorry condition his shirt-front was in and how
his tie had been twisted around under his right ear.
He lay back against the musty cushions, breathing
hard and staring at me out of eyes that were by no
means kindly.

"You couldn't work it!" I said, as I pocketed the
revolver and, having readjusted my own tie, buttoned

my overcoat across a sadly crumpled shirt-front. Then
for the first time the thief spoke.

"D'you know what this'll cost you?" he cried, white
to the lips.

"That's not worrying me," was my calm retort. "I
got what I came after."

He sat forward in his seat with a face that looked
foolishly threatening.

"Don't imagine you can get away with that," he declared. I could afford to smile at his impotent fury.

"Just watch me!" I told him. Then I added more
soberly, with my hand on the door-knob, "And if you
interfere with me after I leave this cab, if you so
much as try to come within ten yards of me to-night,
I'll give you what's coming to you."

I opened the door as I spoke, and dropped easily
from the still moving cab to the pavement. I stood
there for a moment, watching its placid driver as he
went on up the avenue. The glass-windowed door
still swung open, swaying back and forth like a hand
slowly waving me good-by.

Then I looked at my watch, crossed to the University
Club, jumped into a waiting taxi, and dodged back to
the theater, somewhat sore in body but rather well
satisfied in mind.

A peculiar feeling of superiority possessed me as I
presented my door-check and was once more ushered
back to my empty box. During the last hour and a
half that pit full of languid-eyed people had been wit-
nessing a tawdry imitation of adventure. They had
been swallowing a capsule of imitation romance, while

I, between the time of leaving and reentering that garishly lighted foyer, had reveled in adventure at first hand, had taken chances and faced dangers and righted a great wrong.

I felt inarticulately proud of myself as I watched the final curtain come down. This pride became a feeling of elation as I directed my glance toward Alice Churchill, who had risen in the box in front of mine, and was again showering on me the warmth of her friendly smile. I knew I was still destined to be the god from the machine. It was as plain that she was still unconscious of her loss.

I stopped her and her hollow-cheeked brother on their way out, surprising them a little, I suppose, by the unlooked-for cordiality of my greeting.

"Can't you two children take a bite with me at Sherry's?" I amiably suggested. I could see brother and sister exchange glances.

"Benny oughtn't to be out late," she demurred.

"But I've something rather important to talk over," I pleaded.

"And Benny *would* like to get a glimpse of Sherry's again," interposed the thin-cheeked youth just back from the wilds. And without more ado I bundled them into a taxi and carried them off with me, wondering just what would be the best way of bringing up the subject in hand.

I found it much harder, in fact, than I had expected. I was, as time went on, more and more averse to betraying my position, to descending mildly from my pinnacle of superiority, to burning my little pin-wheel of power. I was like a puppy with its first buried bone. I knew what I carried so carefully wrapped up in my waistcoat pocket. I remembered how it had come there, and during that quiet supper hour I was inordinately proud of myself.

I sat looking at the girl with her towering crown of reddish-gold hair. She, in turn, was gazing at her own foolishly distorted reflection in the polished bowl of the chafing-dish from which I had just served her with *capon a la reine*. She sat there gazing at her reflected face, gazing at it with a sort of studious yet impersonal intentness. Then I saw her suddenly lean forward in her chair, still looking at the grotesque image of herself in the polished silver. I could not help noticing her quickly altering expression, the inarticulate gasp of her parted lips, the hand that went suddenly up to her throat. I saw the fingers feel around the base of the compactly slender neck, and the momentary look of stupor that once more swept over her face.

She ate a mouthful of capon, studiously, without speaking. Then she looked up at us again. It was then that her brother Benny for the first time noticed her change of color.

"What's wrong?" he demanded, his thin young face touched suddenly with anxiety.

The girl, when she finally answered him, spoke very quietly. But I could see what a struggle it was costing her.

"Now, Benny, I don't want any fuss," she said, almost under her breath. "I don't want either of you to get excited, for it can't do a bit of good. But my necklace is gone."

"Gone?" gasped Benny. "It can't be!"

"It's gone," she repeated, with her vacant eyes on me as her brother prodded and felt about her skirt, and then even shook out her crumpled opera cloak.

"Does this happen to be it?" I asked, with all the nonchalance at my command. And as I spoke I unwrapped the string of pearls with the pigeon-blood ruby and let them roll on the white damask that lay between us.

She looked at them without moving, her eyes wide with wonder. I could see the color come back into her face. It was quite reward enough to witness the relieving warmth return to those widened eyes, to bask in that lovely and liquid glance of gratitude.

"How," she asked a little weakly, as she reached over and took them up in her fingers, "how did you get them?"

"You lost them in the theater-box during the first act," I told her. Her brother Benny wiped his forehead.

"And it's up to a woman to drop forty thousand dollars and never know it," he cried.

I watched her as she turned them over in her hands. Then she suddenly looked up at me, then down at the pearls, then up at me again.

"*This is not my necklace,*" were the astonishing words that I heard fall from her lips. I knew, of course, that she was mistaken.

"Oh, yes, it is," I quietly assured her.

She shook her head in negation, still staring at me. "What makes you think so?" she asked.

"I don't think it, I know it," was my response. "Those aren't the sort of stones that grow on every bush in this town."

She was once more studying the necklace. And once more she shook her head.

"But I am left-handed," she was explaining, as she still looked down at them, "and I had my clasp, here on the ruby at the back, made to work that way. This clasp is right-handed. Don't you see, it's on the wrong side."

"But you've only got the thing upside down," cried her brother. And I must confess that a disagreeable feeling began to manifest itself in the pit of my stomach as he moved closer beside her and tried to reverse the necklace so that the clasp would stand a left-handed one.

He twisted and turned it fruitlessly for several moments.

"Isn't that the limit?" he finally murmured, sinking back in his chair and regarding me with puzzled eyes. The girl, too, was once more studying my face, as though my movement represented a form of uncouth jocularity which she could not quite comprehend.

"What's the answer, anyway?" asked the mystified youth.

But his bewilderment was as nothing compared to mine. I reached over for the string of pearls with the ruby clasp. I took them and turned them over and over in my hands, weakly, mutely, as though they themselves might in some way solve an enigma which seemed inscrutable. And I had to confess that the whole thing was too much for me. I was still looking down at that lustrous row of pearls, so appealing to the eye in their absolute and perfect graduation, when I heard the younger man at my side call my name aloud.

"Kerfoot!" he said, not exactly in alarm and not precisely in anxiety, yet with a newer note that made me look up sharply.

As I did so I was conscious of the figure so close behind me, so near my chair that even while I had already felt his presence there, I had for the moment taken him for my scrupulously attentive waiter. But as I turned about and looked up at this figure I saw that I was mistaken. My glance fell on a wide-shouldered and rather portly man with quiet and very deepset gray eyes. What disturbed me even more than his presence there at my shoulder was the sense of power, of unparaded superiority, on that impassive yet undeniably intelligent face.

"I want to see you," he said, with an unemotional matter-of-factness that in another would have verged on insolence.

"About what?" I demanded, trying to match his impassivity with my own.

He nodded toward the necklace in my hand.

"About that," he replied.

"What about that?" I languidly inquired.

The portly man at my shoulder did not answer me. Instead he turned and nodded toward a second man, a man standing half a dozen paces behind him, in a damp overcoat and a sadly rumpled shirt-front.

I felt my heart beat faster of a sudden, for it took no second glance to tell me that this second figure was the jewel thief whom I had trailed and cornered in the musty-smelling cab.

I felt the larger man's sudden grip on my shoulder —and his hand seemed to have the strength of a vise —as the smaller man, still pale and disheveled, stepped up to the table. His face was not a pleasant one.

Benny Churchill, whose solicitous eyes bent for a moment on his sister's startled face, suddenly rose to his feet.

"Look here," he said, with a quiet vigor of which I had not dreamed him capable, "there's not going to be any scene here." He turned to the man at my shoulder. "I don't know who you are, but I want you to remember there's a lady at this table. Remember that, please, or I'll be compelled to teach you how to!"

"Sit down!" I told him. "For heaven's sake, sit down, all of you! There's nothing to be gained by heroics. And if we've anything to say, we may as well say it decently."

The two men exchanged glances as I ordered two chairs for them.

"Be so good," I continued, motioning them toward these chairs. "And since we have a problem to discuss, there's no reason we can't discuss it in a semi-civilized manner."

"It's not a problem," said the man at my shoulder, with something disagreeably like a sneer.

"Then by all means don't let's make it one," I protested.

The man behind me was the first to drop into the empty seat on my left. The other man crossed to the farther side of the table, still watching me closely. Then he felt for the chair and slowly sank into it; but not once did he take his eyes from my face. I was glad that our circle had become a compact one, for the five of us were now ranged sufficiently close about the table to fence off our little white-linen kingdom of dissension from the rest of the room.

"That man's armed, remember!" the jewel thief suddenly cried to the stranger on my left. He spoke both warningly and indignantly. His flash of anger, in fact, seemed an uncontrollable one.

"Where's your gun?" said the quiet-eyed man at my side. His own hand was in his pocket, I noticed, and there was a certain malignant line of purpose about his mouth which I did not at all like.

Yet I was able to laugh a little as I put the magazine revolver down on the table; it had memories which were amusing.

The quick motion with which he removed that gun, however, was even more laughable. Yet my returning sense of humor in no way impressed him.

"Where'd you get that gun?" he inquired.

I nodded my head toward the white-faced man opposite me.

"I took it away from your friend there," was my answer.

"And what else did you take?"

There was something impressive about the man's sheer impersonality. It so kept things down to cases.

"This pearl necklace with the ruby clasp," I answered.

"Why?" demanded my interlocutor.

"Because he stole it," was my prompt retort. The big man was silent for a moment.

"From whom?"

"From the lady you have the honor of facing," I answered.

"Where?" was his next question.

I told him. He was again silent for a second or two.

"D'you know who this man is?" he said, with a curt head-nod toward his white-faced colleague.

"Yes," I answered.

"What is he?"

"He's a jewel thief."

The two men stared at each other. Then the man at my side rubbed his chin between a meditative thumb and forefinger. He was plainly puzzled. He began to take on human attributes, and he promptly became a less interesting and a less impressive figure. He looked at Alice Churchill and at her brother, and then back at me again.

Then, having once more absently caressed his chin, he swung about and faced the wondering and silent girl who sat opposite him.

"Excuse me, miss, but would you mind answering a question or two?"

It was her brother who spoke before she had time to answer.

"Wait," he interposed. "Just who are you, anyway?"

The man, for answer, lifted the lapel of his coat and exhibited a silver badge.

"Well, what does that mean?" demanded the quite unimpressed youth.

"That I'm an officer."

"What kind—a detective?"

"Yes."

"For what? For this place?"

"No, for the Maiden Lane Protective Association."

"Well, what's that got to do with us?"

The large-bodied man looked at him a little impatiently.

"You'll understand that when the time comes," was his retort. "Now, young lady," he began again, swinging back to the puzzled girl, "do you say you lost a necklace in that theater-box?"

The girl nodded.

"Yes, I must have," she answered, looking a little frightened.

"And you say it was stolen from you?"

"No, I didn't say that. I had my necklace on when I was in the box—both Benny and I know that."

"And it disappeared?"

"Yes."

"When?"

"I noticed it was gone when I sat down at the table here."

The dominating gentleman turned round to me.

"You saw the necklace from the second box?" he demanded.

"I did," was my answer.

"And you saw it disappear?" he demanded.

"I saw *when* it disappeared," I retorted.

The jewel thief with the crumpled shirt-front tried to break in at this juncture, but the bigger man quickly silenced him with an impatient side swing of the hand.

"When was that?" he continued.

"What difference does it make?" I calmly inquired, resenting the peremptoriness of his interrogations.

He stopped short and looked up at me. Then the first ghost of a smile, a patient and almost sorrowful smile, came to his lips.

"Well, we'll go at it another way. You witnessed this man across the table take the necklace from the young lady?"

"It practically amounts to that."

"That is, you actually detected him commit this crime?"

"I don't think I said that."

"But you assumed he committed this crime?"

"Rather."

"Just when was it committed?"

"During what they call a dark change in the first act."

"You mean the necklace was on before that change and gone when the lights were turned up again?"

"Precisely."

"And the position and actions of this man were suspicious to you?"

"Extremely so."

"In what way?"

"In different ways."

"He had crowded suspiciously close to the wearer of the necklace?"

"He had."

"And his eyes were glued on it during the early part of that act?"

"They certainly were."

"And you watched him?"

"With almost as much interest as he watched the necklace."

"And after the dark change, as you call it, the lady's neck was bare?"

"It was."

"You're sure of this?"

"Positive."

"And what did this man across the table do?"

"Having got what he was after, he hurried out of the theater and made his escape—or tried to make his escape."

"It embarrassed him, I suppose, to have you studying him so closely?"

"He certainly looked embarrassed."

"Of course," admitted my interrogator. Then he sighed deeply, almost contentedly, after which he sat with contemplative and pursed-up lips.

"I guess I've got this whole snarl now," he complacently admitted. "All but one kink."

"What one kink?" demanded Benny Churchill.

The man at my side did not answer him. Instead, he rose to his feet.

"I want you to come with me," he had the effrontery to remark, with a curt head-nod in my direction.

"I much prefer staying here," I retorted. And for the second time he smiled his saddened smile.

"Oh, it's nothing objectionable," he explained. "Nobody's going to hurt you. And we'll be back here in ten minutes."

"But, oddly enough, I have rooted objections to deserting my guests."

"Your guests won't be sorry, I imagine," he replied, as he looked at his silver turnip of a watch. "And we're losing good time."

"Please go," said Alice Churchill, emboldened, apparently, by some instinctive conclusion which she could not, or did not care to, explain. And she was backed up, I noticed, by a nod from her brother.

I also noticed, as I rose to my feet, that I still held the necklace in my hand. I was a little puzzled as to just what to do with it.

"That," said the sagacious stranger, "you'd better leave here. Let the young lady keep it until we get back. And you, Fessant," he went on, turning to the belligerent-lipped jewel thief, "you stay right here and make yourself pleasant. And without bein' rude, you might see that the young lady and her brother stay right here with you."

Then he took me companionably by the arm and led me away.

"What's the exact meaning of all this?" I inquired as we threaded our course out to the cab-stand and went dodging westward along Forty-third Street in a taxi. The rain, I noticed, through the fogged window, was still falling.

"I want you to show me exactly where that man sat in that box," was his answer. "And two minutes in the theater will do it."

"And what good," I inquired, "is that going to do me?"

"It may do you a lot of good," he retorted, as he flung open the cab door.

"I feel rather sorry for you if it doesn't," was my answer as I followed him out. We had drawn up before a desolate-looking stage door over which burned an even more desolate-looking electric bulb. The man turned and looked at me with a short ghost of a grunt, more of disgust than contempt.

"You're pretty nifty, aren't you, for a New York edition of Jesse James?"

And without waiting for my answer he began kicking on the shabby-looking stage door with his foot. He was still kicking there when the door itself was opened by a man in a gray uniform, obviously the night watchman.

"Hello, Tim!" said the one.

"Hello, Bud!" said the other.

"Doorman gone?"

" 'Bout an hour ago!"

Then ensued a moment of silence.

"Burnside say anything was turned in?"

"Didn't hear of it," was the watchman's answer.

"My friend here thinks he's left something in a box. Could you let us through?"

"Sure," was the easy response. "I'll throw on the house-lights for youse. Watch your way!"

He preceded us through a maze of painted canvas and what looked like the backs of gigantic picture-frames. He stepped aside for a moment to turn on a switch. Then he opened a narrow door covered with sheet-iron, and we found ourselves facing the box entrances.

My companion motioned me into the second box while he stepped briskly into that nearer the foot-lights.

"Now, the young lady sat there," he said, placing the gilt chair back against the brass railing. Then he sat down in it, facing the stage. Having done so, he took off his hat and placed it on the box floor. "Now you show me where that man sat."

I placed the chair against the plush-covered parapet and dropped into it.

"Here," I explained, "within two feet of where you are."

"All right!" was his sudden and quite unexpected rejoinder. "That's enough! That'll do!"

He reached down and groped about for his hat before rising from the chair. He brushed it with the sleeve of his coat absently, and then stepped out of the box.

"We'd better be getting back," he called to me from the sheet-iron covered doorway.

"Back to what?" I demanded, as I followed him out

through the canvas-lined maze again, feeling that he was in some way tricking me, resenting the foolish mystery which he was flinging about the whole foolish maneuver.

"Back to those guests of yours and some good old-fashioned common sense," was his retort.

But during the ride back to Sherry's he had nothing further to say to me. His answers to the questions I put to him were either evasive or monosyllabic. He even yawned, yawned openly and audibly, as we drew up at the carriage entrance of that munificently lighted hostelry. He now seemed nothing more than a commonplace man tired out at the completion of a commonplace task. He even seemed a trifle impatient at my delay as I waited to check my hat and coat—a formality in which he did not join me.

"Now, I can give you people just two minutes," he said, as the five of us were once more seated at the same table and he once more consulted his turnip of a watch. "And I guess that's more'n we'll need."

He turned to the wan and tired-eyed girl, who, only too plainly, had not altogether enjoyed her wait.

"You've got the necklace?" he asked.

She held up a hand from which the string of graduated pearls dangled. The man then turned to me.

"You took this string of pearls away from this man?" he asked, with a quick nod toward the jewel thief.

"I assuredly did," was my answer.

"Knowing he had taken them from this young lady earlier in the evening?"

"Your assumption bears every mark of genius!" I assured him.

He turned back to the girl.

"Is that your necklace?" he curtly demanded.

The girl looked at me with clouded and troubled eyes. We all felt, in some foolish way, that the moment was a climactic one.

"No!" she answered, in little more than a whisper.

"You're positive?"

She nodded her head without speaking. The man turned to me.

"Yet you followed this man, assaulted him, and forcibly took that necklace away from him?"

"Hold on!" I cried, angered by that calmly pedagogic manner of his. "I want you to un—"

He stopped me with a sharp move of the hand.

"Don't go over all that!" he said. "It's a waste of time. The point is, that necklace is not your friend's. But I'm going to tell you what it is. It's a duplicate of it, stone for stone. The lady, I think, will agree with me on that. Am I right?"

The girl nodded.

"Then what the devil's this man doing with it?" demanded Benny Churchill, before any of us could speak.

"S'pose you wait and find out who this man is!"

"Well, who is he?" I inquired, resolved that no hand, however artful, was going to pull the wool over my eyes.

"This man," said my unperturbed and big-shouldered friend, "is the pearl-matcher for Cohen and

Greenhut, the Maiden Lane importers. Wait, don't interrupt me. Miss Churchill's necklace, I understand, was one of the finest in this town. His house had an order to duplicate it. He took the first chance, when the pearls had been matched and strung, to see that he'd done his job right."

"And you mean to tell me," I cried, "that he hung over a box-rail and lifted a string of pearls from a lady's neck just to—"

"Hold on there, my friend," cut in the big-limbed man. "He found this lady was going to be in that box wearin' that necklace."

"And having reviewed its chaste beauty, he sneaked out of his own box and ran like a chased cur!"

"Hold your horses now! Can't you see that he thought *you* were the crook? If *you* had a bunch of stones like that on you and a stranger butted in and started trailin' you, wouldn't you do your best to melt away when you had the chance?" demanded the officer. Then he looked at me again with his wearily uplifted eyebrows. "Oh, I guess you were all right as far as you went, but, like most amateurs, you didn't go quite far enough!"

It was Benny Churchill who spoke up before I could answer. His voice, as he spoke, was oddly thin and childlike.

"But why in heaven's name should he want to duplicate my sister's jewelry?"

"For another woman, with more money than brains, or the know-how, or whatever you want to call it," was the impassive response.

I saw the girl across the table from me push the necklace away from her, and leave it lying there in a glimmering heap on the white table. I promptly and quietly reached out and took possession of it, for I still had my own ideas of the situation.

"That's all very well," I cried, "and very interesting. But what I want to know is: *who got the first necklace?*"

The big-framed man looked once more at his watch. Then he looked a little wearily at me.

"I got 'em!"

"You've got them?" echoed both the girl and her brother. It was plain that the inconsequentialities of the last hour had been a little too much for them.

The man thrust a huge hand down in the pocket of his damp and somewhat unshapely overcoat.

"Yes, I got 'em here," he explained as he drew his hand away and held the glimmering string up to the light. "I picked 'em up from the corner of that box where they slipped off the lady's neck."

He rose placidly and ponderously to his feet.

"And I guess that's about all," he added as he squinted through an uncurtained strip of plate glass and slowly turned up his coat collar, "except that some of us outdoor guys'll sure get webfooted if this rain keeps up!"

CHAPTER X

THE THUMB-TAP CLUE

I WAS being followed. Of that there was no longer a shadow of doubt. Move by move and turn by turn, for even longer than I had been openly aware of it, some one had been quietly shadowing me.

Now, if one thing more than another stirs the blood of the man who has occasion to walk by night, it is the discovery that his steps are being dogged. The thought of being watched, of having a possible enemy behind one, wakens a thrill that is ancestral.

So, instead of continuing my busily aimless circuit about that high-spiked iron fence which encloses Gramercy Park, I shot off at a tangent, continuing from its northwest corner in a straight line toward Fourth Avenue and Broadway.

I had thought myself alone in that midnight abode of quietness. Only the dread of a second sleepless night had kept me there, goading me on in my febrile revolutions until weariness should send me stumbling off my circuit like a six-day rider off his wheel.

Once I was in the house-shadows where Twenty-first Street again begins I swung about and waited. I stood there, in a sort of quiet belligerency, watching the figure of the man who had been dogging my steps. I saw him turn southward in the square, as though my flight were a matter of indifference to him. Yet the sudden relieving thought that his movements might have been as aimless as my own was swallowed up by a second and more interesting discovery.

It was the discovery that the man whom I had accepted as following me was in turn being followed by yet another man.

I waited until this strange pair had made a full circuit of the iron-fenced enclosure. Then I turned back into the square, walking southward until I came opposite my own house door. The second man must have seen me as I did so. Apparently suspicious of possible espionage, he loitered with assumed carelessness at the park's southern corner. The first man, the slighter and younger-looking figure of the two, kept on his unheeding way, as though he were the ghost-like competitor in some endless nightmare of a Marathon.

My contemplation of him was interrupted by the advent of a fourth figure, a figure which seemed to bring something sane and reassuring to a situation that was momentarily growing more ridiculous. For the newcomer was McCooey, the patrolman. He swung around to me without speaking, like a ferry swinging into its slip. Then he stood looking impassively up at the impassive November stars.

"Yuh're out late," he finally commented, with that careless ponderosity which is the step-child of unquestioned authority.

"McCooey," I said, "there's a night prowler going around this park of yours. He's doing it for about the one hundred and tenth time. And I wish you'd find out what in heaven he means by it."

"Been disturbin' yuh?" casually asked the law incarnate. Yet he put the question as an indulgent physician might to a patient. McCooey was of that type which it is both a joy and a temptation to mystify.

"He's assaulted my curiosity," I solemnly complained.

"D' yuh mean he's been interferin' wid yuh?" demanded my literal friend.

"I mean he's invaded my peace of mind."

"Then I'll see what he's afther," was the other's answer. And a moment later he was swinging negligently out across the pavement at a line which would converge with the path of the nervously pacing stranger. I could see the two round the corner almost together. I could see McCooey draw nearer and nearer. I could even see that he had turned and spoken to the night walker as they went down the square together past the lights of the Players.

I could see that this night-walker showed neither resentment nor alarm at being so accosted. And I could also see that the meeting of the two was a source of much mystification to the third man, the man who still kept a discreet watch from the street corner on my right.

McCooey swung back to where I stood. He swung back resentfully, like a retriever who had been sent on a blind trail.

"What's he after, anyway?" I irritably inquired.

"He says he's afther sleep!"

"After what?" I demanded.

McCooey blinked up at a sky suddenly reddened by

an East River gas-flare. Then he took a deep and disinterested breath.

"He says he's afther sleep," repeated the patrolman. "Unless he gets her, says he, he's goin to walk
into the East River."

"What's the matter with the man, anyway?" I asked,
for that confession had brought the pacing stranger
into something very close and kindred to me.

"'Tis nothin' much," was the big man's answer.
"Like as not he's been over-eatin' and havin' a bad
night or two."

And with that my friend the patrolman, turning on
his heel, pursued his way through the quiet canyons of
the streets where a thousand happy sleepers knew
nothing of his coming and saw nothing of his going.

I stood there, looking after him as he went. Then
I crossed to the northwest corner of that iron-fenced
enclosure and waited for that youth whom the arm of
wakefulness was swinging about like a stone in a sling.

I deliberately blocked his way as he tried to edge
irritably about me.

"Pardon me," I began. He looked up, like a som-
nambulist suddenly awakened. "Pardon me, but I
think I ought to warn you that you are being followed."

"Am I?"

"Yes; and I think you ought to know it."

"Oh, I know it," was his apathetic response. "I'm
even beginning to get used to it."

He stepped back and leaned against the iron fence.
His face, under the street-lamps, was a very unhappy

looking one. It carried a woebegone impassivity, the impassivity which implied he was so submerged in misery that no further blow could be of consequence to him. And yet, beyond the fixed pallor of that face there was something appealing, some trace of finer things, some touch which told me that he and the nocturnal underworld had nothing in common.

"But are you getting used to the other thing?" I asked.

"What other thing?" was his slow inquiry. I could see the twin fires of some dull fever burning in the depths of his cavernous eyes.

"Going without sleep," I answered. For the second time he stared at me.

"But I'm going to sleep," he answered. "I've got to!"

"We all have to," I platitudinously remarked. "But there are times when we all don't."

He laughed a curious little mirthless laugh.

"Are you ever troubled that way?" he asked.

We stood there facing each other, like two kindred ghosts communing amid the quietness of a catacomb. Then I laughed, but not so bitterly, I hope, as he had done.

"I've walked this square," I told him, "a thousand times to your one."

"I've been doing it here for the last three hours," he quietly confessed.

"And it's done you up," I rejoined. "And what we both need is a quiet smoke and an hour or two with our feet up on something?"

"That's very good of you," he had the grace to admit, as his gaze followed mine toward the house door. "But there are a number of things I've got to think out."

He was a decent sort. There was no doubt of that. But it was equally plain that he was in a bad way about something or other.

"Let's think it out together!" I had the boldness to suggest.

He laughed mirthlessly, though he was already moving southward along the square with me as he began to speak again.

"There is something I've got to think out alone," he told me. He spoke, this time without resentment, and I was glad of it. That unhappy-eyed youth had in some way got a grip, if not on my affection, at least on my interest. And in our infirmity we had a bond of sympathy. We were like two refugees pursued by the same bloodhounds and seeking the same trails of escape. I felt that I was violating no principle of reticence in taking him by the arm.

"But why can't you slip in to my digs," I suggested, "for a smoke and a drop of Bristol Milk?"

I was actually wheedling and coaxing him, as a stubborn child is coaxed.

"Milk!" he murmured. "I never drink milk."

"But, my dear man, Bristol Milk isn't the kind that comes from cows. It's seventy-year old sherry that's been sent on a sea-voyage to Australia and back. It's something that's oil to the throat and music to the senses!"

He looked at me as though the whole width of a Hudson River flowed between us.

"That sounds appealing," he acknowledged. "But I'm in a mess that even Bristol Milk won't wash me out of."

"Well, if it's that bad, it's worth forgetting for an hour or two!" I announced. He laughed again, relaxingly. I took a firmer and more fraternal grip on his arm.

And side by side we went up the steps and through the door into the quietness of that sober-fronted house which I still called by the empty name of home.

In five minutes I had a hickory log ablaze in the fire-place, the library-chairs drawn up, and Criswell, my captive, with his hat and coat off. At his side stood a plate of biscuits and a glass of Bristol Milk. But he seemed to find more consolation in sitting back and peering at the play of the flames. His face was a very tired one. The skin was clammy and dead-looking; and yet from the depths of that fatigue flared the familiar ironic white lights of wakefulness. I think I knew about how he felt.

We sat there without speaking, yet not unconscious of a silent communion of thought. I knew, however, that Bristol Milk was not in the habit of leaving a man long tongued-tied. So I turned to refill his glass. I had noticed that his hands were shaky, just as I had noticed the telltale twitch to one of his eyelids. But when his uncontrolled fingers accidently knocked the glass from the edge of the table, it gave me a bit of a start.

He sat there looking studiously down at the scattered pieces of crystal.

"It's hell!" he suddenly burst out.

"What is?" I inquired.

"Being in this sort of shape!" was his vehement response. I did not permit myself to look at him. Sympathy was not the sort of thing he needed. Seventy-year-old sherry, I felt, was more to the purpose.

"Especially when we haven't any excuse for it," I lazily commented, passing him a second glass, filling it, and turning to watch the fire.

"Warming stuff, that Bristol Milk," he said with a catch of the breath that was too short to be called a sigh. Then, laughing and wiping the sweat from his forehead, he went on with an incoherence that approached that of childhood.

"I've *got an excuse.*"

I waited for a moment or two.

"What is it?"

"That man you saw trailing me around the square, for one thing."

"Even that isn't altogether an excuse," I maintained.

"But it's what he stands for," protested my visitor. He sat staring into the fire for a minute or two. I sat beside him, again conscious of some inarticulate and evasive companionship.

"How did it begin?" I finally asked.

He took a deep breath. Then he closed his eyes. And when he spoke he did so without opening them.

"I don't think I could explain," was his listless answer.

"Make a try at it," I urged. "Let's ventilate the thing, canalize it. Let's throw a little light and order into it."

He moved his head up and down, slowly, as though he had some vague comprehension of the psychology of confession, some knowledge of the advantages of "exteriorating" secret offenses. Then he sat very still and tense.

"But there's no way of ventilating this. There's no way of knocking a window in it. It's—it's only a blank wall."

"Why a blank wall?" I inquired.

He turned and looked past me, with unseeing eyes.

"Because I can't remember," he said in a voice which made it seem that he was speaking more to himself than to me. He looked about him, with a helplessness that was pitiful. "I can't remember!" he repeated, with the forlornness of a frightened child.

"That's exactly what I wanted to get at," I cried, with a pretense at confident and careless intimacy. "So let's clear away in front of the blank wall. Let's at least try a kick or two at it."

"It's no use," he complained.

"Well, let's try," I persisted, with forced cheerfulness. "Let's get at the beginning of things."

"How far back do you want me to go?" he finally asked. He spoke with the weary listlessness of a patient confronted by an unwelcome practitioner.

"Let's begin right at the first," I blithely suggested.

He sat looking at his shaking fingers for a moment or two.

"There's really nothing much to begin at," he tried to explain. "These things don't seem to begin in a minute, or an hour, or a day."

"Of course not," I assented as I waited for him to go on.

"The thing I noticed at the time, about the only thing I even thought of, was that my memory seemed to have a blind spot—a blind spot the same as an eye has."

"Ill?" I asked. "Or overworking?"

"I guess I'd been pounding away pretty hard. I know I had. You see, I wanted to make good in that office. So I must have been biting off more than I could chew."

"What office?" I asked as he came to a stop. He looked up at me with a stare of dazed perplexity.

"Didn't I tell you that?" he asked, massaging his frontal bone with the ends of his unsteady fingers. "Why, I mean John Lockwood's office."

"John Lockwood?" I repeated, with a sudden tightening of the nerves. "Do you mean the railway-investment man, the man who made so many millions up along the northwest coast?"

The youth in the chair nodded. And I made an effort to control my feelings, for John Lockwood, I knew only too well, was the father of Mary Lockwood. He, like myself, had exploited the Frozen North, but had exploited it in a manner very different from mine.

"Go on," I said, after quite a long pause.

"Lockwood brought me down from the Canadian

Northern offices in Winnipeg. He said he'd give me a chance in the East—the chance of my life."

"What were you in his office?"

"I suppose you'd call it private secretary. But I don't think he knew what I was himself."

"And he let you overwork yourself?"

"No, I can't say that. It wasn't his fault. You see, his work this summer kept him out at the coast a good deal of the time. He had an English mining engineer named Carlton looking over some British Columbia interests."

"And you carried on the office work while Lockwood was out west?"

"I did what I could to keep my end of the thing going. But, you see, it was all so new to me. I hadn't got deep enough into the work to organize it the way I wanted to. There were a lot of little things that *couldn't* be organized."

"Why not?"

"Well, this man Carlton, for instance, had Lockwood's office look after his English mail. All his letters had to be sent on to whatever point he reported from."

"Well?"

"When Lockwood was away from the office he deputized me to look after his mail, sign for the registered letters, re-direct telegrams, see that everything went through to the right point. It was quite a heavy mail. Carlton, I guess, was a man of importance, and besides that he was investing for friends at home. Looking after it, of course, was simple enough, but—"

"Wait!" I interrupted. "Has this mail anything to do with our blank wall?"

He looked about at me as though he had seen me for the first time, as though all that while he had been merely thinking aloud.

"Why that *is* the blank wall," he cried.

"How?" I demanded.

"Four weeks ago Lockwood came back from the West. On the same day a registered letter came to the office for young Carlton. That letter held twelve Bank of England notes for a hundred pounds each. About six thousand dollars altogether."

"Where did it come from?"

"From Montreal, from Carlton's own father. He wanted the money forwarded to his son. The older man was on his way back to England. The younger Carlton was looking up certain lands his father wanted to invest in. Young Carlton's movements were rather uncertain, so his father made sure by sending the letter to our office—to Lockwood's office."

"And you were still acting as *poste restante* for the Carlton out in British Columbia?"

"Yes, we'd been receiving and forwarding his mail."

"And?"

"We also received this registered letter from Montreal. That's where the blank wall comes in."

"How?"

"We've no record of that letter ever going out of our office."

He looked at me as though he expected me to be more electrified than I found it possible to be.

"Lost, stolen, or strayed?" I asked.

"That's what I'd give my eye-teeth to know," he solemnly asserted.

"But where do *you* come in?"

His answer was given without the slightest shade of emotion.

"I signed for the letter."

"Then you remember that much?"

"No, I don't remember it. But when they began to investigate through the post-office, I knew my own signature when I saw it."

"With no chance of mistake, or forgery?"

"It was my own signature."

"And you don't even remember getting the letter?"

"I've gone back over that day with draghooks. I've thought over it all night at a stretch, but I can't get one clear idea of what I did."

The force of the situation was at last coming home to me.

"And they're holding you responsible for the disappearance of that letter?"

"Good God, I'm holding myself responsible for it! It's been hanging over me for nearly a month. And I can't stand much more of it!"

"Then let's go back to possibilities. Have you ever checked them over?"

"I've gone over 'em like a scrutineer over a voter's list. I've tested 'em all, one by one; but they all end up at the blank wall."

"Well, before we go back to these possibilities again, how about the personal equation? ,Have you any feeling, any emotional bias, any one inclination about the thing, no matter how ridiculous it may seem?"

He closed his eyes, and appeared to be deep in thought.

"I've always felt one thing," he confessed, "I've always felt—mind you, I only say felt—that when I signed for that Carlton letter, I carried it into Lockwood's own room with his own personal mail, and either gave it to him or left it on his desk."

"What makes you feel that?"

"In the first place, I must have known he'd seen Carlton recently, and had a clearer idea of his address at the time, than I had. In the second place, being registered, it must have impressed me as being comparatively important."

"And Lockwood himself?"

"He says I'm mistaken. He holds I never gave him the letter, or he would have remembered it."

"And circumstances seem to back him up in this?"

"Everything backs him up," was the answer.

"Then let's go back to the possibilities. How about theft? Are you sure every one in the office was reliable?"

"Every one but *me!*" was his bitter retort.

"Then how about its being actually lost inside those four walls?"

"That's scarcely possible. I've gone through every nook and drawer and file. I've gone over the place with a fine-tooth comb, time and time again. I've even gone over my own flat, every pocket and every corner of every room."

"Then you have a home?" I asked.

Again there was the telltale neurasthenic delay before his answer came.

"I was married the same week the letter was lost," was his response.

"And your wife hasn't been able to help you remember?"

"She didn't know of it until a week ago. Then she saw I couldn't sleep, and kept forgetting things, trifling little things that showed I wasn't coordinating properly—such as letting a letter go out unsigned or getting muddled on the safe combination or not remembering whether I'd eaten or not. She said she thought I was in for typhoid or something like that. She went right down to Lockwood and practically accused him of making me overwork. Lockwood had to tell her what had happened. I suppose it was the way it was thrown at her, all in a heap! She went home to her own people that afternoon, without seeing me. I thought it over, and decided there was no use doing anything until—until the mess was cleared up some way or other."

I did not speak for several seconds. The case was not as simple as it had seemed.

"And Lockwood, how does he feel about it?" I finally asked.

"The way any man'd feel!" The acidulated smile that wrinkled his face was significant. "He's having me shadowed!"

"But he *does* nothing!"

"He keeps giving me more time."

"Well, doesn't that imply he still somehow believes in you?"

"He doesn't believe in me," was the slow response.

"Then why doesn't he do something? Why doesn't he act?"

There was a moment's silence. "Because he promised his daughter to give me another week."

Still again I experienced that odd tightening of the nerves. And I had to take a grip on myself, before I could continue.

"You mean Mary Lockwood personally interested herself in your case?"

"Yes."

That would be like Mary Lockwood, I remembered. She would always want to be something more than just; she would want to be merciful—with others. *I* was the only one guilty of an offense which could not be overlooked!

"But why Mary Lockwood?" I asked, for something to say.

"She seemed to think I ought to be given a chance." Criswell spoke with listless heaviness, as though Mary Lockwood's pity, as though any one's pity, were a thing of repugnance to him.

"A matter of thumbs down," I murmured. He looked at me blankly; the idiom had not reached his intelligence. I crossed to the table and poured him out another glass of Bristol Milk.

"You say you did things to show you weren't coordinating properly," I went on. "Now, going back to possibilities, mightn't there have been a touch of aphasia? Mightn't you have done something with that letter and had no memory of what it was?"

"It's not aphasia—it never was that," calmly retorted the unhappy-eyed young man. "You couldn't dignify it with a name like that. And it never amounted to anything serious. I carried on all my office work without a hitch, without one mistake. But, as I told you before, I was working under pressure, and I hadn't been sleeping well. I did the bigger things without a mistake, but I often found I was doing them automatically."

"Then let's go back once more to those possibilities. Could the letter have been misdirected, absent-mindedly? Could it have gone to one of Carlton's addresses?"

"Every address has been canvassed. The thing's been verified through the local post-office, and through the Montreal office. That part of it's as clear as daylight. A letter came to this office of Lockwood's addressed to Carlton. It held six thousand dollars in cash. I received it and signed for it. The man to whom it was addressed never received it. Neither the money nor the letter was ever seen again. And the last record of it ends with *me*. Is it any wonder they've got that gum-shoe man trailing me about every move I make?"

"Wait," I cried, still conjecturing along the field of possibilities. "Why mightn't that letter have come in a second envelope which you removed after its receipt? Why mightn't it have come addressed to Lockwood or the firm?"

"The post-office records show differently. It came to Carlton. I signed for it as an agent of Carlton's. Oh, there's no use going over all that old ground. I've been over it until I thought I was going crazy. I've raked and dug through it, these past three weeks, and nothing's come of it. Nothing *can* come of it, until Lockwood gets tired of waiting for me to prove what I *can't* prove!"

"But, out of all the affair as it happened, out of that whole day when the letter came, isn't there one shred or tatter of memory on which you can try to hang something? Isn't there one thing, no matter how small or how misty, from which you can begin?"

"Not one rational thing! I've tried to build a bridge out into that empty space—that day always seems like empty space to me—I've tried to build it out like a cantilever, but I can't bolt two ideas together. I've tried to picture it; I've tried to visualize it; I've tried to imagine it as I must have lived it. But all I've left is the fool idea of a man hitting his thumb."

"What do you mean by that?" I demanded, sitting up with a jolt.

"I keep seeing somebody, somebody sitting in front of me, holding a letter in his right hand and tapping the thumb of his left hand with it as he talked."

"But who is it? Or who *was* it?"

"I've tried to imagine it was Lockwood."

"Why, you've something right there!" I exultantly cried out. "That's valuable. It's something definite, something concrete, something personal. Let's begin on that."

"It's no use," remarked my companion. His voice, as he spoke, was one of weary unconcern. "I thought the way you do, at first. I felt sure it would lead to something. I kept watching Lockwood, trying to catch him at the trick."

"And?" I prompted.

"I had no chance of making sure. So I went up to his home, and asked for Miss Lockwood herself. I tried to explain how much the whole thing meant to me. I asked her if she's ever noticed her father in the act of tapping his thumbs."

"And had she?"

"She was very patient. She thought it over, and tried to remember, but she decided that I was mistaken. His own daughter, she explained, would have noticed any such mannerism as that. In fact, she ventured to mention the matter to her father. And when John Lockwood found I'd been up to his house, that way, he—well, he rather lost his temper about it all. He accused me of trying to play on his daughter's sympathy, of trying to hide behind a petticoat. Miss Lockwood herself came and saw me again, though, and was fine enough to say that she still believed in me, that she still had faith in me. She said I could always count on her help. But everything she did only seemed to push me further back into the dark, the dark that's worse than hell to me!"

He leaned far forward in the chair, covering his face with his unsteady hands. I had no help to give him.

But as I sat there staring at him I began to see what

he had gone through. Yet more disturbing than the consciousness of this was the thought of what it would eventually lead to, of what it was already leading to, in that broken wreck of a walking ghost, in that terror-hounded neurasthenic who had found a hole in his memory and had kept exploring it, feeling about it as one's tongue-tip keeps fathoming the cave of a lost tooth.

"I went to a doctor, after she left me," the man in the chair was saying through his gaunt fingers as their tips pressed against his eye sockets. "He told me I had to sleep. He gave me trional and bromides and things, but I didn't seem able to assimilate them. Then he told me it was all in my own mind, that I only had to let myself relax. He told me to lie with my hands down at my sides, and sigh, to sigh just once. I lay all night as though I was in a coffin waiting for that sigh, fighting for it, praying for it. But it didn't come."

"Of course it didn't," I told him, for I knew the feeling. "It never does, that way. You ought to have taken a couple of weeks in the Maine woods, or tried fishing up in Temagami, or gone off pounding a golf ball fifteen miles a day."

Then I stopped and looked at him, for some subsidiary part of my brain must have been working even while I was talking.

"By heaven, I believe that girl was mistaken!"

"Mistaken?" he asked.

"Yes, I don't believe any girl really knows her father's little tricks. I'd like to wager that Lockwood *has* the habit of tapping his thumb nail, sometimes, with what he may be holding in his other hand!"

My dispirited friend looked up at me, a little disturbed by the vehemence of my outburst.

"But what's that to me now? What good does it do me, even though he does tap his thumb?"

"Can't you see that this is exploration work, like digging up a lost city? Can't you see that we've got to get down to at least one stone, and follow where that first sign leads?"

I did my best to infect him with some trace of my sudden enthusiasm. I wanted to emotionalize him out of that dead flat monotone of indifference. I jumped to my feet and brought a declamative hand down on the corner of my library table.

"I tell you it does you a lot of good. It's your life-buoy. It's the thing that's got to keep you afloat until your feet are on solid ground again."

"I tried to feel that way about it once," was his listless response. "But it doesn't lead to anything. It only makes me decide I dreamed the whole thing."

I stared down at him as he leaned wearily back in the heavy chair.

"Look here," I said. "I know you're pretty well done up. I know you're sick and tired of the whole hopeless situation, that you've given up trying to think about it. But I want you to act this thing out for me to-night. I want to try to dramatize that situation down in Lockwood's office when you signed for the Carlton letter. I want you to do everything you can to visualize that moment. I want you to get that cantilever bridge stuck out across the gulf, across the gulf from each side, until you touch the middle and give us a chance to bolt 'em together."

I pushed back the chairs, cleared the space on the reading-table, swung the youth about so that he faced this table, and then took one of my own letters from the heavy brass stand beside him. My one object now was to make him "go Berserk."

"This is your room," I told him. "And this is your desk. Remember, you're in your office, hard at work. Be so good, please, as to keep busy."

I crossed the room to the door as I spoke, intent on my impersonation. But I could hear him as he laughed his indulgent and mirthless laugh.

"Now, I'm bringing you this mail matter. And here I have a registered letter addressed to one Carlton. You see it, there? This letter? It's for Carlton, remember. I want you to take it. And sign for it, here. Yes, write down your name—actually write it. Now take the letter. And now think, man, *think*. What do you do after that? What is the next thing? What do you feel is the right thing? The only thing?"

He looked up at me, wonderingly. Then he looked about the room. Then he slowly shook his head from side to side. I had not succeeded in communicating to him any jot of my own mental energy.

"I can't do it," he said, "I can't remember. It doesn't seem to suggest a thing."

"But think, man, think!" I cried out at him. "Use your imagination! Get into the part! Act it! The thing's there in your head, I tell you. It's shut up somewhere there, only you haven't hit the right combination to throw the door open. You can't do a thing in this life, you've never lived an active moment of this life, without a record of it being left there. It may be buried, it may be buried so deep you'll die without digging it up, but it's there, I tell you, if you only go after it!"

"If I was only sure it was there," hesitated the man at the table. "If I only knew just what direction to go! But this doesn't mean anything; it doesn't *get* me anywhere."

"You're not in the part," I cried, with what was almost an ecstasy of impatience. "What you've got to do is *live over* that day. If you can't do that you've got to live over at least one part of it. No; don't think this is all foolishness. It's only going back to a very old law of association. I'm only trying to do something to bring up sight, touch, sound. We both know those are things that act quickest in reviving memory. Can't you see—out of similar conditions I want to catch at something that will suggest the similar action! There's no need telling you that my mind and your mind each has a permanent disposition to do again what it has once done under the same circumstances. There's no use delving into psychology. It's all such ordinary every-day common sense."

He sat looking at me a little blankly as I pounded this out at him. His pallid face, twitching in the light from the fire, was studious, but only passively so. The infection of my rhapsodic effort had not reached him. I knew that, even before he spoke.

"I can see what you're aiming at," he explained. "But no matter how hard I think, I can't get beyond the blank wall. I'm still in this library of yours. And this is still a table and nothing like Lockwood's office desk."

"And that makes it seem rather silly to you?"

"Yes, it *does* seem silly," he acknowledged.

Then a sudden idea fell like a hailstone out of the heavens themselves.

"I know what's the matter," I cried. "I know why you're not acting out the part. It's because you're not on the right stage. You know it's an empty rehearsal—you haven't been able to let yourself go!"

"I'm sorry," he said, with the contrition of a child, and with his repeated hand-gesture of helplessness.

I swung about on him, scarcely hearing the words he was uttering.

"We've got to get into that office," I declared. "We've got to get into Lockwood's own office."

He shook his head, without looking up at me.

"I've been over that office, every nook and cranny of it!" he reiterated.

"But what I want to know is, *can* we get into it?"

"At this time of night?" he asked, apparently a little frightened at the mere idea of it.

"Yes, now," I declared.

"I'd rather not," he finally averred.

"But you still carry those office-keys, don't you?" I asked.

"Yes; I still have my keys. But it wouldn't look right, the way things are. It would be only too easy 'for them to misinterpret a midnight visit of mine to those offices. And they're watching me, every move I make."

"Then let them know you're going to make the move," I maintained. "And then we'll slip down in my car, with no chance of being followed."

He seemed to be turning the matter over in his mind. Then he looked up, as though a sudden light had clarified the whole situation.

"You know Mary Lockwood, don't you?" he demanded.

"Y-yes," I hesitatingly admitted.

"Then wouldn't it be easier for *you* to call her up on the telephone and explain just what you propose doing?"

It was my turn to sit in a brown study. It would be no easy matter, I remembered, to make clear to this stranger my reasons for not caring to converse with Mary Lockwood. I also remembered that the situation confronting me was something which should transcend mere personal issues. And I was in a quandary, until I thought of the ever-dependable Benson.

"I'll have my man call up Lockwood's house," I explained as I rose to my feet, "and announce that we're making an informal visit to those offices."

"But what's that visit for?"

"For the purpose of finding out if John Lockwood really taps his thumbs or not!"

The gray-faced youth stared at me.

"But what good will that do?" he demanded.

"Why, it'll give us the right stage-setting, the right

'props'—something to reach out and grope along. It'll mean the same to your imagination as a brick wall to a bit of ivy." And I stopped and turned to give my instructions to Benson.

"Oh, it's no earthly use!" repeated the man who couldn't remember, in his flat and atonic voice. But instead of answering or arguing with him I put his hat in his hand and held the portière, waiting for him to pass through.

I have often thought that if the decorous and somewhat ponderous figure of Mr. John Lockwood had invaded his own offices on that particular night, he would have been persuaded of the fact that he was confronting two madmen.

For, once we had gained access to those offices and locked the door behind us, I began over again what I had so inadequately attempted in my own library.

During the earlier part of my effort to Belascoize a slumbering mental idea into some approximation to life, I tried to remember my surroundings and the fact that the hour was the unseemly one of almost two o'clock in the morning. But as I seated Criswell at his own office desk and did my utmost to galvanize his tired brain into some semblance of the rôle I had laid out for it, I think he rather lost track of time and place. At the end of ten minutes my face was moist with sweat, and a wave of utter exhaustion swept through me as I saw that, after all my struggle, nothing in that minutely enacted little drama had struck a responsive chord in either his imagination or his memory.

"You don't get anything?" I asked as I dropped back into a chair at the end of my pantomime. No stage-manager, trying to project his personality into an unresponding actor, could have struggled more passionately, more persuasively, more solicitously. But it had been fruitless.

"No, I can't get anything!" said the white-faced Criswell. And I could see that he had honestly tried, that he had strained his very soul, striving to reach up to the light that was denied him. But the matter was not one of mere volition. It was beyond his power. It depended on something external, on something as much outside his conscious control as though it were an angel that must come and touch him on the brow. It was simply that the door of Memory remained locked and barred. We had not hit upon the right combination. But I did not give up.

"Now we're going in to try Lockwood's own office," I told him, with a peremptoriness which made him draw away from me.

"I—I don't think I can go through it again," he faltered. And I could see the lines of mental fatigue deepen on his ashen face.

Yet I proffered him no sympathy; I allowed him no escape from those four imprisoning walls. I had already stirred the pool too deeply. I knew that a relapse into the old impassive hopelessness would now be doubly perilous.

I looked about the room. Three sides of it were lined with book-shelves and every shelf was filled with hundreds of books, thousands of them altogether, from dull and uninteresting-looking treatises on railway building and mining engineering to even more dull-looking consular reports and text-books on matters of finance. The fourth side of the room held two windows. Between these windows, some six feet from the wall, stood Lockwood's rosewood desk. It was a handsome desk, heavily carved, yet like the rest of the furniture, the acme of simplicity. History, I knew, had been made over that oblong of rosewood. It had been and would again be an arena of Napoleonic contention. Yet it stood before me as bare and bald as a prize fighter's platform.

I sat down in the carved swivel chair beside this desk, drew my chair closer to the rosewood, and looked up at Criswell, who, I believe, would have turned and bolted, had he been given the chance. He was, I fancy, even beginning to have suspicions as to my sanity. But in that I saw no objection. It was, I felt, rather an advantage. It would serve to key his nerves up to a still higher pitch—for I still hoped against hope that I might lash him into some form of mental calenture which would drive him into taking the high jump, which would in some way make him clear the blind wall.

"Now, I'm Lockwood, remember," I cried, fixing my eye on him, "and you're Criswell, my private secretary. Have you got that plain?"

He did not answer me. He was, apparently, looking weakly about for a place to sit down.

"Have you got that plain?" I repeated, this time in a voice that was almost thunderous.

"Yes," he finally said. "I understand."

"Then go back into your room there. From that room I want you to bring me a letter. Not any old letter, but one particular letter. I want you to bring me the Carlton registered letter which you signed for. I want you to see it, and feel it, and bring it here."

I threw all the authority of my being into that command. I had to justify both my course and my intelligence. I had to get my man over the high jump, or crawl away humiliated and defeated.

I stared at the man, for he was not moving. I tried to cow him into obedience by the very anger of my look. But it didn't seem to succeed.

"Don't you understand," I cried. "I want you to bring that registered letter in to me, here, now!"

He looked at me a little blankly. Then he passed his hand over his moist forehead.

"But we tried that before," he falteringly complained. "We tried that, and it wouldn't work. I brought the letter in the first time, and you weren't here."

I sat up as though I had been shot. I could feel a tingle of something go up and down my backbone. My God, I thought, the man's actually stumbling on something. The darkness was delivering itself of an idea.

"Yes, we tried that before," I wheedled. "And what happened?"

"You weren't here," he repeated, in tones of such languid detachment that one might have thought of him as under the influence of a hypnotist.

"But I'm here now, so bring me the letter!"

I tried to speak quietly, but I noticed that my voice shook with suppressed excitement. Whether or not the contagion of my hysteria went out to him I can not say. But he suddenly walked out of the room, with the utmost solemnity.

The moment I was alone I did a thing that was both ridiculous and audacious. Jerking open Lockwood's private drawer, I caught up a perfecto from a cigar-box I found there. This perfecto I impertinently and promptly lighted, puffing its aroma about, for it had suddenly come home to me how powerful an aid to memory certain odors may be, how, for instance, the mere smell of a Noah's Ark will carry a man forty years back to a childhood Christmas.

I sat there busily and abstractedly smoking as Criswell came into the room and quietly stepped up to my desk. In his hand he carried a letter. He was solemn enough about it, only his eyes, I noticed, were as empty as though he were giving an exhibition of sleep-walking. He reminded me of a hungry actor trying to look happy over a *papier-mâché* turkey.

"Here's a letter for Carlton, sir," he said to me. "Had I better send it on, or will you look after it?"

I pretended to be preoccupied. Lockwood, I felt, would have been that way, if the scene had indeed ever occurred. Lockwood's own mind must have been busy, otherwise he would have carried away some definite memory of what had happened.

I looked up, quickly and irritably. I took the letter from Criswell's hand, glanced at it, and began absently tapping my left thumb-tip with it as I peered at the secretarial figure before me.

Criswell's face went blank as he saw the movement. It was now not even somnambulistic in intelligence. It maddened me to think he was going to fail me at such a critical moment.

"What are you breaking down for?" I cried. "Why don't you go on?"

He was silent, looking ahead of him.

"I—*I see blue*," he finally said, as though to himself. His face was clammy with sweat.

"What sort of blue?" I prompted. "Blue cloth? Blue sky? Blue ink? Blue *what?*"

"*It's blue*," he repeated, ignoring my interruption. And all his soul seemed writhing and twisting in some terrible travail of mental childbirth.

"I see blue. And you're making it white. You're covering it up. You're turning over white—white—white! Oh, what in God's name is it?"

My spine was again tingling with a thousand electric needles as I watched him. He turned to me with a gesture of piteous appeal.

"What was it?" he implored. "Can't you help me get it—get it before it goes! What was it?"

"It was blue, blue and white," I told him, and as I said it I realized what madhouse jargon it would have sounded to any outsider.

He sank into a chair, and let his head fall forward on his hands. He did not speak for several seconds.

"And there are two hills covered with snow." he slowly intoned.

My heart sank a little as I heard him. I knew I had overtaxed his strength. He was wandering off again into irrelevancies. He had missed the high jump.

"That's all right, old man," I tried to console him. "There's no use overdoing this. You sit there for a while and calm down."

As I sank into a chair on the other side of the desk, defeated, staring wearily about that book-lined room that was housing so indeterminate a tragedy, the door on my left was thrown open. Through it stepped a woman in an ivory-tinted dinner gown over which was thrown a cloth-of-gold cloak.

I sat there blinking up at her, for it was Mary Lockwood herself. It was not so much her sudden appearance as the words she spoke to the huddled figure on the other side of the desk that startled me.

"You were right," she said, with a self-obliterating intensity of purpose. "Father taps his thumbs. I saw him do it an hour ago!"

I sat staring at her as she stood in the center of the room, a tower of ivory and gold against the dull and mottled colors of the book-lined wall. I waited for her to speak. Then out of the mottled colors that confronted my eye, out of the faded yellows and rusty browns, the dull greens and brighter reds, and the gilt of countless titles, my gaze rested on a near-by oblong of blue.

I looked at it without quite seeing it. Then it came capriciously home to me that blue had been the color that Criswell had mentioned.

But after all blue is only blue, I vacuously told myself as I got up and crossed the room. Then I saw the white streak at the top of the book, and for no adequate reason my heart suddenly leaped up into my throat.

I snatched at that thing of blue and white, like a man overboard snatching at a life-line. I jerked it from its resting-place and crossed to the desk-top with it.

On its blue title page I read: "Report of the Commissioner of the North West Mounted Police, 1898."

The volume, I could see at a glance, was a Canadian Government Blue Book. It was a volume which I myself had exploited, in my own time, and for my own ends. But those ends, I remembered as I took up the book and shook it, belonged now to a world that seemed very foolish and very far-away. Then, having shaken the volume as a terrier shakes a rat, I turned it over and looked through it. This I did with a slowly sinking heart.

It held nothing of significance. Yet I took it up and shook it and riffled through its leaves once more, to make sure. Then between what I saw to be the eighteenth and nineteenth pages of that section which bore the title "The Report of Inspector Moodie," I came upon a photographic insert, a tint-block photo-engraving. It carried the inscription: "The Summit of Laurier Pass Looking Westward." What made me suddenly stop breathing was the fact that this photograph showed two hills covered with snow.

"Criswell!" I called out, so sharply that it must

have sounded like a scream to the bewildered woman in the cloth-of-gold cloak.

"Yes," he answered in his far-away voice.

"Was John Lockwood ever interested in Northern British Columbia? Did he happen to have any claims or interests or plans that would make him look up trails in a Police Patrol report?"

"I don't know," was the wearily indifferent answer.

"Think, man!" I called out at him. *"Think!"*

"I can't think," he complained.

"Wouldn't he have to look up roads to a new mining-camp in that district?" I persisted.

"Yes, I think he did," was the slow response. Then the speaker looked up at me. His stupor was almost that of intoxication. His wandering eye peered un-steadily down at the Blue Book as I once more riffled through its pages, from back to front. I saw his wavering glance grow steady, his whole face change. I put the book down on the desk-top, with the picture of Laurier Pass uppermost under the flat white light.

I saw the man's eyes gradually dilate, and his body rise, as though some unseen hydraulic machinery were slowly and evenly elevating it.

"Why, there's the blue! There's the white!" he gasped.

"Go on!" I cried. "Go on!"

"And those are the two hills covered with snow! That's it! I see it! I see it, now! That's the book John Lockwood was going through *when I handed him the letter!"*

"What letter?" I insisted.

"Carlton's letter," he proclaimed.

"Then where is it?" I asked, sick at heart. I looked from Criswell to the girl in the gold cloak as she crossed the room to the book-shelf and stooped over the space from which I had so feverishly snatched the Blue Book. I saw her brush the dust from her finger-tips, stoop lower, and again reach in between the shelves. Then I looked back at Criswell, for I could hear his voice rise almost to a scream.

"I remember! I see it now! And he's got to remember! He's got to remember!"

I shook my head, hopelessly, as he flung himself down in the chair, sobbing out that foolish cry, over and over again.

"Yes, he's got to remember," I could hear Mary Lockwood say as she turned and faced us.

"But what will make him?" I asked, as her studiously impersonal gaze met mine.

"This will," she announced as she held out her hand. I saw then, for the first time, that in this hand she was holding a heavily inscribed and R-stamped envelope.

"What's that?" demanded Criswell, staring hard.

"It's your lost letter," answered Mary Lockwood. "How it fell out, I don't know. But we *do* know, now, that father shut this letter up in that book. And the Lockwoods, I'm afraid," she continued with an odd little quaver in her voice, "will have a very, very great deal to ask your forgiveness for. I'm sorry, Mr. Criswell, terribly sorry this ever happened. But I'm glad, terribly glad, that it has turned out the way it has."

There was a moment of quite unbroken silence. Then Criswell turned to me.

"It's *you* I've got to thank for all this," he finally blustered out, with moist yet happy eyes, as he did his best to wring my hand off. "It's you who've—who've reinstated me!"

We were standing there in a sort of triangle, very awkward and ill-at-ease, until I found the courage to break the silence.

"But I don't seem to have been able to reinstate myself, Criswell," I said as I turned and met Mary Lockwood's level gaze. She looked at me out of those intrepid and unequivocating eyes of hers, for a full half minute. Then she turned slowly away. She didn't speak. But there was something that looked strangely like unhappiness in her face as she groped toward the door, which Criswell, I noticed, opened for her.

CHAPTER XI

"**I** HOPE you slept well, sir," said Benson, as I sat down to my breakfast of iced Casaba and eggs O'Brien, a long month later.

"Like a top, thank you," I was able to announce to that anxious-eyed old retainer of mine.

"That sounds like old times, sir," ventured Benson, caressing his own knuckle-joints very much as though he were shaking hands with himself.

"It *feels* like old times," I briskly acknowledged. "And this morning, Benson, I'd like you to clear out my study and get that clutter of Shang and Ming bronzes off my writing-desk."

"Very good, sir."

"And order up a ream or two of that Wistaria Bond I used to use. For I feel like work again, Benson, and that's a feeling which I don't think we ought to neglect."

"Quite so, sir," acquiesced Benson, with an approving wag of the head which he made small effort to conceal.

It was the truth that I had spoken to Benson. The drought seemed to have ended. The old psychasthenic inertia had slipped away. Life, for some unaccountable reason or other, still again seemed wonderful to me, touched with some undefined promise of high adventure, crowned once more with the fugitive wine-glow of romance. Gramercy Square, from my front windows, looked like something that Maxfield Parrish might have drawn. A milk-wagon, just beyond the corner, made me suddenly think of Phaethon and his coursers of the stellar trails. I felt an itching to get back to my desk, to shake out the wings of creation. I wanted to write once more. It would never again be about those impossible Alaskan demigods of the earlier days, but about real men and women, about the people I had met and known and struggled into an understanding of. Life, I began to feel, was a game, a great game, a game well worth watching, doubly well worth trying to interpret.

So when I settled down that day I wrote feverishly and I wrote joyously. I wrote until my fingers were cramped and my head was empty. I surrendered to a blithe logorrhea that left me contentedly limp and lax and in need of an hour or two of open air.

So I sallied forth, humming as I went. It was a sparkling afternoon of earliest spring, and as I paced the quiet streets I turned pleasantly over in that half-torpid brain of mine certain ideas as to the value of dramatic surprise, together with a carefully registered self-caution as to the author's over-use of the long arm of Coincidence.

Coincidences, I told myself, were things which popped up altogether too often on the printed page, and occurred altogether too seldom in actual life. It was a lazy man's way of reaching his end, that trick of

riding the bumpers of Invention, of swinging and dan-
gling from the over-wrenched arm-socket of Coincidence. It was good enough for the glib and delusive
coggery of the moving-pictures, but—

And then I stopped short. I stopped short, confronted by one of those calamitous street-accidents
only too common in any of our twentieth-century
cities where speed and greed have come to weigh life
so lightly.

I scarcely know which I noticed first, the spick-and-
span cloverleaf roadster sparkling in its coat of Nile-
green enamel, or the girl who seemed to step directly
in its path as it went humming along the smooth and
polished asphalt. But by one of those miraculously
rapid calculations of which the human mind is quite
often capable I realized that this same softly-hum-
ming car was predestined to come more or less vio-
lently into contact with that frail and seemingly hesitating figure.

My first impulse was to turn away, to avoid a
spectacle which instinct told me would be horrible.
For still again I felt the beak of cowardice spearing
my vitals. I had the odynephobiac's dread of blood.
It unmanned me; it sickened my soul. And I would
at least have covered my face with my hands, to blot
out the scene, had I not suddenly remembered that
other and strangely similar occasion when a car came
into violent collision with a human body. And it had
been my car. On that occasion, I only too well knew,
I had proved unpardonably vacillating and craven. I
had run away from the horror I should have faced

like a man. And I had paid for my cowardice, paid for it at the incredibly extortionate price of my self-respect and my peace of mind.

So this time I compelled myself to face the music. I steeled myself to stand by, even as the moving car struck the hesitating body and threw it to the pavement. My heart jumped up into my throat, like a ball-valve, and I shouted aloud, in mortal terror, for I could see where the skirted body trailed in under the running-gear of the Nile-green roadster, dragging along the pavement as the two white hands clung frantically to the green-painted spring-leaves. But I didn't run away. Instead of running away, in fact, I did exactly the opposite. I swung out to the side of the fallen girl, who stiffened in my arms as I picked her up. Then I spread my overcoat out along the curb, and placed the inert body on top of it, for in my first unreasoning panic I assumed that the woman was dead. I could see salivia streaked with blood drooling from her parted lips. It was horrible. And I had just made sure that she was still alive, that she was still breathing, when I became conscious of the fact that a second man, who had run along beside the car shaking his fist up at its driver, was standing close beside me. He was an elderly man, a venerable-looking man, a man with silvery hair and a meek and threadbare aspect. He was wringing his hands and moaning in his misery as he stared down at the girl stretched out on my overcoat.

"They've killed her!" he cried aloud. "O God, they've killed her!"

"Do you know this girl?" I demanded as I did my best to loosen the throat of her shirt-waist.

"Yes—yes! She's my Babbie. She's my niece. She's all I have," was his reply. "But they've killed her."

"Acting that way won't help things!" I told him, almost angrily. Then I looked up, still angrily, to see what had become of the Nile-green car. It had drawn in close beside the curb, not thirty feet away. I could see a woman stepping down from the driving-seat. All I noticed, at first, was that her face seemed very white, and that as she turned and moved toward us her left hand was pressed tight against her breast. It struck me, even in that moment of tension, as an indescribably dramatic gesture.

Then the long arm of the goddess known as Coincidence swung up and smote me full in the face, as solidly as a blacksmith's hammer smites an anvil. For the woman I saw walking white-faced yet determined toward where I knelt at the curb-side was Mary Lockwood herself.

I stood up and faced her in the cruel clarity of the slanting afternoon sunlight. For only a moment, I noticed, her stricken eyes rested on the figure of the woman lying along the curb-edge. Then they rose to my face. In those eyes, as she stared at me, I could read the question, the awful question, which her lips left unuttered. Yet it was not fear; it was not cowardice, that I saw written on that tragically colorless brow. It was more a dumb protest against injustice without bounds, a passionate and unarticulated pleading for some delivering sentence which she knew could not be given to her.

"No, she's not dead," I said in answer to that unspoken question. "She may not even be seriously hurt. But—"

I stared down at the telltale saliva streaked with blood. But the silvery-haired old man at my side put an end to any such efforts at prevarication.

"She's killed," he excitedly proclaimed.

"She's no such thing," I just as excitedly retorted.

"But you saw what they did to her?" he demanded, clutching at my shoulder. "You saw it. They ran her down, like a dog. They've ruined her; they've broken her body, for life!"

I could see Mary Lockwood's hand go out, as though in search for support. She was breathing almost as quickly, by this time, as the reviving girl on the curb-edge.

"Shut up," I curtly commanded the old man as he started in once more on his declamations, for the customary city crowd was already beginning to cluster about us. "It isn't talk we want now. We must get this girl where she can be taken care of."

It was then that Mary Lockwood spoke for the first time. Her voice was tremulous, but the gloved hand that hung at her side was no longer shaking.

"Couldn't I take her home?" she asked me. "To my home?"

I was busy pushing back the crowd.

"No," I told her, "a hospital's best. I'll put her in your car there. Then you run her over to the Roosevelt. That's even better than waiting for an ambulance."

I stooped over the injured girl again and felt her pulse. It struck me as an amazingly strong and steady pulse for any one in such a predicament. And her respiration, I noticed, was very close to normal. I examined each side of her face, and inspected her lips and even her tongue-tip, to see if some cut or abrasion there couldn't account for that disturbing streak of blood. But I could find neither cut nor bruise, and by this time the old man was again making himself heard.

"You'll take her to no pest-house," he was excitedly proclaiming. "She'll come home with me—what's left of her. She *must* come home with me!"

Mary Lockwood stared at him with her tragic and still slightly bewildered eyes.

"Very well," she quietly announced. "I'll take her home. I'll take you both home."

And at this the old man seemed immensely relieved.

"Where is it you want to go?" I rather impatiently demanded of him. For I'd decided to get them away from there, for Mary's sake, before the inevitable patrolman or reporter happened along.

"On the other side of Brooklyn," explained the bereft one, with a vague hand-wave toward the east. I had to push back the crowd again, before I was able to gather the limp form up from its asphalted resting-place.

"And what's your name?" I demanded as the old

man came shuffling along beside us on our way to the waiting car.

"Crotty," he announced. "Zachary Crotty."

It wasn't until I'd placed the injured girl in the softly-upholstered car-seat that that name of "Crotty," sent like a torpedo across the open spaces of distraction, exploded against the hull-plates of memory.

Crotty! The very name of Crotty took my thoughts suddenly winging back to yet another street-accident, an accident in which I myself had figured so actively and so unfortunately. For Crotty was the name of the man, I remembered, who had confirmed my chauffeur Latreille's verdict as to the victim of that never-to-be-forgotten Hallow-e'en affair. Crotty was the individual who had brought word to Latreille that we had really killed a man. And Crotty was not a remarkably common name. And now, oddly enough, he was figuring in another accident of almost the same nature.

Something prompted me to reach in and feel the hand of the still comatose girl. That hand, I noticed, was warm to the touch. Then I turned and inspected the venerable-looking old man who was now weeping volubly into a large cotton handkerchief.

"You'll have to give us your street and number," I told him, as a mask to cover that continued inspection of mine.

He did so, between sobs. And as he did so I failed to detect any trace of actual tears on his face. What was more, I felt sure that the eye periodically concealed by the noisily-flourished handkerchief was a chronically roving eye, an unstable eye, an eye that seemed averse to meeting your own honestly inquiring glance.

That discovery, or perhaps I ought to say that suspicion, caused me to turn to Mary, who was already in her place in the driving-seat.

"Wouldn't it be better if I went with you?" I asked her, stung to the heart by the mute suffering which I could only too plainly see on her milk-white face.

"No," she told me as she motioned for the girl's uncle to climb into the car. "This is something I've got to do myself."

"And it's something that'll have to be paid for, and well paid for," declaimed our silvery-haired old friend as he stowed away his cotton handkerchief and took up his slightly triumphant position in that Nile-green roadster.

It was not so much this statement, I think, as the crushed and hopeless look in Mary Lockwood's eyes that prompted me to lean in across the car-door and meet the gaze of those eyes as they stared so unseeingly down at me.

"I wish you'd let me go with you," I begged, putting my pride in my pocket.

"What good would that do?" she demanded, with a touch of bitterness in her voice. Her foot, I could see, was already pressing down on the starter-knob.

"I might be able to help you," I rather inadequately ventured. Even as I spoke, however, I caught sight of the blue-clad figure of a patrolman pushing his way through the crowd along the curb. I imagine that Mary also caught sight of that figure, for a shadow passed across her face and the pulse of the engine increased to a drone.

"I can't wait," she said in a sort of guilty gasp. "This girl needs help. And she needs it quickly."

Unconsciously my eyes fell to the other girl sitting back so limply in the padded seat. She was, clearly, coming round again. But as she drifted past my line of vision with the movement of the car I made a trivial and yet a slightly perplexing discovery. I noticed that the relaxed hand posed so impassively along the door-top bore a distinct yellow stain between the tips of the first and second fingers. That yellow stain, I knew, was customarily brought about by the use of cigarettes. It was a mark peculiar to the habitual smoker. Yet the meek and drab-colored figure that I had lifted into that car-seat could scarcely be accepted as a consumer of "coffin-nails." It left a wrinkle which the iron of Reason found hard to eradicate.

It left me squinting after that departing roadster, in fact, with something more than perplexity nibbling at my heart. I was oppressed by a feeling of undefined conspiracies weaving themselves about the tragic-eyed girl in the Nile-green car. And a sudden ache to follow after that girl, to stand between her and certain activities which she could never comprehend, took possession of me.

Any such pursuit, however, was not as easy as it promised. For I first had to explain to that inquiring patrolman that the accident had been a trivial one, that I hadn't even bothered about taking the license-number of the car, and that I could be found at my home in Gramercy Square in case any further information might be deemed necessary. Then, once clear of the neighborhood, I hesitated between two possible courses. One was to get in touch with Mary's father over the phone, with John Lockwood. The other was to hurry down to Police Headquarters and talk things over with my good friend Lieutenant Belton. But either movement, I remembered, would have stood distasteful to Mary herself. It meant publicity, and publicity was one thing to be avoided. So I solved the problem by taking an altogether different tack. I did what deep down in my heart I had been wanting to do all along. I hailed a passing taxicab, hopped in, and made straight for that hinterland district of Brooklyn where Crotty had described his home as standing.

I didn't drive directly to that home, but dismissed my driver at a near-by corner and approached the house on foot. There was no longer any Nile-green car in sight. And the house itself, I noticed, was a distinctly unattractive-looking one, a shabby one, even a sordid one. I stood in the shadow of the side-entrance to one of those gilt-lettered corner-saloons which loom like aromatic oases out of man's most dismal Saharas, studying that altogether repellent house-front. And as I stood there making careful note of its minutest characteristics a figure came briskly down its broken sandstone steps.

What made me catch my breath, however, was the fact that the figure was that of a man, and the man was Latreille, my ex-chauffeur. And still again, I remembered, the long arm of Coincidence was reaching out and plucking me by the sleeve.

But I didn't linger there to meditate over this abstraction, for I noticed that Latreille, sauntering along the opposite side of the street, had signaled to two other men leisurely approaching my caravansary from the near-by corner. One of these, I saw, was the old man known as Crotty. And it was obvious that within two minutes' time they would converge somewhere disagreeably close to the spot where I stood.

So I backed discreetly and quietly through the side-entrance of that many-odored beer-parlor. There I encountered an Hibernian bartender with an empty tray and an exceptionally evil eye. I detained him, however, with a fraternal hand on his sleeve.

"Sister," I hurriedly explained, "I've got a date with a rib here. Can you put me under cover?"

It was patois, I felt sure, which would reach his understanding. But it wasn't until he beheld the five-spot which I'd slid up on his tray that the look of world-weary cynicism vanished from his face.

"Sure," he said as he promptly and impassively pocketed the bill. Then without a word or the blink of an eye he pushed in past a room crowded with round tables on iron pedestals, took the key out of a door opening in the rear wall, thrust it into my fingers, and offhandedly motioned me inside.

I stepped in through that door and closed and locked it. Then I inspected my quarters. They were eloquent enough of sordid and ugly adventure. They smelt of sour liquor and stale cigar-smoke, with a vague over-tone of orris and patchouli. On one side of the room was an imitation Turkish couch, on the other an untidy washstand and a charred-edged card-table. Half-way between these there was a "speak-easy," a small sliding wall-panel through which liquid refreshments might be served without any undue inter-ruption to the privacy of those partaking of the same. This speak-easy, I noticed as I slid it back the merest trifle, opened on the "beer parlor," at the immediate rear of the bar-room itself, the "parlor" where the thirsty guest might sit at one of the little round tables and consume his "suds" or his fusel-oil whisky at his leisure. And the whole place impressed me as the sort of thing that still made civilization a mockery and suburban recreation a viper that crawled on its belly.

I was, in fact, still peering through my little speak-easy slit in the wall when I became conscious of the three figures that came sidling into that empty room with the little round tables. I could see them distinct-ly. There was the silvery-haired old Crotty; there was Latreille; and there was a rather unkempt and furtive-eyed individual who very promptly and unmistakably impressed me as a drug-addict. And repugnant as eavesdropping was to me, I couldn't help leaning close to my speak-easy crevice and listening to that worthy trio as they seated themselves within six feet of where I stood, Latreille and old Crotty with their backs to me, the untidy individual whom they addressed as The Doc sitting facing the wall that shielded me.

"Swell kipping!" contentedly murmured one of

that trio, out of their momentary silence. And at that I promptly pricked up my ears, for I knew that swell kipping in the vernacular of the underworld stood for easy harvesting.

"What'll it be, boys?" interrupted a voice which I recognized as the bartender's.

"Bourbon," barked Latreille.

"A slug o' square-face, Mickey," companionably announced the old gentleman known as Crotty.

"Deep beer," sighed he who was designated as The Doc. Then came the sound of a match being struck, the scrape of a chair-leg, and the clump of a fist on the table-top, followed by a quietly contented laugh.

"It's a pipe!" announced a solemnly exultant voice. And I knew the speaker to be my distinguished ex-chauffeur. "It's sure one grand little cinch!"

"Nothing's a cinch until you get the goods in your jeans," contended Crotty, with the not unnatural skepticism of age.

"But didn't she hand her hundred and ten over to The Doc, just to cover running-expenses? Ain't that worth rememberin'? And ain't she got the fear o' Gawd thrown into her? And ain't she comin' back to-night wit' that wine-jelly and old Port and her own check-book?"

This allocution was followed by an appreciative silence.

"But it's old Lockwood who's got o' come across," that individual known as The Doc finally reminded his confrères.

This brought a snort of contempt from Latreille.

"I tell you again old Lockwood'll fight you to the drop of the hat. The girl's your meat. She's your mark. You've got her! And if you've only got the brains to milk her right she's good for forty thousand. She's weakened already. She's on the skids. And she's got a pile of her own to pull from!"

"Forty thousand?" echoed the other, with a smack of the lips.

"That's thirteen thousand a-piece," amended Latreille largely, "with one over for Car-Step Sadie."

"Cut out that name," commanded Crotty.

"Well, Babbie then, if that suits you better. And it's a landslide for her!"

"Ain't she earned it?" demanded her silvery-haired old guardian.

"Strikes me as being pretty good pay for gettin' bunted over with a play-car and not even a shin-bruise."

"Well, ain't her trainin' worth something, in this work?"

"Sure it is—but how 'n hell did she get that blood streakin' across her face so nice and life-like?"

The silvery-haired old gentleman chuckled as he put down his glass of square-face.

"That's sure our Babbie's one little grand-stand play! You see, she keeps the pulp exposed in one o' her back teeth. Then a little suck with her tongue over it makes it bleed, on a half-minute notice. That's how she worked the hemorrhage-game with old Bronchial Bill all last winter, before the beak sent him up the river."

I stood there, leaning against the soiled shelf across which must have passed so much of the liquid that cheers depressed humanity. But never before, I feel sure, did anything quite so cheering come through that sordid little speak-easy. I was no longer afraid of that malignant-looking trio so contentedly exulting over their ill-gotten victory.

"Well, it's a cinch," went on the droning voice, "if The Doc'll only cut out the dope for a couple o' days and your Babbie doesn't get to buckin' over the foot-board!"

"It ain't Babbie I'm worryin' over," explained old Crotty. "That girl'll do what's expected of her. She's got to. I've wised her up on that. What's worryin' me more is that cuff-shooter who butted in over there on the Island."

Still again I could hear Latreille's little snort of open contempt.

"Well, you can put that bug out of your head," quietly averred my ex-chauffeur. "You seem to 've forgotten that guy, Zachy. That's the boob we un-loaded the Senator's town car on. And that's the Hindoo I framed, away back on Hallow-e'en Night. You remember that, don't you?"

I leaned closer, with my heart pounding under my midriff and a singing in my ears. But old Crotty didn't seem to remember.

"On Hallow-e'en Night?" he ruminated aloud.

"Why, the stiff I asked you to stand ready to give the glad word to, if he happened round for any habeas-corpus song and dance!" prompted the somewhat impatient voice of Latreille. "Don't you mind, back on last Hallow-e'en, how the Big Hill boys stuffed that suit of old clothes with straw and rags, and then stuck it up in the street? And how we hit that dummy, and how I made the chicken-hearted pen-wiper think that he'd killed a man and coyoted off the scene?"

I don't know what old Crotty's reply to those questions were. I wasn't interested in his reply. It wasn't even rage that swept through me as I stood listening to those only too enraging words.

The first thing that I felt was a sense of relief, a vague yet vast consciousness of deliverance, like a sleepy lifer with a governor's pardon being waved in his face. I was no longer afraid for Mary. I was no longer afraid of life, afraid of myself, afraid of my fellows. My slate was clean. And above all, I was in no way any longer afraid of Latreille. *I* was the chicken-hearted pen-wiper—and I hated him for that word—who had been "framed." *I* was the over-timorous victim of their sweet-scented conspiracies. *I* was the boob who had been made to shuffle and suffer and sweat. But that time was over and done with, forever. And the great wave of relief that swept through me surged back again, this time crested with anger, and then still again towered and broke in a misty rush of pity for Mary Lockwood. I thought of her as something soft and feathered in the triple coils of those three reptilious conspirators, as something clean and timid and fragile, being slowly slathered over by the fangs which were to fasten themselves upon her innocence, which were to feed upon her goodness of heart. And I decided that *she* would never have to go through what I had been compelled to go through.

I didn't wait for more. There was, in fact, nothing more to wait for, so far as I and my world were concerned. I had found out all I wanted to find out. Yet I had to stand there for a full minute, coercing myself to calmness. Then I tiptoed across the room to a second door which stood in the rear wall, unlocked it, and stepped out into the narrow and none too well-lighted hallway. This led to a washroom which in turn opened on another narrow passageway. And from this I was able to circle back into the barroom itself.

I didn't tarry to make any explanations to the worthy called Mickey, or to advertise my exit to his even worthier friends. I slipped quietly and quickly out of that unclean street-corner fester-spot, veered off across the street where the early spring twilight was already settling down, and went straight to the house which I knew to be Crotty's.

I didn't even wait to ring. I tried the door, found it unlocked, and stepped inside. There, no sign of life confronted me. But that didn't for a moment deter my explorations. I quietly investigated the ground floor, found it as unprepossessing as its proprietor, and proceeded noiselessly up the narrow stairway for an examination of the upper regions.

It wasn't until I reached the head of the stairs that I came to a stop. For there I could hear the muffled but unmistakable sound of somebody moving about.

It took me several minutes to determine the source of these movements. But once I had made sure of my ground I advanced to the door at the back of the half-darkened hall and swung it open.

On the far side of the room into which I stood staring I saw a girl in house-slippers and a faded rose-colored *peignoir* thrown over a none too clean night-dress of soiled linen. In one hand she held a lighted cigarette. With the other hand she was stirring something in a small graniteware stew-pan over a gas-heater. Her hair was down and her shoulders were bare. But all her attention seemed concentrated on that savory stew, which she sniffed at hungrily, almost childishly, between puffs on her cigarette. Then she fell to stirring her pot again, with obvious satisfaction.

I had the door shut behind me, in fact, before she so much as surmised that any one else was in the room with her. And when she looked up and saw me there her eyes slowly widened and she slowly and deliberately put her spoon down on the soiled dresser-top beside her. It wasn't exactly fear that I saw creep into her face. It was more the craft of the long-harried and case-hardened fugitive.

"Bab," I said, addressing her in the language which I imagined would most forcibly appeal to her. "I don't want to butt in on your slough. But time's precious and I'm going to talk plain."

"Shoot!" she said after a moment of hesitation followed by another moment of silent appraisal.

"The cops are rounding up The Doc and old Crotty for claim faking. They're also coming here, Bab, to gather up a girl called Car-Step Sadie for dummy-chucking under the car of that Lockwood woman and bleeding her for one hundred and ten bones, and—"

"Those bulls 've got nuttin' on me!" broke out the disturbingly dishabille figure in soiled linen, as she stood staring at me with a sort of mouse-like hostility in her crafty young eyes.

"But they're bringing a police-surgeon along with 'em," I went glibly on, "for they claim, Bab, you've got a hollow tooth you can start bleeding any time you need to stall on that internal-injury stuff. And they've dug up a couple of cases that aren't going to sound any too good over in the District Attorney's office. Now, I'm not here to give advice. This is merely a rumble. And you can do what you like about it. But if you're wise, you'll slide while the sliding is good."

She stood once more silently studying me.

"What's all this to yuh, anyway?" she suddenly demanded.

"It's so little, my dear," I airily acknowledged, "that you can do exactly as you like about it. But—"

"Where's The Doc?" was her next quick question. "Where's Crotty?"

I had to think fast.

"They've ducked," I asserted, amazed at my own newly-discovered facility in fictioneering.

"Who said they'd ducked?"

"Do you know Mickey's, over there on the corner?" I ventured.

She nodded as she darted across the room and

threw aside the faded *peignoir*. The movement made my thoughts flash back to another and earlier scene, to the scene wherein one Vinnie Brunelle had played the leading rôle.

"Latreille," I explained to the girl across the room, "dropped in at Mickey's and tipped Crotty and The Doc off, not more than a quarter of an hour ago."

"And they rabbited off wit'out throwin' me a sign?" she indignantly demanded.

"They did," I prevaricated.

She suddenly stopped, swinging about and viewing me with open suspicion.

"Where'd yuh ever know that Latreille guy?" she demanded.

"Latreille worked with me, for months," I declared, speaking with more truth, in fact, than I had intended.

"Then me for the tall timber!" announced that hard-faced little adventuress as she began to scramble into her clothes.

"Don't you want me to get you a taxi?" I inquired, backing discreetly away until I stood in the open door.

"Taxi nuttin'!" she retorted through the shower of soiled lingerie that cascaded about her writhing white shoulders. "What d'yuh take me for, anyway? A ostrich? When I get under cover, I go there me own way, and not wit' all Brooklyn bawlin' me out!"

And she went her own way. She went, indeed, much more expeditiously than I had anticipated, for in five minutes' time she was dressed and booted and hatted and scurrying off through the now darkened streets. Which trail she took and what cover she sought didn't in the least interest me once I had made sure of the fact she was faring in an opposite direction to Mickey's thirst-appeasing caravansary. But she went. She shook the dust of that house off her febrile young heels; and that was the one thing I desired of her. For that night, I knew, still held a problem or two for me which would be trying enough without the presence of the redoubtable Lady Babbie and her sanguinary bicuspid.

Yet once she was clear of that house, I decided to follow her example. This, however, was not so easy as it had promised to be. For I had scarcely reached the foot of the stairway when I heard the sound of voices outside the street door. And I promptly recognized them as Crotty's and Latreille's.

That discovery sent me groping hurriedly backward into the darkened hallway. By the time the door opened I had felt my way to a second flight of steps which obviously led to the basement. I could hear the voice of the man known as The Doc, for the three men were now advancing, and advancing none too quietly, into their musty-aired harborage. But my own flight down those basement stairs was quiet enough, for I realized now the expediency of slipping away and putting in a call for help.

It was only after a good deal of groping about, however, that I was able to reach the door opening on the basement-area, directly under the street-steps. A huge brass key, fortunately, stood in place there. So as I passed out I took the trouble to relock that door after me and pocket the key.

In five minutes I had found a side-street grocery-store with a sufficiently sequestered telephone. And by means of this telephone I promptly called up Headquarters and asked for Lieutenant Belton.

He listened to what I had to say with much more interest than I had anticipated.

"Witter," he called back over the wire, "I believe you've stumbled across something big."

"Then supposing you stumble over here after it," was my prompt suggestion. But Belton wasn't to be stampeded into the over-hasty action of the amateur.

"If that isn't that bunch Headquarters has been wanting to interview for the last three months, I miss my one best bet. But in this business, Witter, you've got to *know*. So I'll slip over to the Bureau and look up mugs and records. If that faint-spiller is Bad Nadeau, *alias* Car-Step Sadie, there's no doubt about your man being Crotty."

"She *is* Car-Step Sadie," I told him.

"Then we'll be out there with bells on," he calmly announced.

"But what do you expect me to do, in the meantime?" I somewhat peevishly demanded.

"Just keep 'em guessing," he tranquilly retorted, "keep 'em guessing until we amble over there and take 'em off your hands!"

That was easy enough to say, I remembered as I made my way back to Crotty's broken-faced abode, but the problem of holding that unsavory trio in subjection didn't impress me as an over-trivial one. Yet I went back with a new fortitude stiffening my backbone, for I knew that whatever might happen that night, I now had the Law on my side.

That casual little flicker of confidence, however, was not destined to sustain me for long. A new complication suddenly confronted me. For as I guardedly approached the house from which I'd sent Bab Nadeau scampering off into the night I noticed the Nile-green car already drawn up close beside the curb. And this car, I further noticed, was empty.

So it was with a perceptibly quickened pulse that I sidled down into the unclean area, unearthed my brass key, and let myself silently into the unlighted basement. Then I just as quietly piloted my way in through the darkness, found the stairway, and ascended to the ground floor.

The moment I reached the hallway I could hear the sound of voices through a door on my left. I could hear Mary Lockwood's voice, and then the throaty tones of that opianic old impostor known as The Doc. . . . "No doubt of the fact at all, my dear young lady. The spine has been injured, very seriously injured. Whether or not it will result in paralysis I can't tell until I consult with my colleague, Doctor Emmanuel Paschall. But we must count on the poor girl being helpless for life, Crotty, helpless for life!"

This was followed by a moment or two of silence. And I could imagine what that moment or two was costing Mary Lockwood.

"But I want to see the girl," she said in a somewhat desperate voice. "I *must* see her."

"All in good time, my dear, all in good time," temporized her bland old torturer. This was followed by a lower mumble of voices from which I could glean nothing intelligible. But those three conspirators must have consulted together, for after a moment of silence I caught the sound of steps crossing the floor.

"He'll just slip up and make sure the patient can be seen," I heard the suave old rascal intone. And I had merely time to edge back and dodge about the basement stairhead as the room-door was flung open and Latreille stepped out in the hall. The door closed again as he vanished above-stairs.

When he returned, he didn't step back into the room, but waited outside and knocked on the closed door. This brought old Crotty out in answer to the summons. Just what passed between that worthy trio, immured in their whispering consultation in that half-lighted hallway, failed to reach my ears. But this in no way disturbed me, for I knew well enough that Latreille had at least passed on to them the alarming news that their much needed patient was no longer under that roof. And what was more, I knew that this discovery would serve to bring things to a somewhat speedier climax than we had all anticipated. There was a sort of covert decisiveness about their movements, in fact, as they stepped back into the room and swung the door shut behind them. So I crept closer, listening intently. But it was only patches and shreds of their talk that I could overhear. I caught enough, however, to know they were protesting that their patient was too weak to be interviewed. I could hear Crotty feelingly exclaim that it wasn't kind words which could help this poor child now, but only something much more substantial, and much more mundane.

"Yes, it's only money that can talk in a case like this," pointedly concurred The Doc, clearly spurred on to a more open boldness of advance. And there were further parleyings and arguments and lugubrious enumerations of possibilities from the man of medicine. I knew well enough what they were doing. They were conjointly and cunningly brow-beating and intimidating that solitary girl who, even while she must have gathered some inkling of their worldliness, comprehended nothing of the wider plot they were weaving about her. And I further knew that they were winning their point, for I could hear her stifled little gasp of final surrender.

"Very well," her strained voice said. "I'll give you the check."

This pregnant sentence was followed by an equally pregnant silence. Then came a series of small noises, among which I could distinguish the scrape of a chair-leg and steps crossing the floor. And I surmised that Mary was seating herself at a desk or table, to make out and sign the precious little slip of paper which they were so unctuously conspiring for. So it was at this precise moment that I decided to interfere.

I opened the door, as quietly as I could, and stepped into the room.

It was Latreille who first saw me. The other two men were too intently watching the girl at the desk. They were still watching her as she slowly rose from her chair, with a blue-tinted oblong of paper between her fingers. And at the same moment that Mary Lock-wood stood up Latreille did the same. He rose slowly, with his eyes fixed on my face, backing just as slowly away as he continued to stare at me. But that retreat, I very promptly realized, wasn't prompted by any sense of fear.

"Mary," I called out sharply to the girl who still stood staring down at the slip of blue paper.

She looked up as she heard that call, peering at me with half incredulous and slightly startled eyes. I don't know whether she was glad or sorry to see me there. Perhaps it was both. But she neither moved nor spoke.

"Mary," I cried out to her, "don't give that up!"

I moved toward her, but she in turn moved away from me until she stood close beside the ever watchful Latreille.

"This is something which you don't understand," she said, much more calmly than I had expected.

"But I *do*," I hotly contended.

"It's something which you can't possibly under-stand," she repeated in tones which threw a gulf yawning between us.

"But it's *you* who don't," I still tried to tell her. "These three here are claim fakers; nothing but crimi-nals. They're bleeding you! They're blackmailing you!"

A brief but portentous silence fell on that room as the bewildered girl looked from one face to the other. But it lasted only a moment. The tableau was sud-

denly broken by a movement from Latreille. And it
was a quick and cat-like movement. With one sweep
of the hand he reached out and snatched the oblong of
blue paper from Mary Lockwood's fingers. And as I
beheld that movement a little alarm-gong somewhere
up at the peak of my brain went off with a clang.
Some remote cave-man ancestor of mine stirred in his
grave. I saw red.

With one unreasoned and unreasoning spring I
reached Latreille, crying to the girl as I went: "Get
out of this house! Get out—quick!"

That was all I said. It was all I had a chance to
say, for Latreille was suddenly taking up all my attention. That sauve brigand, instead of retreating, caught
and held the slip of paper between his teeth and squared
for combat. And combat was what he got.

We struck and countered and clenched and went to
the floor together, still striking blindly at each other's
faces as we threshed and rolled about there. We sent
a chair spinning, and a table went over like a nine-
pin. We wheezed and gasped and clumped against the
baseboard and flopped again out into open space. Yet
I tore that slip of paper from between Latreille's teeth,
and macerated it between my own, as we continued to
pound and thump and writhe about the dusty floor.
And I think I would have worsted Latreille, if I'd been
given half a chance, for into that onslaught of mine
went the pent-up fury of many weeks and months
of self-corroding hate. But that worthy known as The
Doc deemed it wise to take a hand in the struggle. His
interference assumed the form of a blow with a chair-

back, a blow which must have stunned me for a moment or two, for when I was able to think clearly again Latreille had me pinned down, with one knee on my chest and old Crotty stationed at the door with a Colt revolver in his hand. The next moment Latreille forced my wrists down in front of me, jerked a handkerchief from my pocket, and with it tied my crossed hands close together. Then he turned and curtly motioned to Crotty.

"Here," he commanded. "Bring that gun and guard this pin-head! If he tries anything, let him have it, and have it good!"

Slowly and deliberately Latreille rose to his feet. He paused for a moment to wipe the blood and dust from his face. Then he turned to Mary Lockwood, who stood with her back against the wall and her tightly clenched fists pressed close to her sides. She was very white, white to the lips. But it wasn't fear that held her there. It was a sort of colorless heat of indignation, a fusing of rage and watchfulness which she seemed at a loss to express in either word or action.

"Now you," barked out Latreille, motioning her to the desk, "make good on that paper. And do it quick!"

Mary surveyed him, silently, studiously, deliberately. He was, apparently, something startlingly new in her career, something which she seemed unable to fathom. But he'd by no means intimidated her. For, instead of answering him, she spoke to me.

"Witter," she called out, watching her enemy as she spoke. "Witter, what do you want me to do?"

I remembered Lieutenant Belton and his message. I

remembered my own helplessness, and the character of the men confronting us. And I remembered that time was a factor in Mary's favor and mine.

"Do what he tells you," I called up to her. And I knew that she had stepped slowly across to the desk again. Yet what she did there I failed to understand, for my attention was once more centered on the old scoundrel covering me with the Colt revolver and repeatedly and blasphemously threatening to plug me through the heart if I so much as made one finger-move to get off that floor. So I lay there studying him. I studied his posture. I studied the position of his weapon. I studied my own length of limb. I studied the furniture overturned about the room. And then I once more studied old Crotty.

Then I laughed aloud. As I did so I suddenly twisted my head and stared toward the door.

"*Smash it in, Sam!*" I shouted exultantly, and with all the strength of my lungs.

It startled them all, as I had intended it should. But it also did something else which I had expected it to do. It caused Crotty to glance quickly over his shoulder toward the door in question. And at the precise moment that he essayed this movement I ventured one of my own.

I brought my outstretched leg up, in one quick and vicious kick. I brought my boot-sole in one stinging blow against the stock of the firearm and the fingers clustered about it. And the result was practically what I had anticipated. It sent the revolver cascading up into the air, like a circus-tumbler doing a double-twister over an elephant's back. There was the bark of an exploding cartridge as it went. But I had both timed and placed its fall, and before either one of that startled couple could make a move I had given a quick twist and roll along the dusty floor and caught up the fallen weapon in my own pinioned right hand. Another quick wrench and twist freed my bound wrist, and before even a second shout of warning could escape from any of them I was on my feet with the revolver balanced in my right hand and fire in my eye.

"Back up, every one o' you," I commanded. For I was hot now, hot as a hornet. And if one of that worthy trio had ventured a move not in harmony with my orders I am morally certain that I should have sent a bullet through him. They too must have been equally assured of my determination, for side by side they backed away, with their hands slightly above their heads, like praying Brahmans, until the wall itself stopped their retreat.

"Stand closer," I told them. And they shuffled and side-stepped shoulder to shoulder, ludicrously, like the rawest of rookies on their first day of drill. As I stood contemplating them, with disgust on my face, I was interrupted by the voice of Mary.

"Witter," she demanded in a voice throaty with excitement yet not untouched with some strange exultation which I couldn't take time to analyze, "what shall I do this time?"

I couldn't turn and face her, for I still had to keep that unsavory trio under inspection.

"I want you to go down to your car," I told her

over my shoulder, "and get in it, and then go straight
home. And then—"

"That's absurd," she interrupted.

"I want you to do it."

"But I don't intend to," she said, ignoring my mas-
terfulness.

"Why?"

"I've been too cowardly about this already. It's
been quite bad enough, without leaving you here like
that. So be good enough to tell me what I can do."

I liked her for that, and I was on the point of telling her so, when down below I heard the quick stamp
and clump of feet. And I felt in my bones that it
must be Belton and his men. Then I remembered
Mary and her question.

"I'll tell you what you can do," I said, pointing toward Latreille. "You can ask this man what it was
I ran down in my car last Hallow-e'en."

She was moving forward, with a face quite without
fear by this time. But her brow clouded, at that speech
of mine, and she came to a sudden stop.

"I don't need to ask him," she slowly acknowledged.

"Why not?"

"Because I know already."

"*He* told you?" I demanded, with a vicious and
quite involuntary jab of my barrel-end into one of
Latreille's intercostal spaces.

"Not directly," replied the ever-truthful Mary. "But
it was through him that I found out. I know now it
was through him."

"I thought so," I snorted. "And through him you're

now going to find out that he was a liar and a slanderer. So be good enough to explain to her, Latreille, that it was a straw-stuffed dummy we ran down, a street-crowd's scare-crow, and nothing else!"

Latreille didn't answer me. He merely stood there with studious and half-closed eyes, a serpent-like squint of venom on his colorless face. It was, in fact, old Crotty who broke the silence.

"We'll do our talkin', young fellow, when the right time comes. And when we do, you're goin' to pay for an outrage like this, for an unprovoked assault on decent citizens!"

"Well, the time's come right now," I promptly announced, for I had caught the sound of Belton's quick step on the stairs. And the next moment the door swung open and that stalwart officer stood staring intently yet cautiously about the corner of the jamb. He stood there squinting in, in fact, for several seconds, calmly inspecting each face and factor of the situation. It wasn't until he stepped in through the open door, however, that I noticed the ugly-looking service-revolver in his own right hand.

"That's the bunch we want, all right," proclaimed the officer of law and order as he turned back to the still open door. "Come up, boys, and take 'em down," he called cheerfully and companionably out through the darkness.

Mary, at the answering tumult of those quick-thumping feet, crept a little closer to my side. Alarm, I suppose, had at last seeped through and crumbled the last of her Lockwood pride. The flash of waiting firearms, the strange faces, the still stranger experiences of that night, seemed to have brought about some final and unlooked for subjugation of her spirit. At least, so I thought.

"Couldn't you take me away, Witter?" she asked a little weakly and also a little wistfully. Yet there was something about the very tone of her voice which sent a thrill through my tired body. And that thrill gave me boldness enough to reach out a proprietory arm and let the weight of her body rest against it.

"You won't want us, will you, Belton?" I demanded, and that long-legged young officer stared about at us abstractedly, for a moment or two, before replying. When he turned away he did so to hide what seemed to be a slowly widening smile.

"*These* are the folks I want," he retorted, with a hand-wave toward his three prisoners. And without wasting further breath or time on them I helped Mary out and down to the Nile-green roadster.

"No; let me," she said as she noticed my movement to mount to the driver's seat. But she was silent for several minutes as we threaded our way out through the quiet and shadowy streets.

"Witter," she said at last and with a gulp, "you must think I'm an—an awful coward."

"*I* was the coward," I proclaimed out of my sudden misery of mind. For there were certain things which would be terribly hard to forget.

"You?" she cried. "After what I've just seen? After what you've saved me from? Oh, how you must despise me!"

"No," I said with a gulp of my own. "That's not the word."

"It's not," she absently agreed.

"It's not," I repeated, "for I love you!"

She made no response to that foolish and untimely declaration. All her attention, in fact, seemed directed toward her driving.

"But I was so cowardly in that other thing," she persisted, out of this second silence. "Judging without understanding, condemning something I was only too ready to do myself!"

"And it made you hate me?"

"No—no. I hate myself!" And her gesture was one of protest, passionate protest.

"But you *must* have hated me."

"Witter," she said, speaking quite low and leaning a little closer to the wheel as she spoke, as though all her thoughts were on the shadowy road ahead of her, "I never hated you—never! I couldn't even make myself."

"Why?" I asked, scarcely knowing I had spoken.

"Because *I've always loved you*," she said in a whisper, big with bravery. And I heard a silvery little bell begin to ring in my heart, like a bird in an orchard, heralding spring.

"Stop the car!" I suddenly commanded, once the real, the glorious meaning of those six words of Mary's had sunk through to that strange core of things we call our Soul.

"What for?" demanded Mary, mechanically releasing the clutch and throwing the brake-pedal down.

She sat staring startled into my face as we came to a stop. "What *for?*" she repeated.

"Because we must never run anything down again," I solemnly informed her.

"But I don't see," she began, "why—"

"It's because I'm going to kiss you, my beloved," I said as I reached out for her. "And something tells me, Mary, that it's going to be a terribly long one!"

THE END

www.ingramcontent.com/pod-product-compliance
Lightning Source LLC
Chambersburg PA
CBHW032204030726
47494CB00020B/450